HEARTTHROB
OR
HEART-TWISTER?

//////////////

"I'm not sure what it is you want me to do," Fran said.

"My daughter's not happy," Brannigan said. "I want you to fix that."

"If I could fix unhappiness, I'd be a very busy psychologist."

He rose from the chair. "Well, I suppose I'd better be getting back. Goodnight." Brannigan gave her a smoldering glance.

"Tell me one thing," Fran said. "Is it my imagination, or are you all the time coming on to me?"

He grinned. "Sorry," he said as he walked out. "Habit."

For a second there, she almost liked the man.

DEADLY CONFIDENTIAL

JANICE HARRELL

HarperPaperbacks
A Division of HarperCollinsPublishers

HarperPaperbacks   *A Division of* HarperCollins*Publishers*
10 East 53rd Street, New York, N.Y. 10022

Cover photo by Herman Estevez

First printing: January 1992

Printed in the United States of America

HarperPaperbacks and colophon are trademarks of HarperCollins*Publishers*

10 9 8 7 6 5 4 3 2 1

one / / /

I hammered the nail into the wall, ignoring the shower of paint flakes that fell to the carpet, then stood back to admire my work. The crisp Ph.D. diploma and the license to practice psychology in the state of North Carolina looked impressive. Not that I was a believer in the Wizard of Oz theory of education that says a degree is better than brains—but I had worked hard for those bits of sheepskin, and in my eyes they had charm. To add to the effect I had hung up my Phi Beta Kappa certificate, the certificate for completing my internship, my B.A. (magna cum laude), and my M.A.—everything except my Girl Scout merit badges.

I dropped the hammer and fell into my big blue overstuffed chair. My new office was small but cozy. It had just enough room for me and one slender, not very excited patient. In addition to the overstuffed blue chair, it was furnished with a hundred pounds of psychology books, the worm-eaten Empire desk that my mother had picked up for a song in the Paris Flea Market, a philodendron in a brass pot, and a large economy-sized box of Kleenex.

After getting those diplomas up, I should have been able to enjoy a few moments of simple satisfaction, but instead I was hyperventilating. It came over me that way sometimes, the fear of failure. It was sort of like morning sickness, except I never had anything to show for it nine months later. Right at the moment I was remembering my aunt Alicia, a harmless old biddy who had passed her days painting watercolors of zinnias. I had a strong and overpowering premonition that I was going to turn out just like her. Forget making Phi Beta Kappa, forget the Ph.D.—none of that counted. I was suddenly convinced that I was going to spend my days collecting quarterly checks from my trust fund just the way she had. Obviously, I would never get any patients.

It may have been my father's fault that I suffered from this irrational anxiety. He was the one who had been so scathing on the subject of aunt Alicia. And even though he had been dead for five years I hadn't quite outdistanced his voice with its mystical power to intimidate. I patted myself on the chest and practiced breathing deeply.

It wasn't as if I were the only one to get cold feet about setting up a practice, I told myself. It was perfectly normal. In fact, when I had bought the blue chair I had murmured something anxious about hoping the practice would go okay and the salesman had said in a bored voice, "All the young doctors say that."

Fear of failure was a common problem. I understood that. I just wished it would go away and let me breathe.

Brack Prideaux, the child psychologist whose office was adjacent to mine, chose this moment to stick in his head. He was a big man, built like a prize-fighter run slightly to seed. A scar ran through one of his eyebrows, and his nose looked as if it had once met with a fist. His clear gray eyes with friendly lines at the corners made me want to tell him all my troubles, but I quashed the impulse. I wanted to at least try to make a good impression on my new colleagues. No sense baring all my personal insecurities at this point.

"How's it coming?" he asked. "I've been tied up all morning, or I'd have offered to help."

"I could use a vacuum," I said. Housekeeping worked better than Valium for me when it came to dealing with anxiety.

"Try Mrs. Smythe."

"Yeah." I sprang out of the cushy chair. "I will. I'll do that."

I found Mrs. Smythe, the secretary, at her post in the front office. She was muttering, and at first I wasn't able to make her out, but then I heard her say quite clearly, "I'll show him. He thinks he's so smart. He'll never find you here!"

As near as I could make out, she was talking to the red-and-white picnic cooler beneath her desk. It hit me that my inspection of the office of Psychological Associates before signing on had been a shade cursory. If Mrs. Smythe went around talking to picnic coolers, who was to say that next she might not be skipping off to Tijuana with the office receipts?

"Uh, Mrs. Smythe, is everything all right?"

She looked up at me, her face flushed. "Oh, hello, dear. I'm so flustered, I don't half know what I'm doing. Somebody stole my blueberry yogurt out of the refrigerator again last week."

I clucked sympathetically.

"Last week it was my carrot curls!" she went on energetically. "So from now on I'm keeping my lunch right under my desk. When a person's on a diet and practically about to faint with hunger and that person goes to the fridge and finds her lunch gone—well!"

Mrs. Smythe was not exactly fat, but her comfortable bosom, her stomach, and her hips formed a series of plump curves. She had the waved blond hair I associated with dolls, a doll's guileless blue eyes, and a wattle of crepey skin at the neck. I wondered who had ripped off her carrots. Chocolate cake I could have understood, but carrot curls? It argued a perverted taste.

"But never mind about that now," she said hastily. "Look at this!" She donned the glasses that were secured around her neck with a thin chain. "I'm so glad you came in because if I don't tell somebody, I'm just going to bust, that's all." Opening her big black appointment book with a flourish, she stabbed at one of the names with her index finger.

I peered over her shoulder and read the name— Merris Brannigan.

"That's James Brannigan's daughter," she said. "James Brannigan's coming here! On Monday. Isn't it exciting? I've never met a real movie star before, have you? I can't wait to tell my grandchildren!"

"But he probably won't come, will he? I mean, won't there be a mother or somebody to bring her?"

"Her mother died under Tragic Circumstances last year," said Mrs. Smythe triumphantly. "I'm sure he'll be the one to bring her in. I read in *Personalities* that he's a devoted father." She gave me a conspiratorial look. "Do you want me to buzz you when they get here so you can see him?"

"That's okay, you don't have to. I think I can manage to wander over in the direction of the waiting room at"—I paused to peer closely at her book—"eleven-thirty on Monday."

Movie stars are no different from ordinary people. That's my way of looking at it. Still, I had to admit to being curious about James Brannigan. Did he have pores like the rest of us mortals? And chewed nails? Or was he celluloid smooth the way he looked up on the movie screen? I could understand Mrs. Smythe's excitement, all right. I had every intention of checking him out myself. Purely in the spirit of scientific inquiry, of course.

"I wonder if he'd mind if I asked for his autograph," Mrs. Smythe mused.

At last she managed to fix her attention on my query about the vacuum cleaner and she directed me to the hall closet. I was in the process of uncoiling the vacuum's hose and rolling it out when a door opened suddenly down the hall, and Avise MacBride appeared. A sleek handsome woman, her dark hair pulled into a French twist, she was the sort who normally moved slowly like a fully robed

Supreme Court justice, but now she dodged the vacuum coils in a neat quarterback-type maneuver and swept past me to the window in the hall where Mrs. Smythe collected fees from patients. With a slight uneasiness, I noticed her fists were tightly clenched. "I cannot understand why you didn't let me know my two o'clock had canceled," she said.

I heard Mrs. Smythe say, "It just slipped my mind. Things have been so hectic."

For hectic, I thought, read carrot curl theft and the rumored approach of James Brannigan.

Avise's musical voice began to climb the scale in an ominous way. "I waste enough time waiting for patients who simply don't show up without having to wait for people who have called to cancel. For forty minutes I sat there expecting the patient to walk in at any minute."

"I'm sorry," began Mrs. Smythe.

Avise cut her off abruptly. "I defy anyone to write a report under those circumstances. I suppose you think that my time isn't as valuable as Dr. Finch's or Dr. Miller's? Is that what you think? All I ask for is a little simple consideration. I don't think it's too much to expect you to let me know right away when a patient cancels."

"Gracious, I am sorry!" said Mrs. Smythe, surprised.

Avise turned on her heel and swept past me once more. The rims of her eyelids were pink and her mouth was working. However, she managed to close her office door behind her before, no doubt, bursting into tears.

"Jeez," I breathed. But there was more to come.

Avise had no sooner disappeared into her office than Dr. Miller emerged from his. "If you can't handle this job, Mrs. Smythe, just say so," he sputtered, "and we'll find someone who can. Was it too much trouble to ring me when my two-fifteen arrived? An office cannot be run in this sort of slapdash way. We need order around here. Organization. If our present system isn't working smoothly, we may have to rip it out and begin again with a younger woman at the desk."

"I'm sorry." Mrs. Smythe cringed. "It won't happen again, Dr. Miller."

I crept back to my office dragging the vacuum. I wondered what could be going on with Avise and Miller that a relatively minor glitch in the office could whip them up into a fury. I realized that I didn't yet know much about my new co-workers. I had been introduced to everyone when I came to look over the place and sign the lease, but I hadn't gotten much beyond introductions. I had no way of knowing whether this display of temperament was a fair sample of what I could expect from now on. I hoped not.

I tapped on Brack Prideaux's half-open door.

"Come in," he called.

I found him leaning back in his swivel chair. "My three and four o'clock have both canceled," he said. "Chicken pox epidemic. If this keeps up I'll end up on the soup line."

I picked my way among the blocks, small metal trucks, and plastic farm animals that littered the floor.

His office was easily three times larger than mine and had two windows where mine had none. On the wall, neatly arranged on shelves, were some anatomically correct rag dolls for interviewing suspected victims of child molesting. Under them was a plentiful assortment of dolls of every sex, color, and age so that any family, no matter how nontraditional or reconstituted, could be represented in play. In the corner, a round mahogany table was piled high with board games, everything from checkers to that standby of child therapy, The Talking, Feeling, Doing Game.

Prideaux's desk was heavily littered with file folders and papers and next to it was a big leather recliner where, presumably, the parents of hyperactive children were allowed to collapse. It was a big office, but not too big for all that he had in it.

"Nice office," I said.

"I could use some more room. A pool table would be good. Pool's great for breaking the ice with adolescents."

I settled myself into his leather recliner. "I sometimes wonder if I should go back and do a postdoc in child." Anything rather than facing up to beginning a practice in the here and now, I thought.

"If you end up doing that, I have one word of advice for you. Don't get swivel chairs. That's a basic when you're working with kids. I only wish someone had told me. Do you know how many times the average kid can spin around in these things? And as for the hyperactive kid—unbelievable."

"Why don't you get a different kind of chair?"

He looked sheepish. "I kind of like swivel chairs."
He spun around.

"I was wondering if you could fill me in on some
of the people around here," I said. "When I went to
get the vacuum, Miller and Avise were out there
yelling."

"Couldn't have been Avise," he said. "Avise
doesn't yell. Not her style."

"Well, no. Cold, deadly politeness is more like it.
But she was furious all right. And Miller was so
flipped out his glasses nearly fell off. Just because
Mrs. S. slipped up on keeping them posted about
their patients canceling."

"Speaking of patients, I think you'd better go see
some school counselors, take some pediatricians to
lunch. You need to be developing your referral
sources, or you'll never be able to pay the overhead
around here."

"I've already made a couple of appointments." I
noticed he seemed to be trying to divert the subject
from Avise and Miller. This did not discourage me. In
nursery school, I had nearly drowned myself once
trying to get a better look at the class tadpoles. Ever
since then people had been complaining that I was
overly inquisitive, but it had done nothing to
improve my character. It was too late now for me to
start heeding delicate hints.

"What do you think is going on with Avise and
Miller?" I persisted. "Are they coming apart at the
seams or what?"

"Let's just say there are currents and crosscur-
rents around here. But that shouldn't bother you. If

we were afraid of a little messy emotion, we wouldn't be in psychology, right?"

"Maybe," I said doubtfully. "But I think it's better if it's just the patients who are falling apart. There's something else about Miller. I've noticed that everybody calls him Dr. Miller, but they call you Brack. Why is that?"

"A question," said Prideaux, leaning back and staring at the ceiling, "with deep metaphysical and ontological overtones. Is it because Miller is short? Is it because he is deeply insecure? Is it because he is a pompous ass?" He shrugged. "I don't know. But he's Dr. Miller to everyone. Not to Avise, of course."

"Are you telling me that Avise and Miller are close?"

Brack looked at me in surprise. "They used to be married. I thought you knew."

Not only did I not know, I was astonished. Maybe I had a limited imagination, but I couldn't believe anybody would want to marry Miller. He was a decidedly unappetizing specimen with his red face, skimpy reddish hair, and forty pounds of excess flaccid flesh.

"So, what does she call him? Honeybunch?"

Brack grinned. "As far as I can tell a strategically placed 'uh' stands in for his name. Things are kind of tense between those two."

"Why does she keep on working here, then? I'd think she'd want to put lots of distance between her and him."

"Miller gives her free rent. And he does her supervision free. She's just certified on the M.A. level so she's got to have somebody sign off on her reports. It's not easy for her. She ain't getting rich doing disability testing for the government, and I think she's got an invalid mother somewhere she has to support. I guess every bit helps."

"Sounds sticky."

"Yeah, it's pretty bad. And the worst of it is I get the feeling the setup is Miller's way of trying to keep Avise under his thumb. You know, it's like they're divorced, but he hates to let her really get away."

I was beginning to see why Avise's nervous system might be shorting out.

"Miller sounds horrible," I said.

"What do you expect? This is a guy who describes himself as a 'creative deal maker.'"

"Huh? Run that by me again."

"He owns this building." Brack made a sweeping gesture that almost threw him off balance in the swivel chair. "He owns lots of buildings. He fancies himself some kind of financial whiz. Don't you think financial whizzes are generally simple character disorders?" He tilted his head. "That's been my experience, anyway."

I forbore mentioning that I come from a long line of financial whizzes.

"I hope I'm not going to have to sit around here and watch while he tightens the screws on Avise," I said.

"Oh, well, with any luck they'll save all that for private. I expect this stuff you saw was an isolated incident. For one thing, Mrs. Smythe is usually pretty reliable. I wonder what made her slip up?"

"I know the answer to that one." I got myself comfortable for a nice schmooze. "Get this. James Brannigan might be coming to the office, *this* office, on Monday!"

"Thrilling." Prideaux eyed me dubiously. "I perceive from the trill of suppressed joy in your voice that you're a fan and I suppose you and Mrs. Smythe will want to get together to discuss the nuances of his development, his oeuvre, his juvenilia as compared to his blue and rose periods."

"You're going to sit there being superior and tell me you don't go to movies?"

"Only black-and-white films with subtitles. Ah, *Last Year at Marienbad*," he sighed. "They don't make them like that anymore."

"I wonder why he's bringing his daughter to see Miller. You'd think somebody like that would go to Feininger's for a workup." Feininger's was the town's prestigious private psychiatric hospital. It was traditional to a fault, Freudian to the core, extremely expensive, and world-renowned. I knew for a fact that ambitious medical school graduates from as far away as Venezuela vied for the sought-after Feininger internships. Feininger's was a major name in the field of mental health.

It was Feininger's that, together with a nearby state hospital and a veterans' psychiatric hospital, assured that, incredible as it seems, about a quarter of the population of Bailey City worked in mental health, whether as therapists, nurses, purveyors of linens, or simply cutters of grass and trimmers of hedges. The mental health industry was one of the town's largest employers. As I had realized when I decided to locate in Bailey City. This town was not the place for the psychologist who didn't want to talk shop.

"My guess is that Brannigan probably did take her to Feininger's for a workup," Brack said, "but Feininger's sends a lot of their neurology cases to Miller. He's got close ties over there. Until a year ago he was clinical director of their adult unit. And whatever you might think of him, he's one of the best neuropsychologists in the country. He wrote the book."

"Don't I know it. *Miller on Testing.*" I chewed on a knuckle and wondered if I would ever be a world authority on anything. "I wonder what's wrong with Brannigan's daughter."

"I guess that's what Miller is supposed to find out. I wouldn't jump to conclusions though. Feininger's would run a complete battery of tests on a hangnail. Once you set foot in there, they never want to let you go. An average anxiety attack is good for two years of treatment, and then it's 'now that you're so much better, let's talk about analysis.'"

"That would be a lovely change from St. Luke's. You should have seen the way they whipped people in and out of there."

"Is that where you did your internship? Well, naturally they get them out fast. St. Luke's is mostly a charity ward, isn't it? But if you can pay what Feininger's charges, you get long, loving treatment."

I saw that he was sneaking looks at his Dictaphone, and it occurred to me that he must be wanting to dictate his notes from the last session before it faded entirely from his mind.

"I'd better go. I don't want to keep you from your work."

He smiled. "No problem." But he didn't try to persuade me to stay. Later I wondered if he had decided he had said too much about the undercurrents at the office, but at the time I left feeling pretty pleased with myself. I had gotten a fair amount of information about my co-workers for a first reconnaissance.

When I returned to my office, I was surprised to see that an elderly man was sitting in my patient's chair. I squeezed past him to get to my desk—perhaps a mistake, I thought an instant later, since that put him between me and the door and he looked none too reliable. A yellow drip of egg could be perceived on his shirt collar, and red veins made an intricate pattern on his nose. His hair fell in damp strands over a bony forehead and he had a dusty, neglected air, as if a bad housekeeper had stuck him behind a door and forgotten about him. I glanced hastily at the appointment book lying open beside my calendar and confirmed that no name had appeared in the two o'clock slot since last I looked. Of course, in view of Mrs. Smythe's present confused state, perhaps that meant nothing.

"I'm Dr. Fellowes," I said. "Are you here to see me?"

"Sure thing, sweetie," he replied in a creaky voice. "I know everybody around here. Ask 'em. 'Melvin knows us,' they'll say. What they don't figure is that I know them better than they think. Some people are so hoity-toity, if you asked 'em to the White House, they'd make out they were slumming, but all the time they're no better than they should be. No better than they should be. No better. I know." He nodded wisely.

I realized he might not remember whom he had come to see.

"Ms. MacBride," I suggested. "Are you here to see Ms. MacBride? I can get Mrs. Smythe to buzz her for us."

"Oh, I know all about Ms. MacBride."

"Are you her patient?" I persisted, reaching hopefully for the phone.

"Did I say I was her patient? I did not. I just said it was you I came to see, didn't I? I don't like Miss Hoity-Toity MacBride. And the others aren't any better."

"Excuse me. What did you say your name was?" I dialed the front desk.

"I didn't say." He folded his arms over his chest. "That's for me to know and for you to find out, right, sister? Everybody's got secrets. Even old Melvin."

"Mrs. Smythe? I have a Mr., uh, Melvin in here. Does he belong to someone else?"

"Oh, dear, oh, dear, oh, dear. This is just one of those days!" The receiver clicked, and she was gone.

"Betcha you've got a secret or two," the old man said. "A pretty girl like you. We've all got something we wouldn't want to see in the newspaper, now don't we? Like that big guy. Ask him if he ever served time, heh?"

"Big guy" could only mean Brack Prideaux, but I

knew this man couldn't be Prideaux's patient since Prideaux saw only children. I wondered what Mrs. Smythe was doing, if anything, to help me cope with Melvin. "Dr. Miller?" I prompted. "Have you come to see Dr. Miller?"

"I've known him for years. Yep, we go way back. Old Melvin knows a few things, I can tell you. Ask Dr. Hotshot Miller about that girl he killed, heh? I know all about it, yes, indeed."

I began to feel rather as if I had the Ancient Mariner on my hands.

Suddenly, the reassuring bulk of Lyman Finch appeared at my door, his jolly face beaming. "Mr. Mawson!" he said with every appearance of pleasure. "Ms. MacBride is waiting for you. We don't want to disappoint Ms. MacBride, now, do we?"

"Bitch," muttered Mr. Mawson.

Finch all but lifted him out of the seat and then guided him through the door, saying, "Here we go. That's the way." It was easy for me to see why Mrs. Smythe had sent Dr. Finch to deal with the problem. He was a big, broad-shouldered man, but he had the compelling, cheerful manner of a kindergarten teacher.

After he had delivered Mr. Mawson to Avise's office, Finch stopped back by my office. He was wiping his forehead with a handkerchief, but his good cheer was undiminished. "It's enough to make you give up booze, isn't it?"

"Korsakoff's syndrome?"

"Yup. Sad case. The man was an accountant before he pickled his brain with bourbon. In fact, it's his old firm that does the office books for us. The son has taken over the business, of course. I'm afraid Melvin has become quite a problem. I've advised Tom Mawson to apply for disability for his father and then try to get him into a halfway house. Unfortunately, I'm afraid no halfway house will be able to keep him. He'd be wandering off and into mischief in no time."

"He was trying to persuade me that everybody in the building has a criminal past."

Finch looked at me sharply. "Well, I don't need to tell you not to believe a thing he says." He stowed the handkerchief in his pocket and took his leave of me.

two ///

The next morning, I kept
an appointment with a school counselor even though
her school was in a poor district and it was hard to feel
optimistic about many referrals coming from that direction. I didn't get back to the office until after noon, and
by then most of the staff were already in the lounge
eating their bag lunches. Mrs. Smythe had a carton of
yogurt gripped between her knees and was absent-
mindedly ladling spoonfuls into her mouth. She was
deeply engrossed in the issue of *Personalities* that featured James Brannigan's face on the cover. Avise, sitting
next to her on the couch, managed to look stately while
eating a piece of stuffed pita bread—no mean feat. I
noticed that she was not above stealing the occasional
glance at Mrs. Smythe's magazine.

Brack Prideaux and Lyman Finch were eating
sandwiches at the table. Now that Finch was no
longer wrestling a Korsakoff's syndrome patient out
of my office, I saw that his resemblance to Santa
Claus was pronounced. The big round belly and the
broad, beaming face needed only a red velvet jump-
suit to complete the look.

When I came in, I could not escape the impression that everyone in the room was disappointed to see me, which was a small blow to my vanity. Smiling uncertainly I went over to the refrigerator. I wondered if my canned pâté had escaped the depredations of the yogurt snatcher.

When I reached the fridge, however, I was brought up short by a cartoon taped to the door. I recognized at once that it was a caricature of Miller. I was conscious of a faint rustling in the room as everyone shifted positions behind me. The cartoon was clearly the center of some interest and I guessed that everyone was waiting for my reaction to it.

It was an amazing piece of work. It had Miller's scanty hair, his glasses, his soft pudginess, and his pompous three-piece suit. But there was more to it than that. Looking at it, you got hints of Miller's characteristic manner, a sort of bustling indignation. It was there in the slight pursing of the lips and the attitude of the arms. Sketchy as the drawing was, it gave an amazingly vivid sense of the man. In its own way it was a minor masterpiece. Drawn with fluid, confident black-ink lines, its only color was a purple ring around Miller's mouth.

It took a moment for me to realize that the purple was intended to be blueberry juice.

I snickered involuntarily, then glanced guiltily behind me. It would be awkward if Miller walked in and caught me giggling. Now I guessed why everyone had seemed disappointed to see me. They had been hoping for Miller. I retrieved my pâté and moved over to the couch to join the rest of the conspirators. They all looked at me with suspicious blandness.

Prideaux was obviously struggling to keep a straight face. "Pâté, huh?" he said, raising his eyebrows. "Nice."

"Got it from the deli," I said. No use passing myself off as a gourmet cook. It would only lead to later disillusionment.

No one mentioned the drawing.

I spread some pâté on a cracker and craned my neck to read over Mrs. Smythe's shoulder at her magazine. "God, look at that," I said. "He's gorgeous!" It was a black-and-white shot of Brannigan surprised by a flash bulb outside a New York bistro. Not even his eyes opened comically wide in shock could dispel the impression that this was a good-looking man.

"He's a dream, all right." Mrs. Smythe sighed. "I like this part here, where the interviewer says that women find him attractive because of his keen intellect."

"Sure they do," I said derisively.

To my astonishment, the stately Avise blushed. The number of women who can work up a full blush after the age of thirty is minuscule and it was hard for me to take my eyes off her, but I returned my gaze to the magazine. "I suppose those teeth are capped," I said.

"I for one don't like seeing a man degraded into a sex object," said Prideaux.

"But I've always craved to be a sex object," Finch protested.

"Never mind, Lyman," Prideaux said. "It's not too late. That new Porsche will bring them on in droves."

I tried to imagine the huge Finch and his round stomach shoehorned into a Porsche and pursued by eager women, but I couldn't manage it.

"That reminds me of a story I heard at a hypnosis workshop last week," said Prideaux. "It seems there was a farmer whose prize rooster was clearly getting past it—"

Prideaux's story came to an abrupt end when Miller stepped into the room. No one had the presence of mind to keep talking, so we all watched Miller walk toward the refrigerator in the sort of silence in which the proverbial pin drops. I found myself hoping it was true that people never recognize caricatures of themselves.

Miller froze as he spotted the drawing. His red face paled and took on a sickly yellow cast. "What is the meaning of this?"

In a single motion he swept his hand down the refrigerator, ripped off the drawing, then crumpled it and threw it to the floor.

With the paper lying at his feet, his eyes raked over us all. I felt as guilty as if I had drawn the cartoon.

"I suppose I could demand to know who is responsible for this," he said menacingly. "But I believe I know." He turned back toward the door, dusting his suit jacket with his hands as if wiping the whole distasteful episode from his body. Although Miller invariably wore three-piece suits, the dignified effect was undercut somewhat by his argyle socks and pink tie. "I am on my way to an important luncheon with Senator Adamson. Otherwise we could no doubt have an interesting discussion about the passive-aggressive qualities of this sort of prankster." Then he strutted out, reminding me momentarily of the old rooster in Prideaux's joke.

An uneasy silence fell.

"Oh, dear," fluttered Mrs. Smythe, "I hope he doesn't think I did it."

"Now, Edith, why would he think that?" Finch opened his sandwich and examined the lettuce.

"You heard what he said, Dr. Finch. He said he thinks he knows who did it."

Finch made a deprecating sound. "I expect he thinks he can stampede the culprit into confessing by pretending he knows who did it." He bit into his sandwich. "Stupid of him," he added.

I walked over, bent to pick up the crumpled drawing, and smoothed it out. "It's very good," I said.

"I hope you aren't expecting the artist to take a bow." Prideaux grinned.

What with moving into a new house and at the same time trying to get a practice going, the decisions to be made were giving me an all but permanent stiffening of my neck and shoulder muscles. Should I sign up for flood insurance? Termite insurance? Earthquake insurance? An agent had already called me and had left me with the feeling that I was living recklessly by not insuring myself against these hazards. It made me long for the olden days when people were content to trust in Divine Providence. In the end I decided on a comprehensive policy with a liability rider for the office, reasoning that there was always the possibility my brass-potted philodendron might fall on someone's foot.

Another thing I spent a lot of time pondering was my yellow pages listing. The cost was exorbitant, but at the moment that didn't seem important. I longed to pay extra for bold type and many column inches. In fact, in my current weakened state of mind, if a sales representative could have suggested a battery-powered ad that flashed my name in cerise and fuchsia, I would have signed in a minute. I was in the grip of panic. Luckily, it occurred to me to get a ruler and measure everyone else's yellow pages ad. After I had done that, I felt calm enough to limit myself to a small ad consonant with my professional dignity. After all, I told myself, I didn't want the ad to be so big that it looked as if I were desperate.

There were other decisions, equally momentous. Should I build my practice in the traditional way, depending on referrals from fellow professionals and grateful patients? Or should I ride the wave of the future and take out a quarter-page ad in the newspaper? I was paralyzed with indecision.

My nerves were so on edge, I suppose I might have packed my bags and fled back to school for a postdoc at once if I hadn't known it would mean another six months of not being able to find my can opener. There were even moments when I felt that crazy Aunt Alicia didn't have such a bad setup. Painting watercolors of flowers, picking up one's quarterly checks at the bank—was it such a bad life?

I was so preoccupied that I might not have given

the caricature of Miller another thought had I not gone to the big shopping center that evening to pick up some sponges and light bulbs.

The Art of Bailey City Schools said a sign suspended over the standing bulletin boards in the corner of the mall. I walked by, admiring the display. I had a certain professional interest since figure drawings are a standard part of diagnostic tests. I was glad to see that the pictures were normal. The second graders' self-portraits, for example, had none of the large teeth and heavy shading that I remembered from the drawings of some of the sad, frightened children I had met during my rotation at a children's inpatient unit. And the melodramatic crayon sketches of motorcycles, rearing horses, and rock stars that made up the high-school entries were standard fixtures of the adolescent imagination.

All my professional interest faded, however, when my gaze fell on a set of line drawings that were startlingly familiar. I put down my shopping bag on a nearby bench and groped inside my purse until I found the caricature of Miller that I had rescued from the floor of the office. My glance moved from the drawing in my hands to the ones posted on the bulletin board. No question—they had been drawn by the same hand. I inched up closer and peered at the pen-and-ink drawings. One showed a teacher standing at a blackboard. Another seemed to be a sketch of a student. Although the two drawings were not exactly caricatures, the artist obviously had a keen eye for what makes someone distinctive. The teacher in the drawing stared at the class with a pop-eyed earnestness that surely had to be taken from life. And the sketch of the student, sprawled over some steps with his books, showed a loose-jointed, large-eared fellow who, I sensed, must sprawl somewhere in the flesh. In tiny block letters in the right-hand corner was the signature Tim Miller.

Tim Miller? My first thought was that he must be Miller's son, but I distinctly remembered Miller's telling me that he had no family.

Could the artist be a patient, maybe? Miller was a common enough name. Someone in therapy with Miller might have powerful feelings toward him that would account for the malice I had seen in the caricature. I looked closely at the drawings but could form no opinion about whether the artist might or might not be a patient. I remembered something an old professor of mine had once said, that figure drawings are not much good in diagnosis if your subject can actually draw. A drawing that looks like anxiety neurosis might mean only that the artist has studied Munch. Stick figures, instead of indicating infantilism, might reflect only your artist's admiration of Klee. Tricky. And these pictures showed a sureness of line and composition that was almost professional. With someone as gifted as this Tim Miller, the diagnostic ground shifted under your feet. I hesitated to draw any conclusions at all about his state of mind.

Besides, if Tim were a patient of Miller's, how had his drawing got into the lounge? As far as I knew, patients didn't go in there. So, who had taped the caricature on the refrigerator door?

three ///

Thursday, I found myself once more in my overstuffed blue chair, brooding on my lack of patients. I had left the door of my office open in the hope that someone might come in and interrupt me, but unfortunately no one did.

The offices around me hummed and vibrated with useful activity. Retarded and disabled citizens moved with regularity into Avise's office for tests to see if they were retarded or disabled enough to rate government assistance. Children arrived clutching at their mothers' skirts and departed Prideaux's office chewing on oversize cookies. Finch's and Miller's office doors were out of my line of vision, but I was dismally certain that they, too, were getting a steady stream of patients.

I began to daydream about going back for my postdoc. Perhaps it had been rash of me, I decided, to begin my career without actually specializing in anything. Yes, specialization was the key. Perhaps in child. I liked children. Or neuropsych. I had a solid background in that already. Imperceptibly, my thought about graduate school shaded into warm and sleepy thoughts about buttercups and miscellaneous baby wildlife. Gradually, with a twinge of annoyance, I became aware that an unmistakable sound was intruding on my daydream. The imaginary buttercups faded away. The stout, soundproof doors of the offices could not muffle a disagreement going on up the hall. I wondered if someone's patient was getting out of hand. At St. Luke's it had not been unheard of for a patient to produce a razor and go for a therapist's throat. I sat stiffly, wondering if I should do something, when suddenly a door slammed.

I got up and peeked down the hall. A tall young man was standing outside Miller's office holding his hand to his face. He seemed to be disoriented because instead of turning left toward the waiting room, he began walking unsteadily in my direction.

"Are you all right?" I asked him.

He looked at me with dazed brown eyes. "He hit me," he said thickly.

When he took his hand away from his face, I could see the clear mark of a hand. Either Miller had slapped this kid, or he had produced the most convincing case of stigmata I had ever seen.

I wondered if Miller was having a psychotic break. Judging by his behavior so far it seemed all too likely. But if he was cracking up, I wasn't sure what I should do about it. "Is someone coming to pick you up?" I asked the boy.

"What? Oh, no. I have the car."

"Come on in and sit down a minute. Do you want a soft drink or something? I could go down and get you one."

He obediently moved into my office and plopped down in my big blue chair. "I guess I am sort of shook up," he admitted.

Now that the mark of the hand was slowly fading from the boy's face, I could see that he was really quite attractive, tall with blond hair, high arched eyebrows, and clear brown eyes.

"Were you in with Dr. Miller just now?"

"What? Oh, no." He grinned suddenly. "I'm not a patient. I'm Tim Miller, Dr. Miller and Avise's kid."

I noted that even Miller's son referred to him as Dr. Miller. Very strange. And what about Miller's comment that he had no family? I wonder how he classified a son if not as family.

"You must be the new psychologist," he said. "I'm sorry I can't remember your name."

"Fran. Fran Fellowes." I looked at him curiously. "Do you go to Bailey City High School? I think I've seen some of your pen-and-ink drawings on display. I liked them a lot."

"Yeah, they weren't bad. You saw them at the shopping center, huh?"

I reached for my pocketbook and pulled out the caricature of Miller. "I liked this one, too."

He flushed.

"Is that what that scene with your father was about? Did he figure out that you did the caricature?"

"Huh? Oh, no. He'd never figure that out," he said contemptuously. "I'd have to sign it first. He couldn't tell a Tiepolo from a toothpaste commercial, my dad. You know, he actually told me one time that art is a sign of neurosis." He threw his hands up help-lessly. "What happened just now is he started falling to pieces when I told him what I thought of him." Tim's lips tightened. "Mom told me he wasn't going to come across with any money for college, so I fig-ured I didn't have anything to lose by putting in my pitch in person. But he says he's not going to give me a penny. He's rolling in it, too. You know where Finch's kids go to school? One's at Virginia Episcopal and one's up at Andover. And I'm slogging away down here at Bailey City High in an art program that stinks. They can hardly even scrape together money for paint and paper, and the only course they even offer is commercial art, which mostly means copying things out of magazines."

"Those drawings of yours didn't look like copies."

"Yeah, well, Miss Simpson is okay. She lets me do pretty much what I want. She thinks I ought to study abroad." He gave a bitter snort. "She knows my father's a big name in psychology. Naturally, I don't go telling her he's disowned me."

"I guess a lot of parents aren't very understand-ing when their kids want to be artists," I said.

"That's not it. He just hates me, that's all."

I might have dismissed that statement as the self-dramatization of an emotional adolescent if what I had already seen of Miller hadn't made it seem plau-sible.

Tim got up and smoothed his hair self-consciously with one hand. "I'd better get going."

There was a soft knock on my half-open door, and Brack Prideaux came in. He was surprised to see

Tim but managed to cover it pretty well. "I was just coming to ask Fran if she'd join me for lunch, Tim. Want to make it a threesome?"

"No thanks, Dr. Prideaux. I'm going to go over to a friend's house. Tommy Hvidding's father's a lawyer, and I think he'll be able to tell me if I can sue my dad for the money for college. I guess you know Dad's saying he won't give me a penny."

"Was that the ruckus I heard just now?"

"Yeah. I told him what I thought of him all right," Tim said with some satisfaction, "and he hit me."

"Next time hit him back," advised Prideaux.

Tim grinned. "I don't think he's going to let me get that close."

The door closed behind Tim. "What do you mean, telling that kid to hit his father?" I asked. "I'm surprised at you—encouraging domestic violence. The kid is easily a foot taller than his dad, too. But passing over your moral position, which stinks, don't you think that if he hauls off and whops his father, it'll hurt his chances of getting money for college?"

"Miller's not going to give him any money." Prideaux perched on the edge of my desk. "He hates that kid."

"That's funny. He seemed like a nice enough kid to me."

"Ah, but you know how that is, fair Frances. We love or hate people not according to their desserts but according to the capacity of our own hearts. Miller, having a raisin-size heart, finds it amazingly easy to hate Tim."

"Miller sounds pretty strange."

"He's strange, all right. But not, unfortunately, certifiable." He slid off the desk. "Tim's a good kid. He should belong to somebody who appreciates him." Under his piratical eyebrows, his eyes were bright with sympathy.

Over lunch, I learned that Brack had his own share of family troubles. His wife had run off with a scuba-diving instructor three years before.

"God knows what was going on with her," he said. "When I think about it now, it's like I'm watching a film of somebody else's life. You know, the kind where you can tell in the first frame that the girl is going to leave the poor sucker but he's just too dense to know it."

I was sympathetic. I had had my share of emotional upheavals, but so far I had always been the one to leave. It was a ploy I believed basic to survival.

"What about you?" he inquired. "Ever been married?"

"Me? I'm still practically in the first blush of girlhood."

"Ever been tempted?"

"I'm not ready to dwindle into a wife," I said primly.

He smiled at me. "Tell me about your father."

I gave him a doubtful look. "You're not one of those types who psychoanalyzes a person over a cup of coffee, are you?"

"Perish the thought. Your father is a bit overbearing, huh?"

"You knew him! Okay, I admit it. I may have a

slight wariness based on personal experience. I'm not sure that's a bad thing."

Prideaux ran his fingers swiftly through his hair. "Sheesh, no. I'm the last one to be telling people to plunge into matrimony. Still, I like to think I'm not soured on the whole idea." He gave me a charming smile, and I felt my toes stiffen. The problem with Brack Prideaux was that underneath his banter was a daunting intensity. I sensed that he was not a guy you could have a lighthearted affair with. If you started out sharing something simple, like a bed, the next thing you knew you'd be sharing something frighteningly permanent, like a mortgage.

"Still thinking of going back for a postdoc?" He reached for the pepper.

I mentally gave him points for picking up on the slight but telling rigor in my joints. Brack Prideaux was no dummy.

"I don't know. Maybe I should do whatever Finch is doing." I sliced my egg roll in half. "Finch of the Porsche and the two kids in expensive schools." I began to delicately pick out the vegetables, which is my idea of stringent dieting. "So tell me what he specializes in. Whatever it is, I'm sure I'd adore it."

"You don't want to do what Finch does. He tests all those rising young men at CCE and Marlin's to see if they have executive potential."

"Nah! You're making that up."

"I'm not. It sounds boring, but think about the economics of it. Companies have money, ordinary people don't. So—make your deals with companies."

"Wait a minute. If that's what he does, why don't

I ever see any executive types sitting in the waiting room with their *Wall Street Journals*?"

"Because he does all the testing over at the company and stores it on a computer. He only uses his office for seeing private patients in the afternoon. He's always pretty booked up."

"Do you think he'd like to send his overflow to me?" My sharp pang of envy felt like heartburn. "What's his secret?"

"He has a television show. You ought to try to catch it sometime. It's not bad. He takes a topic of everyday interest—divorce, say, or achievement anxiety—and gives a friendly little talk. Sometimes he has a panel for discussion. You can see the beauty of it as a practice-building technique. Once a week Lyman beams his friendly face out to the folks in television land, radiating good cheer until he seems like a member of the family. Naturally when those folks start having problems, they think of Uncle Lyman and give him a call."

"Okay, now I see how Finch stays busy. How do you do it?"

"No secret. I'm just a solid, well-qualified practitioner, that's all. I'm not saying it wasn't tough at first but now I've got some contacts at Division of Social Services, I play golf with two pediatricians, and I have a lot of grateful patients out there."

Our little chat had done nothing to perk me up. Everyone seemed to be making a go of it and I couldn't even get started.

When I got back to my office, Miller was sitting in my big blue chair. With repulsion I noticed little tufts of reddish hair on his freckled hands and the way the skin under his eyes was slightly darkened. Edging carefully past him to get to my desk, I decided that if I ever rented another office, it would have two doors, one in back as an escape hatch. There was something claustrophobic about this tiny room with its big chair almost blocking the only exit.

"I don't believe I've had a chance to welcome you personally," Miller said.

I sat down and inclined my head noncommittally.

He evidently took this as wanton encouragement because he immediately put his hand on my thigh. I stared down at it in sheer surprise. It may seem odd that I had reached the advanced age of twenty-seven without ever having felt the moist, soft hand of an older man on my thigh, but there it was. I had led a sheltered life. I was so taken aback that for a moment I could not speak.

However, it clearly was a mistake not to have given him a karate chop at once because immediately his hand began to creep upward. I was momentarily so staggered by his closeness and his smell—a mixture of musky after-shave, onions, and garlic—that I could scarcely catch my breath. It was like being touched by a slug. Then unexpectedly, he lunged at me. His plump knee was pressed beside me on the blue chair pinching my thigh painfully and I felt the heat of his thigh and the weight of his body and his hot breath as his face pressed close to mine.

Panicking, with nausea welling up in my throat, I pushed him away. He fell against my desk and the philodendron wobbled on its base and fell off the desk. I stared at the crumbs of potting soil spilled on the carpet and felt tears sting my eyes. He had messed up my philodendron, the creep.

"My dear!" he said thickly. His plump arms reached for me. I quickly picked up the brass pot and held it in both my hands, ready to pitch at him. "Get out of my office!"

He compressed his mouth and the inside of his lips showed at the corners. "No need to treat me like a criminal. You gave me the distinct impression—"

"I'm going to make a distinct impression in your skull if you don't get out of this office by the time I count to three." I spoke between clenched teeth. "One—" I said ominously.

He sprang for the door. "You have a problem, Fran. Do you know that? You ought to consider therapy."

Lucky for him, this was his exit line. I was so angry, I couldn't answer for what I might have done next if he hadn't got out. If there is one sort of creep I despise above all, it is the one who tries to blame his victim. *I* was the one with the problem? Sure.

I kicked the door shut behind him and collapsed in my chair, suddenly drained after the huge rush of adrenaline. To think that when that toad stepped in my office I had actually felt almost sorry for him.

The buzzer on my desk rang and I picked up the phone.

"Dr. Fellowes?" said Mrs. Smythe's voice. "Dr. Miller would like you to step into his office for a minute, if you don't mind."

"Said the spider to the fly," I muttered.

"What did you say, dear?"

"Tell him I got his message."

I tapped my fingernail on my planter thoughtfully. Miller was my landlord. I wondered if he was about to try some funny business with my lease in revenge for my fighting him off. If he did, he would find out about written contracts and consumer protection laws. When I had left my last true love, Jason, I had promised myself that I would never again let some man determine what I did. If it was beginning to look as if this might not be quite the supportive setting I needed while trying to get my fledgling practice off the ground, nevertheless, I was inclined to stand and fight. If Miller wanted to make it extremely worth my while to break that lease, maybe, just maybe I would consider it. But damned if I was going to let a creep like him order me about.

I went to his office and threw open the door.

"You sent me a message?" I said coldly.

"Come in. Sit down, girl." He stroked his tie. "I need to discuss a business proposition with you. I didn't get a chance just now in your office with all the fuss."

"Fuss" was one way of putting it. I rather preferred the term "criminal assault."

I smiled at him thinly. "I'll stand, thank you." I stood in the doorway, being careful, this time, to provide an escape route.

"As you wish," he said. "Um, have you ever heard of Continental Health? One of the most progressive and, indeed, largest health care organizations in this country. I am in the process of negotiating with them at this very time." The skin at his neck bulged as his Adam's apple moved. "You're the first to know. Yes, it is not generally known, but Continental Health will be offering its packages of HMO health plans in Bailey City as early as next year, and it is obviously in our best interest to restructure the practice to meet this challenge."

Unwillingly, I took a step into his office. The instincts handed down to me from generations of my merchant forebears told me that Miller's attention had turned from sex to something that interested him more fundamentally—money. A telltale tingling of those instincts also told me he was about to make me an offer I couldn't refuse. Already I could almost feel his knife at my throat.

I hadn't heard of Continental Health, but the term *HMO* rang a bell. Even in the ivory towers of graduate school I had heard about these health insurance plans in which a business makes a deal with a group of doctors or with a mental health group to provide all the care for its employees at a reduced rate.

The military had cut just such a deal with a group in Norfolk, the site of a huge naval installation. I didn't have all the grisly details, but I presumed that therapists in competing practices had been reduced to selling matches on the street corners.

"I interest you, I see." Miller smiled. "Now, I believe I can put together a bid that will induce Continental Health to sign our group on as a Preferred Provider for the mental health segment of their plan."

"But we don't have a group," I pointed out. "We just rent offices in the same building and share a secretary. That's not what I'd call a group."

"I just said we would have to restructure, didn't I? We would have to become a group, naturally. I, of course, would supply the necessary capital and would serve as the senior coordinator."

Naturally.

"I'm not sure you're familiar with the way these setups work," Miller went on. "The entire purpose is cost containment. The emphasis, then, is toward short-term therapy. I, as senior coordinator, and Dr. Finch as well, would do all the intake interviews and decide how long each patient should be seen and by whom." He smiled again. "Triage."

I had always associated triage with ruthless decisions made in times of war. I had a feeling the connotations were somewhat similar in this case.

"But then we would all be working for you," I said.

"Not on salary," he hastened to add. "You would get your therapy fee, as usual. The only difference would be that I would pick up the overhead."

"The only difference?"

"Well, practically the only difference. There would be certain legal distinctions, naturally."

"About this cost containment." I came straight to the point. "How much would we get paid for a therapy hour?"

"Twenty dollars."

"Twenty dollars!"

He raised a finger for emphasis. "But remember, you would have no overhead. It's not a bad deal at all, really."

Not for you, I thought. I had no doubt that the senior coordinator's fee would be three or four times that of the peons who did the therapy. But I chose my words carefully. I pulled my chair as far away from him as I could and sat down in it. "But what if you have difficulty interesting your colleagues in this, uh, proposition."

"I think they'll see the advantages. Continental Health estimates that it will take over sixty percent of the local market in health insurance. I needn't point out that this would deal a devastating blow to those who are not signed on with the organization defined as Preferred Provider. Their practices could be wiped out."

The prospect seemed to afford him peculiar satisfaction.

"But you may not be able to get anybody to come in with you," I pointed out. "In that case you wouldn't be in a position to make any bid at all to Continental Health."

"Oh, I'm not worried about that. Avise will come in with me, and I can always fill in the gaps with M.A. people and school psychologists, counselors, and such." He waved a hand carelessly.

I was surprised at how quickly the mention of money had cleared my brain.

"But these health organizations are extremely sophisticated about people's qualifications," I said. "Someone told me they go over everyone with incredibly exaggerated care before signing them on. Do you think that the sort of people you have in mind will meet their standards?"

"Finch and I will provide supervision, naturally, so I doubt that will be a problem."

Unspoken was the obvious thought, *What do they expect for twenty dollars an hour?*

He smiled sunnily at me. "I thought it only fair to make my offer to you and the others first."

"Kind of you," I murmured.

He rose. At the same time I reached for the paperweight on his desk, and holding it in my right hand, I smiled back at him sweetly.

"I hope you aren't going to let this little contretemps between us just now affect your decision. I'm not holding any grudges. We can still be friends and, of course, business associates," he said. "Think about it."

I didn't bother to reply. I closed the door behind me and stood for a moment in the hall reflecting on the laws forbidding homicide. Bastard, I thought.

four ///

Brack was on his way into his office with a cup of coffee when he spotted me in the hall and hesitated. "Are you okay?"

No doubt my uneven color, my ragged breathing, and the fact that I was trembling like an aspen had clued him in that something was amiss. "I'm not sure," I said honestly.

He motioned me into his office with a nod. Soon I was sinking all too willingly into his comfortable reclining chair, ready to babble on about my troubles.

"You look pretty shaken up," he said sympathetically. "You haven't gotten any bad news, have you?"

I hardly knew where to start. I took a deep breath. "For one thing, Miller assaulted me just now in my own office."

"Are you serious?"

"Of course, I'm serious. I always sound flip when I'm unnerved. It's my version of hysteria."

"What happened exactly?"

"I was just sitting there and he jumped me. In a flash I was pinned under him in that stupid soft chair, his knee was grinding into my thigh, and I could smell everything he'd had for lunch. It'll probably put me off Italian food permanently," I said bitterly.

"Good grief! Just out of the blue like that, he jumped you?"

"Don't start!" I warned him. "Miller gave me some line about how I'd encouraged him and all I can say is that if you seriously think I encouraged a nasty piece of work like Miller you must think I'm awfully hard up."

"You know I didn't mean that, Fran. I was just trying to get the picture. Miller is so uptight. It's just hard to imagine him letting go enough to do something like that. I mean, it's more like something in a movie."

"Do you think I'm making it all up?" I asked in a dangerous tone.

"Of course not." He looked stung.

"I'm sorry, Brack. This has really gotten to me. I feel absolutely unclean and I guess I'm snapping at everybody in sight. You know how when people treat you like dirt some crazy little voice inside tells you that you must deserve it?"

"Yeah, I've noticed that. Well, what do you want to do about it? What can you do about it?"

"I *want* to kill him," I said bitterly. "But the impracticality of it, unfortunately, strikes me forcibly. They still put people in jail for murder. But I swear, after I threw him off, I picked up my brass planter and if he had taken another step in my direction, I expect they'd be taking my mug shot at this very moment."

Brack's face darkened. "If I thought you had a

prayer of making an assault case stick, I'd say go with it. Why should he get away with something like this? You can bet if some patient came in and assaulted Miller, the cops would be here in a minute."

"Then on top of making me feel defiled, not to mention putting me off garlic, he lays on all this stuff about Continental Health."

I could see by Brack's expression that he didn't know what I was talking about.

"You mean he hasn't told you about Continental Health?" I lost no time filling Brack in on Miller's plan to sell us all to Continental Health for twenty bucks an hour.

To my surprise, he was not disturbed by what I had to say about Miller's plan. He leaned back in his chair. "I don't take the whole thing seriously. Come on, Fran, you've got to see that Miller's acting erratically. I mean, I don't suppose he's routinely been jumping on top of colleagues since the year one. Word would have been bound to get around. He must be coming unglued. I expect it has to do with Avise seeing other men. After years of being divorced, she's finally starting to have other relationships, and Miller just can't handle it. It's as if he's trying to maintain the illusion that they're still in some sense married."

"But the bid to Continental Health—"

"Don't you see? His assault on you, his threats—I suppose you would call what he said about Continental Health a threat?"

"I certainly would."

"These are just efforts to assert his masculinity, to cover up his fears of inadequacy and loss."

I didn't doubt it for a minute. But Brack was thinking like a psychologist. I was thinking like a businessperson. Brack didn't seem to fully understand the nature of Miller's threat. Since Mrs. Smythe took care of the billing for the office, Brack probably did not realize how much of his business depended on insurance payments or what blow would be dealt to it if Miller put his plan into effect.

I took a sheet of paper from his desk and, speaking slowly in words of one syllable, explained to him exactly what the effects would be if Continental Health took over sixty percent of the local health insurance market and signed on Miller as its exclusive provider of psychological services. "Don't you see?" I concluded. "Chances are it would cut your business by sixty percent!"

"Well, of course that would be bad. But it probably won't happen. If it did, we'd make out somehow. I could live on less. People do. But what I'm trying to say is, I don't really think it's going to come to that. When Miller is finally able to deal with this business of Avise, he'll drop the blustering and start acting like a normal human being. Or as close as Miller can come to approximating a normal human being. I'll tell you something—he doesn't like dealing with people. I can't picture him in the kind of setup you're describing. With this triage business, he'd have to see patients all day. He'd hate it. Why do you think he went into testing and administration? To get away from patients."

"I hope you're right."

After I left his office, it occurred to me that there

was a fundamental difference between Brack's point of view and mine. It wasn't just that the natural tenor of Brack's personality was optimistic while I habitually kept an eye peeled for the next disaster. There was a real difference in our situations. Since Brack was busy all the time, it was hard for him to imagine his practice shriveling. Substantial change is always difficult to envision. It's so much easier to believe that life will always go on as usual. I daresay that back at the dawn of time, when a caveman innovator came up with the wheel, the majority of the village sat about chewing on their dinosaur bones muttering deprecatingly, "Just a fad."

But from my perspective, it was easy to imagine disaster. I had had a good taste of what a shortage of patients was like, and it was all too easy for me to believe that it could go on forever, that Miller could cut off my fledgling practice before it even developed.

I heard no more of Miller's plan for the remainder of the week. And no one stormed out of his or her office incandescent with rage the way I would have expected they would if he had put his proposition to all and sundry. I concluded that Brack had been right about Miller. His threatening flourishes had probably been his way of dealing with my repulsion of his advances.

After what had happened, I could scarcely quell a shudder as I walked past the man's closed office door. At the most unpredictable times, I would have a flashback to that awful moment when I was pinned under him. I felt as if I had been the unwilling participant to some unspeakable sexual perversion, and I couldn't shake the image from my brain. I was still horrified when I recalled the terrible helplessness I had felt during the first shock of Miller's assault on me. I couldn't forgive myself for those two or three seconds when I had been immobilized by my own surprise and disgust, seconds when Miller in his delusion apparently concluded that I welcomed his onslaught. The very thought of it made my flesh creep.

I thought a lot about what had happened the day Miller jumped me, and I finally persuaded myself that he had not actually intended to do me any harm. I was ready to believe that I had been the victim of the most incredible social ineptness it had ever been my misfortune to encounter. I acknowledged that it was even remotely possible that Miller actually believed this was how men went about making passes at women. After the way I had reacted, I did not really think he would try it again.

But I suppose Miller had succeeded in reawakened my memories of being a helpless child because in spite of all this, I ended up doing something I was really ashamed of. I went to a sporting goods store and bought several pounds of lead shot. When I repotted my philodendron, I poured the shot in as a drainage layer, under the potting soil.

Sometimes in the days that followed, I often looked at that philodendron and blushed. As a supposedly grown-up psychologist, I was embarrassed that I felt the need to have a plant that should have been registered as a lethal weapon. What it said about my inner sense of security, I didn't even like to think.

Luckily, I soon had more immediately pressing things to think of. The following Monday, my first patient crossed the threshold, referred by his high-school counselor. He propped his boots on my desk and lit a cigarette. Since I had no windows, I could only hope that the air-conditioning was up to meeting the challenge of the smoke that billowed from his mouth. I backed away a little and regarded him with professional compassion. With his black hair stiffened by mousse until it resembled an LP record shattered by a terrorist attack and with his full upper lip lifted into a sneer, he had all the winsome charm of the young Attila. But I was keen to understand him. If I were able to help this boy, the counselor would send more cases my way. I would have established my first solid source of referrals.

"You seem to be having some difficulties at school, Mark," I said in a soothing voice. "Would you like to tell me about them?"

"They keep throwing me out is all."

"You don't enjoy school?"

"I hate it. Bunch of assholes."

"What would you rather be doing?" I asked, placing the tips of my fingers together.

"I want to make a lot of money like my brother-in-law. He's an optometrist. Glasses. You know. I want a Maserati, or maybe a Ferrari. Right now I've got a Harley Davidson. One fantastic set of wheels. But a guy doesn't stay sixteen forever, you know. You gotta move up. Get something with a little class."

I looked thoughtfully at his unfocused eyes. With his sense of style and his values, this boy could have gone far in a homicidally oriented motorcycle gang. The problem was that he had been born into a respectable, if materialistic, middle-class family.

"Do you do drugs much?" I asked.

"What do you think I am? Nah. Maybe a little speed, a little crack. Nothing major. I like to keep my head straight because I don't want to trash my Harley, you get me?"

With a surge of disappointment I realized that there was no way this kid could be treated outside a tightly secure inpatient drug-rehabilitation center. That was what I was going to have to tell his parents even though it meant saying good-bye to my first and only patient. I listened to how his teachers, his girlfriends, and his parents were always on his case, then I said, "I'll give your parents a call. You might be happier in some alternative school situation. I think we'd better consider a drug-rehabilitation clinic. I'll find out about what's available in this area, and then we'll talk about it."

"Drug rehab? No way!" he said angrily. "Look, lady, I don't have a drug problem. You've got it all wrong. I can stop anytime I want. You don't know what you're talking about, hear me? Where do you think you get off talking about sending me to rehab?" His voice grew shrill. "You don't know your ass from your elbow, you headshrinkers. Lock me up? That'll be the day!"

After he slammed the door behind him, I noticed smoke rising from my wastebasket. When I prodded the papers, I saw a tongue of flame. Coughing, I swiftly threw the hefty volume Principles of Preventive Psychiatry onto the fire to smother it. Then, grabbing the wastebasket, I rushed out to the bathroom, gingerly fished out the slightly charred book, and doused the remaining fire with water. As I was coming back out of the bathroom in a cloud of smoke holding the wastebasket full of sodden ashes, I ran into Brack.

He took in the situation in a glance. "You don't want to build a practice with that kind of kid," he advised. "You'd end up dead."

I pushed the hair out of my eyes, realizing too late that this probably left a streak of ash over my forehead. "That had occurred to me," I said.

I took the smoky trash can outside to the dumpster. That was how I happened to be coming back through the waiting room just after James Brannigan arrived with his daughter.

I must have been more shaken than I had realized by my first sociopathic patient because the sight of the Brannigan family seemed to do odd things to my respiratory system. I had trouble getting my breath. James Brannigan looked so familiar yet was so out of my own plane of existence that I felt as strong a shock as if the face on the dollar bill had said hello.

Brannigan's eyelashes were thicker and his skin clearer than that of ordinary mortals. He was dark, with a slightly aquiline nose and the broad decisive planes in his cheekbones and jaw that the camera loves. Without being precisely pretty, he nevertheless made you think that the myth of Narcissus might be based on a true story. It was a face you could have looked at all day.

His daughter stood beside him, her fairness a foil to his dark good looks. She was simply the most beautiful teenager I had ever seen, a girl with corn-silk blond hair and eyes that flashed periwinkle blue. Against the prosaic background of the office with its standard beige carpet and curtains, the beauty of the Brannigans flamed out, as exotic as if a Bedouin chieftain, his person adorned with gold coins and his Arabian steed tasseled in scarlet, had galloped up in front of Mrs. Smythe's window.

Staring, I stopped suddenly just inside the door, uncomfortably aware of the ashes distributed carelessly over my person.

"D-Doctor Fellowes," stuttered Mrs. Smythe, looking at me in dismay. "What happened to you?"

"Just a little accident. My last patient must have dropped a lit cigarette into my trash."

"You should post a No Smoking sign."

"Yes, I think I'll do that."

"Dr. Miller is running a few minutes behind," she told Brannigan. "But I'm sure he'll be with you shortly if you'll just have a seat. I hope you won't think I'm being presumptuous, Mr. Brannigan, but my granddaughter would just love to have your autograph. Do you think you could sign something for me?"

"Sure. Do you have something here?" Brannigan had a low, husky voice, one that seemed to purr "Come to me" and made knees turn to jellied madrilene.

Mrs. Smythe produced a copy of *Personalities.* As Brannigan signed it, I made my way cautiously past him. I was convinced that unless I speedily took myself out of range, I would end up asking for his autograph myself, which was strictly against my principles. Movie stars were, after all, only ordinary people who happened to make movies. If I only had a minute to regulate my heartbeat, I was sure I would remember that.

I went to the bathroom and washed the ashes off myself as best I could, then headed to the staff lounge. I intended to treat myself to something chocolate out of the snack machine. I figured that after what I'd been through, I deserved it.

I was sitting on the couch unwrapping a Hershey bar when James Brannigan came in and dropped some coins into the drink machine. The can came down with a clunk.

"Does that kind of thing happen to you very often?" he asked. "The fire, I mean."

I had difficulty concentrating on what he was saying because I was mesmerized by his face. There was something else about him, too. Far from behaving like the average nervous parent, he had the manner of a man about to slip into bed with a woman he has taken for granted for a long time.

I choked a little on my candy bar. "I told somebody he needed to be in drug rehabilitation before he was ready to hear it," I said. "The fire was his revenge, I think."

He looked me up and down. "So you're sup-

posed to wait for the magic moment to tell him or
something?"

"It can be tricky," I admitted. "With drugs, while
you're waiting for the right moment, the patient
could end up dead."

The way he stood carelessly and spoke softly, as
if he expected me to strain to hear him, made me
intensely uncomfortable. And much to my annoyance, I realized that I was straining to hear him.

"They said I could wait for Merris. But it'll be an
hour, an hour and a half. Had lunch yet?" he asked.

I looked at the candy bar in my hand. "Well, no,
but—"

"Let's go."

It never occurred to me to refuse. My feet would
have scurried on without me, whatever my mouth
had said. "All right. I have to get my pocketbook."

In my office I paused for a moment to collect
myself, and I recognized that whatever signals
Brannigan was giving off, this was no romantic
encounter. It was not even a social encounter. To be
sure, there were men who found me attractive. The
small freckles on the bridge of my nose had come in
for some favorable comment, and men gazing into
my eyes had often remarked on the gold flecks in the
hazel. My legs were first-rate. I did not kid myself,
however, that I was the sort of world-class beauty
who would attract the likes of James Brannigan. It
had to be as a psychologist that I interested him, not
as a woman. I wondered what he wanted.

We drove in his rented car to a nearby restaurant
called Sharkey's. Before we got out of the car,

Brannigan put on large mirrored sunglasses and a funky porkpie hat. The two additions obscured enough of him that the most anyone could have confidently said was that he looked an awful lot like James Brannigan. I sympathized. People who come to town seeking psychiatric help for their children don't want the news splashed all over the tabloids.

Sharkey's was almost empty since it was still early for lunch. We chose a section so steeped in gloom that Brannigan was forced to take off his sunglasses in order to grope his way to a booth. A small candle sputtered in a red glass on the table, giving negligible illumination.

Brannigan wasted no time on small talk. "Tell me about this guy Miller," he said as soon as we sat down.

I blinked, a bit thrown by the sudden question. "He's thought to be good," I said. "He wrote one of the standard texts on neuropsychological testing."

The waitress appeared, looked at Brannigan and then stared. The light was dim enough that the clipboard on which she took orders had its own light attached. Under such circumstances she could hardly have been sure of recognizing her own mother, but she made a game attempt to get a better look at him by moving the little candle closer to the rear of the table.

"No, don't move it," I said, blocking the candle with my hand. "It's just fine right there. We'll both have omelettes, please."

"What would you like to drink, sir?" she said,

hungrily eyeing Brannigan's corner of the booth.

"My brother will have the caffeine-free cola, and I'll have the same," I interposed. "We're in rather a hurry, so if you don't mind, would you step on it?"

She left, casting a regretful glance behind her.

"Your brother?"

"I had the idea you didn't want to be recognized."

"I like caffeine," he grumbled. "I live on caffeine."

I ignored his complaint. Now that my head was cool and the darkness hid his thick eyelashes, it was easier to treat Brannigan as an ordinary fellow human being. "You were asking me about Miller," I said. "Well, he's good. You can feel confident he'll do a thorough job. He may not look very prepossessing, but that doesn't matter. Some of the best people in the business are absolute toads."

"You don't like him," he said.

"No-o," I said slowly.

Of course, to say that I didn't like Miller was a gross understatement. Merely to be in the same room with him made my flesh creep. But I couldn't figure out why I had revealed even that much to Brannigan. My first and most professional instinct had been to say something vague and diplomatic. The only explanation I could think of for why I had told him the blunt if understated truth was that he seemed to have pulled it out of me. I had the oddest feeling that he was pleased with my answer.

"What's your name?" asked Brannigan. "Your first name."

"Fran," I admitted reluctantly.

"James." He smiled. As if I didn't know his name. "Okay, Fran, tell me. What's this Miller like? What makes him tick? That's your business, isn't it? Figuring out what makes people tick."

"Why do you want to know? I've only been in the office a couple of days. I don't know him very well."

He fiddled with the salt and pepper. "Why don't you like him?"

"If you want to know the truth, he's just kind of a creep." I added, "I think he likes to watch people squirm because it makes him feel more important."

I ended up telling Brannigan about the incident of the caricature. I did not, however, tell him about Miller's slapping his son Tim around or about his attack on me. That sort of stuff was bound to alarm him—his beautiful daughter even now was alone with Miller.

Not that I thought there would be any problem in that way. If Miller was in the habit of assaulting underage patients, he was more unglued than I thought he was.

"Also, he's a snob," I added.

"You don't like snobs."

"Can't stand them."

I could make out in the gloom that he was putting on his sunglasses and pulling his cap down to his ears as the waitress returned with our omelettes. She peered at him wide-eyed and was quickly succeeded by another girl bearing rolls in a basket. It was beginning to look as if every member of the staff would show up at our table if I didn't put a stop to it. A few minutes later a third girl appeared to ask if everything was all right.

"Fine," I said. "And could you see that we aren't disturbed? We have a lot of work to do."

She reluctantly disappeared.

"Do you always have your working lunches in total darkness?" asked Brannigan.

"I don't do that kind of work, Mr. Brannigan," I said sweetly. "Listen, I'm only trying to help."

"You make me look so dumb," he grumbled.

"You should worry. In a few days you go home but I have to live down the rest of my life that I have an eccentric, deaf, and dumb brother who wears funny hats."

His teeth flashed white in the darkness. "How'd you get into this psychology business, huh?"

The question had very much the flavor of "What's a nice girl like you doing in a dump like this" and I found myself bristling.

"The usual way. Went to school and then just kept on going to school."

"You know what I mean." He took off the sunglasses and leaned back against the seat. I could see the whites of his eyes as he looked at me. "How come crazy people? What's the appeal? I don't get it."

"You don't think people are interesting?"

"Some of them."

I took a deep breath. "It's this way—I had this father who thought he owned the world, especially that he owned me. He was a very strong personality." I shrugged. "It's hard to describe. I mean, you'd think that sort of person went out with the nineteenth century."

"Oh, I've known a few," Brannigan said. "Mostly directors."

"Yes, well, the thing is my father had"—I hesitated, searching for words—"a fair amount of power. On top of it, he was like some wind off the desert." I laughed mirthlessly. "He leveled everything and wiped out all independent life. It was his way."

"You seemed to have survived okay."

"Thank you," I said. "Anyway, I suppose I got interested in psychology by way of my father. I kept asking myself why he was the way he was? And especially—why do people let him get away with it?"

"Got it figured out?"

I smiled. "Still working on it. Guess I'll be well adjusted in my next life."

"You're the first shrink I've known that had a sense of humor."

"Ah, but how many shrinks have you known?"

"More than I'd like. Look, I want you to see Merris."

I stared at him in surprise. "But I thought she was coming in on a neuropsych consult." Already, I could imagine Miller's rage—perfectly justifiable in this case—at my stealing his patient.

"She doesn't need more testing. Feininger's is giving her the works. Just talk to her, or whatever it is you people do."

"You mean take her as a therapy patient?"

"Yeah."

"But aren't you going to be in town for just a short while?"

"So see her a short while."

"I'm not following you. Why do you want me to see her?"

"I like you."

Even though the intelligent part of my mind told me James Brannigan was not interested in me as a woman, a more primitive part of me grew warm at the compliment.

He moved the candle to the middle of the table and I caught my breath a little as the perfect planes of his face came into view.

It was a struggle to maintain a professional demeanor. "What seems to be bothering her?" I asked.

"Her mother died. She needs somebody to talk to."

"Is that why she's being tested at Feininger's? This is a grief reaction we're talking about?"

"I guess." He rubbed the side of his nose with his finger. "Look, I don't want her to have any more testing. I just want her to talk to somebody."

If this was a grief reaction, I asked myself, why the neuropsychological testing? None of this made sense. But who was I to complain? I, who had had only one official patient so far and that one an aspiring arsonist.

Even though I was desperate for patients, however, a few qualms persisted.

"You know, when a therapist sees an adolescent," I said carefully, "he or she doesn't go and tell the parents what the patient says. The therapy session is private. I can maybe give you a prognosis, give you some idea of what kind of treatment would be good and how long it would take, but I'm not going to inform on Merris. Therapy doesn't work that way."

"You've got it wrong. That's not what I'm after." I detected a note of amusement in his voice. "Just talk to her," he said.

"But how long do you expect to be here? When do you have to get back to your work?"

"We start shooting in September. I'm taking the summer off to get Merris straightened out."

I had to admit that my reaction to Brannigan was very odd. I always had said I couldn't stand men who were dictatorial. But in spite of myself, I found myself responding to Brannigan like a sailboat to a following wind. Something about his arrogant tone set my blood running fast. His was a game I knew how to play, the game of sparring with the high-handed male. I'd had lots of practice at it, after all.

Seeing Merris could be interesting from a professional standpoint, too, I reminded myself. I had begun to be a little curious about what she was like. Was that arrogance of Brannigan's carried on a dominant gene? I shot him a curious look. "Just book the appointment with Mrs. Smythe."

When we got back to the office, Avise MacBride was in the waiting room picking up one of her patients. She was wearing a classically simple dress of pale blue crepe studded with covered buttons in a row down her back, and her bearing, as usual, was queenly. But seeing us, she spoiled the regal effect somewhat when she nervously lifted her hand to check her hair. "Hullo, James."

"Hi, Avise. How are you getting along?"

"Splendidly. You know I went back to get my master's in psychology?"

Brannigan scuffed his tennis shoe idly against the carpet. "No, I didn't know. You like the work?"

"Love it." She gave a silvery laugh. "I guess you could say I've found myself." Her bell-like tones were worthy of better lines.

A door opened in the hallway and Miller's voice sounded in the silence. Avise swallowed convulsively, then turned quickly to her patient. "Mr. Brown?" A stout black man stood up. "Would you follow me?" Then, leading Mr. Brown, she moved with measured steps down the hall.

"I didn't realize you knew Avise," I said. I was wondering what to make of the little tableau I had just witnessed.

"It was a long time ago." He looked away.

Miller came into the waiting room with Merris at his side—it was beauty and the beast. But the beast was wearing such an ingratiating smile that I hardly recognized him.

"I'll need to schedule another hour with Merris, Mr. Brannigan," Miller was saying. "Will that be convenient?"

Brannigan shoved his hands in his pockets. "When?"

"Anytime. Just tell Mrs. Smythe when you can make it, and she will rearrange my other appointments to accommodate you. I know you're a very busy man."

Mrs. Smythe's face appeared at her window. I realized Brannigan would probably book an hour with me at the same time he booked the follow-up visit with Miller. I began to regret I hadn't given special instructions to Mrs. Smythe. I hated to think that even now she might be murmuring, "Dr. Fellowes? Oh, she can take Merris at any time. Her appointment book is absolutely empty."

When Brannigan finished with Mrs. Smythe, Miller was still standing by, keen to be of service. "If you have any questions, any questions at all, don't hesitate to ask," he urged. "Mrs. Smythe will give you my home phone number, and please do feel free to call at any time."

Brannigan shot him a look of ill-concealed loathing and turned abruptly on his heel and fled the office. Merris, obviously mystified, followed him. I went after them.

As I quietly closed the office door behind me, I observed that Brannigan was every bit as good-looking standing in the full glare of the lot. The faint crow's-feet that were now evident at the corners of his eyes did not detract from his appeal one whit. Merris was already halfway across the parking lot, obviously plenty eager to put the offices of Psychological Associates well behind her. But Brannigan paused a moment at the curb and stared across the street, looking troubled.

I wasn't sure what had caused his self-confidence to waver so perceptibly. Was it meeting up with Avise, who was evidently an old friend, and maybe something more? Or was it merely his evident hatred of Miller? Then suddenly he put on his mirrored sunglasses and the troubled look vanished behind them. He was once again very much the movie star traveling incognito. I noticed that even though he was dressed as inconspicuously as possible in a colorless cotton sweater and tight jeans, his drab clothes only pointed up the quality of the product contained within. But maybe, to do him justice, the effect wasn't deliberate. Maybe he had hoped to remain inconspicuous.

"So, did you get it all set up with Mrs. Smythe?" I asked.

He stared at me as if seeing me for the first time. "Oh, yeah. All set. Merris'll be coming around. I'll mention it to her when we get home."

"Is there anything else I ought to know before I see her?" I asked.

"Nah." A brief smile lit his face. "You two are going to like each other."

"I hope I can help," I said.

When I stepped back into the office, Miller was still in the waiting room. The man looked as cheerful as if he had spent the morning evicting widows and orphans. He was actually rubbing his hands together in satisfaction. "You notice, Fran, that I know how to deal with people like that."

I edged toward the hall, but I tried at the same time to assume a respectful look, something that has never come easy to me.

"In my experience," he burbled, "people who have risen to the top of their professions invariably have a great deal on their minds and are grateful when you recognize their special needs. They like to feel you are ready to go the extra mile." His pale eyes misted nostalgically. "I remember when I treated—I won't say who—but anyway, a well-known opera singer, absolutely topflight singer. She said to me, 'Dr. Miller, you're always there for me.' That's what I aim for. I have many demands on my time, you see, being something of an authority. And since I work under pressure myself, I flatter myself that I understand these people better than most."

I made a noncommittal noise all the while wondering what he expected. A rousing chorus of "For He's a Jolly Good Fellow"?

The office door opened then, letting in a blast of hot air, and Tim Miller came in. I wondered momentarily if I had made a mistake in not buying that earthquake insurance. With Tim and his irate father less than a leap apart, catastrophe seemed imminent. Indeed, when I glanced uneasily at Miller, he was puffing up like a startled reptile, his chest, nostrils, and cheeks expanding at the sight of Tim. I would have much preferred not to be standing between the two of them.

Mrs. Smythe stuck her head out the window as if on cue. "Dr. Jim Feininger for you, Dr. Miller, on line four," she said. As far as I was concerned, no deus ex machina had ever been a more welcome interruption. Miller pivoted on one foot and without speaking stalked to his office. The door slammed behind him with a muffled thud, the carpet and the acoustic ceiling drinking up the noise.

Miller was adept at conveying his venom without saying a word, I noticed. The smell of his revolting after-shave lingered on the air.

"I guess he's still mad," I offered.

Tim ignored the comment. "Who was that girl?" he asked.

I was impressed by his coolness. His father's rage seemed to have had no effect on him at all. He was evidently one of those plucky souls who could have watched *Friday the Thirteenth* while partaking heartily of popcorn. I myself was a bundle of nerves.

"The girl I saw in the parking lot," he insisted. "The blonde. Is she a patient or something?"

"The girl? That's Merris Brannigan. Beautiful, isn't she?"

"You know her?"

"Don't look at me." I was amused. "I don't have her phone number. I don't have her address either."

"I wonder who would?" His eyes narrowed in speculation.

"Dunno." I grinned at him. "Good luck."

A few minutes later, as I was futilely searching the hall closet for a feather duster, I learned that it had taken Tim only a few minutes to figure out who would have Merris's phone number. He was standing at Mrs. Smythe's window, dangling a set of car keys on one finger.

"She must have dropped them when she was getting in the car," he was telling Mrs. Smythe earnestly. "I tried to get her attention, but they drove off too fast. I thought that if you knew where she lived, I'd just run them on by there."

I caught his eye while Mrs. Smythe was looking up the address. He did not even bother to look embarrassed. He just grinned at me, proof, if I needed it, that the adolescent sex drive is a magnificent natural force.

I finally gave up on finding a feather duster and improvised by using paper towels instead. Not that there was much dust in my office as of yet, but I felt less anxious if I kept busy. As I ran a wad of paper towels over my desk surface and flicked it at my books, I found myself wondering again where Brannigan knew Avise from. I should have asked him. It would have seemed perfectly natural at the time. But I couldn't very well ask now, which was too bad because something was obviously going on. If Brannigan and Avise were such old pals, why had he asked me about Miller? Avise, as Miller's ex-wife, would obviously have been a much better source.

It had been a long day and at the end of it I was glad to pull into my own driveway. My house was in the posh section of Bailey City known informally as Doctor's Row, owing to the fact that only physicians had the wherewithal to afford it. The real estate agent had assured me in a hushed voice that the venerable Dr. Feininger himself had a mini-estate somewhere in the general neighborhood, though just where these hallowed grounds were I had never bothered to find out. I had concentrated my attention rather on finding a suitably lavish place to call my own. I think it was an assertion of my identity, as much as anything, that made me buy the house on Doctor's Row. I had lived in squalor with a fellow graduate student for the past year and had come to associate the love affair with the recyclable cans stacked in our hallway and the attendants hosing out body bags on the other side of the street. The apartment Jason and I had lived in had been just across from the city morgue. That had given me bad dreams just at first but had not bothered Jason in the slightest. His compassion was strictly geographical. That is, he worried terrifically about the death squads in El Salvador but was not at all bothered by the poor suckers being carted into the morgue any more than he worried about my picking up his dirty underwear off the bathroom floor. I knew he would have been horrified by the decadent luxury of my new house and thinking of that gave me a certain morbid satisfaction.

There were fringe goodies, as well. I had been brought up in a large house with tall ceilings and in some ways this place felt like coming home. I had plenty of air to breathe. I suppose, if I had kept a diary, I might have labeled this chapter of my life "return from squalor." Or maybe "escape from Jason." It amounted to the same thing.

After my exhausting day bemoaning my empty schedule book, I was in no shape to cook, so I called out for pizza. When the doorbell rang, I mentally congratulated Mamma Baroni's on a swift delivery, but it turned out to be Brannigan, leaning with an outstretched arm against the doorframe. He looked infuriatingly cool.

"I thought you were the pizza," I said.

"You don't have to sound so disappointed." He

stepped inside.

"How on earth did you find out where I live?"

"Your name's on the mailbox." He threw himself onto my couch with total lack of concern for the well-being of the springs.

I looked out disbelievingly at the mailbox, then reluctantly closed the front door.

"I'm next door. Rented the place for the summer." He flung his arms out on the back of the sofa. "Nice place you have here."

It was a nice place. But the place next door was even nicer, three stories complete with a large patio and a swimming pool. That would be the one Brannigan had rented. If I had thought about it, I suppose I could have predicted that he would somehow land in these posh precincts. For one thing, there weren't any other palatial houses in Bailey City as far as I knew. But it did seem bad luck that he should turn up right next door to me. I had been doubtful when I saw that empty house, but the real estate agent had assured me that house wasn't really a rental. The owners were only away for the year, he had said. Any tenant would be eminently suitable and definitely short term. It was my bad luck that Brannigan had fit the bill.

I was glad that a tall hedge separated our properties. The last thing I wanted was to feel that Brannigan was watching my every move. The way he was doing now, for instance.

"Business must be good." His eyes flickered to the Persian rug on which I had taken my first steps over a quarter of a century before.

"Family money," I explained briefly. "Fellowes Hotels." I could not believe I had said that. I hardly ever mentioned the family hotels. What was it about Brannigan that he had this effect on me? Why did I need to prove to him that I was somebody? The slip did not improve my spirits. "Want a beer?" I asked gloomily.

"Sure."

The doorbell rang again. This time it *was* the pizza. I was so rattled, I tipped the boy five dollars.

I looked at the big pizza box. Not much hope of pretending there wasn't enough for two. The pizza place had flatly refused to deliver a small pizza, and this one was the size of a cartwheel. "Want some?" I asked. I didn't want Brannigan sitting there on my couch, and I most emphatically didn't want him to stay for dinner. I had a hard day. I didn't figure I was up to dealing with Brannigan's questions and his unblinking gaze. The only problem was I couldn't seem to settle on a polite but firm way to get rid of him. Thus do wimps get swept along by more powerful and decisive personalities.

I went to get beer, napkins, and paper plates. Then I sat down at the other side of the coffee table and chewed on a piece of pizza. I wasn't hungry. Something odd was going on, and I knew I wasn't going to have any peace until I had figured out what it was.

Watching Brannigan under my lashes, I imagined myself writing a psychological report on him. "The patient presented as an exceptionally good-looking male in his late thirties. Dressed in his usual costume of tight blue jeans and a drab, textured shirt, he has the habit of hunching his shoulders and looking down as if he were shy, a quite deceptive impression. His manner is superficially amiable but he gives few clues as to what he is thinking." Those who hold that the eyes are the mirror of the soul, I thought, should have tried to read Brannigan's—black-lashed, brown, and opaque.

"Tell me," I said, "why did Feininger's refer Merris to Miller? What makes them suspect something neurological?"

"They didn't. I was the one who asked for the testing." For a moment or two, Brannigan was fully occupied dealing with wayward strings of mozzarella.

It was funny how easy it was for me to imagine him telling all those eminent doctors at Feininger's what to do. Neurological testing? No problem, Mr. Brannigan. Yessir, Mr. Brannigan, we'll set it right up.

What was it about him, anyway? His manner was low-key, yet I had the feeling he expected everyone would do just what he wanted and that he wasn't often disappointed. Not that any particular magical charm would be needed for him to get his way at Feininger's. His name and fame should have done the trick. Anyone can be affected by that kind of thing. Me, for instance. And I have such a fine character.

I cleared my throat. "You suspect some kind of organic involvement, then? I mean, you think there might be something wrong with her brain?"

"Sometimes she can't sleep, can't concentrate. Thought we'd better have it checked out." He licked tomato sauce off his fingers.

"Exactly why are you so interested in Miller?"

His eyebrows lifted a fraction. "Am I interested in Miller? I don't know. Guess I'm curious. He's kind of a funny-looking little guy, isn't he?"

"I guess." Of course we can't all look like movie stars. Abruptly I said, "Where do you know Avise from?" I found myself holding my breath awaiting his reply. It was ridiculous.

He shot me an amused look. "Now who's curious? What difference does it make?"

"It's just that you two seem to come from such different . . ." My voice trailed off. I had thought it would be awkward to ask about Avise and I had been right. I only hoped he didn't think I had some very personal interest in the question. His self-esteem needed no buttressing. "Naturally," I concluded with what dignity I could muster, "I wondered where you two had met."

"Avise used to do some acting. We worked together in New York, long time ago—getting on to eighteen years I guess it must be."

I was intrigued by this sudden revelation. "Avise was an actress?" Once the idea was suggested to me, I found it made surprising sense. She was too dignified to be true. It was as if she were acting out someone's idea of what a therapist should be.

"Some people thought she had talent," said Brannigan, "but looks like she found something she liked better than acting."

Suddenly, I put my finger on what had seemed false about that little scene I had witnessed in the waiting room. Avise had been going out of her way to convince Brannigan she was happy. No equivocation at all, either. Just "look how happy and successful I am," when in reality her situation stank. Miller had her under his thumb and she was writhing. I think I sensed the wrongness of it at the time. The super-happy facade so commonly seen at high-school reunions is, in normal life, used mostly when meeting divorced spouses and ex-lovers. That was what had made me feel she and Brannigan were something more than old friends.

"Did you two live together?"

He nodded.

My imagination reeled a second as I thought of what it would be like to go from Brannigan's bed to Miller's. The shock of a contrast like that could be fatal.

"Is that why you didn't ask her what you wanted to know about Miller?" I went on doggedly. "Because you two had been involved?"

"What is this, the third degree?"

I felt hot color rise to my face. It was true that I had been asking an awful lot of nosy questions. "I don't know," I said. "Something about this whole setup strikes me as peculiar."

"I like that!" He gave me an amused glance. "You people are always saying people ought to get help, but when I try to do it you act as if I'm up to no good."

He had a point. After all, what was so strange about a father getting therapy for his bereaved daughter? The expense of therapy was obviously no problem for him. And maybe Merris needed some-body to talk to. Maybe it was as simple as that.

Except what was going on with Brannigan fixing it for her to have testing? What made him jump to the conclusion she needed a neurological workup just because she was a little absentminded? I would imagine that most parents would think first of drugs.

"Anyway," I said, "for whatever reason, you didn't like to ask Avise about Miller, huh? That's why you took me out to lunch and pumped me."

"What's this thing you've got about Miller, Fran? I don't give a damn about Miller. I was just making conversation. Haven't you ever had a guy take you out to lunch just for the hell of it?"

Checkmate. I sighed. "Is that why you came over here tonight? For the pleasure of my company?"

"Actually, I thought I'd fill you in on some of the background about Merris. Is that okay?"

"Oh." I was conscious of mild disappointment. What did I want from him anyway? "Sure," I said. "That's fine. You said that the problem was a grief reaction, right?"

"Merris's mother killed herself."

I was taken aback. "I'm sorry."

"I thought you might already know about it. She jumped out of an eighth-floor window at Feininger's." He wiped his fingers on his napkin. "That's why I don't like to see Merris feeling down. It worries me."

"Well, I can see why you're concerned." I frowned. "In a case like that you have to worry about identification with the mother, longing to rejoin her—"

He interrupted me. "Merris doesn't know it was suicide. We sent her to Switzerland the morning I got word. I mean, it was, like, zap—I get the news and Merris is on the plane. I figured that was the only way. I knew it was going to be all over the newspapers and I didn't want her to have to read that junk. And the pictures, God." He made an involuntary gesture of disgust. "Anyway, we fixed it so she was out of the country before it hit the news. She thinks Jessica died in a car accident, and that's the way I want to keep it."

"Are you sure she doesn't know?"

"It's like I just told you. She's been in Switzerland ever since it happened. With Rosemary—that's my secretary—and Isaacs, my bodyguard. They've both been with me since the year one and I'd trust them before I'd trust myself. Believe me, I was glad I had somebody I could count on. It was a nightmare." His expression grew bleak. "The way it turned out, it worked out pretty well because I was working in Italy and Spain last summer. A couple of weeks afterward I flew over, and I got to see a lot of Merris, more than if she'd been in the States."

"She didn't even go to the funeral?"

"We didn't have a funeral. It would have been a circus. Just a private burial and a memorial service in Lucerne. Naturally, Merris went to that." He picked up a slice of pizza. "Anyway, now that we're back in the States, the whole story's long since blown over."

"Aren't you afraid she'll find it out from somebody else? What about when they interview you?

Wouldn't it come up?"

He shrugged. "When the movie's released—I'll worry about it then. I figure if she finds out later, it won't matter so much. She was fourteen when it happened. She's fifteen now. Every day that goes by she's tougher."

Brannigan didn't sound a bit like a concerned parent asking for help. I wondered where I came in. "I'm not sure what it is you want me to do," I said finally.

"Merris isn't happy. I want you to fix that."

I smiled.

"What's so funny?"

"If I could fix unhappiness, I would be a very busy psychologist."

He wiped his hands carefully. "Good pizza. I'd better be getting back now."

I walked with him to the door.

"Good night." He gave me a smoldering glance.

"Wait a minute. Stop right there." I was aware that there was a desperate note in my voice, but I didn't much care. "Tell me one thing. Is it my imagination, or are you all the time coming on to me?"

He grinned. "Sorry." He thrust his hands into his pockets as he walked out onto the porch. "Habit."

For a second there, I almost liked the man.

five ///

At ten o'clock the next morning, Mrs. Smythe buzzed me that Merris had arrived and I went to collect her. To my relief there was no sign of her father. I wanted to do a good job with Merris and I knew her father was capable of being a distraction of the highest order.

She followed me back to my office, sat down, and looked at me, the blue in her eyes neatly matching the blue pattern of the chintz. Her small nose and her delicate chin seemed to have been designed by God for the covers of magazines. I was so struck by the utter perfection of her looks that for a minute I didn't say anything.

"Is anything wrong?" she asked.

"Sorry. It's just that the last person who sat in that chair wore boots and had breath like a burning tire." I paused. "I'm Dr. Fellowes, and in case you're wondering, I don't report back to your father about what you tell me. He only pays the bills. So you don't have to worry about that. Is there anything in particular on your mind that you'd like to talk about today? Is anything bothering you?"

"What's bothering me is that I'm being carried around to see all these doctors, and that people ask me dumb questions and tell me to do dumb things like arrange blocks and tell stories about pictures. This is summer vacation? No thanks."

I could understand her point of view, all right. "Why do you think your father brought you here?"

"I don't know." She wrinkled her nose. "I thought at first it was because he was afraid I was going to kill myself like my mother did."

I fiddled with the paperweight on my desk. So it was just as I had suspected. Brannigan hadn't been able to keep the truth from her after all. "I was told that you didn't know how your mother died." I looked up at her. "How did you find out?"

"Simple. I knew everybody was hiding something from me, so I just looked up the obit in *The New York Times* at the library in Zurich. Then I tracked down the news story of the inquest."

I scribbled on my notepad: Intelligent, resourceful fifteen-year-old.

"What's that you're writing down?"

"Just that you're a smart kid."

"Suicide while the balance of the mind was disturbed. That's what the inquest said." Tears began to roll down her face, and I handed her the box of tissues.

"You feel sad about that," I said.

"Of course you feel sad when your mother dies." She blew her nose. "You're going to try to tell me there's something sick about that? But mostly I'm mad. She was at this dumb hospital. They were supposed to be taking care of her, and they blew it. Daddy should have sued them."

I was surprised that I hadn't considered that aspect of the matter before. What was a suicidal patient doing near an eighth-floor window? I began to think I would like to see the inquest report myself.

She blew her nose again and hiccuped. "I was really surprised when Dad brought me to this same dopey hospital, Feininger's. Anybody can see they don't know what they're doing. You wouldn't believe how it gets to me to be around that place, thinking about Mamma."

"Why don't you tell your father how you feel?"

"It's this way—I don't want him to know that I know about Mamma. You see? I figure if he's all this worried about me when he doesn't even know that I know, how is he going to act when he finds out I do know?"

"I see your point. But I think if it upsets you to be around Feininger's, you ought to tell your father. He could take you somewhere else."

I wonder why he didn't, I thought. Even if Brannigan didn't blame Feininger's for his wife's death, the hospital and grounds were bound to have sad associations for him as well as for Merris. Sure, Feininger's was world-famous, but it wasn't the only decent hospital in the world.

"Do you ever worry that you might kill yourself?" I asked.

"Oh, I think about it, sure. I don't mean I think about killing myself. I just mean I sometimes ask myself if I could end up like Mamma. But I don't think so. I'm not much like her. She was a very sensitive person. Anybody could hurt her feelings. She sort of went to extremes, too. When she was up she was just plain gaga with happiness, and when she was down, she cried an awful lot. Everybody's always said I'm more like my dad. Dad and I don't get our feelings hurt—we just get mad."

This looked to me like a healthy identification with the father. It also looked like normal grief, a smart kid coping pretty well with an unhappy reality. Either I was reading Merris entirely wrong, or Feininger's was wasting its time doing a battery of tests on her.

"Merris, I want you to do me a favor," I said. "I promised your father I wouldn't give you any tests, and I'm not going to—not exactly. I just want you to look at these ink blots and tell me what they remind you of."

I pulled out my Rorschach cards and spent the next forty-five minutes scribbling notes like mad. There's nothing more exhausting to record than the Rorschach of an intelligent, verbal, imaginative subject. A subject who is hiding something or repressing something might look at card six and draw a blank, giving the therapist's writing hand a short break. I have known subjects to draw blanks on three or four successive cards, which is pathological, but very restful for the tester. But Merris never drew a blank. She produced associations freely, saw beautifully integrated wholes as well as common details, gave movement responses as well as some color, and came out with one or two originals along with the populars.

When we had finished, I shook my right hand in the hope of restoring feeling to the fingers.

"I've done those ink blots before with Dr. Miller," Merris said, "but I said I'd do it again for you because I kind of like to. It's fun."

I wiggled my fingers, trusting I would regain the full use of them by nightfall. I smiled weakly. "How do you like it here in Bailey City? Aside from being dragged over to Feininger's, I mean."

"Oh, I like it. I've met this boy. I can't tell you how great it is to talk to a regular American boy again. Tim Miller—doesn't that sound incredibly American?" She stretched out luxuriously in the chair. "You can't imagine, after a whole year of guys named Wolf and Zi-Zi and Jean-Pierre! Anyway, I asked Tim to come over sometime and swim in our pool."

"Is he going to do that?"

"Sure. He doesn't have a pool. Besides"—she gave me a frank glance with those blue eyes—"to tell you the truth, I usually don't have any trouble getting boys to pay attention to me."

That I could believe. "Well, our time is up now," I said.

She stood up. When she shook the pale hair off her shoulders, it moved with the heavy, fluid motion of those silken fringes seen in Victorian parlors. I found myself hoping that this girl was not going to add complications to Tim Miller's already difficult life.

"Am I supposed to come back and see you again?" she asked. "Or what?"

"Why don't you talk that over with your father and the two of you can decide."

After she left, I painstakingly scored the Rorschach. I did everything with it but make it sing "Dixie" in A minor. Being fresh out of school, I had a natural horror of pronouncing someone normal only to have her later proclaim to all and sundry that she could plug herself into light sockets. But no matter how I looked at the data it said, "Bright, normal kid." I wondered what Feininger's was making of their complete battery. Were they scratching their heads the way I was and wondering why this girl's father had brought her thousands of miles for treatment? Or were they persuading themselves that they saw problems that only years of exceedingly expensive therapy could fix?

Before I left the office that evening, I lifted Brannigan's phone number out of Mrs. Smythe's appointment book. I thought a little chat was in order.

I worked on keeping my indignation warm as I drove home. What did Brannigan mean by dragging his daughter all over getting her tested when there was nothing wrong? He was up to something. I was sure of that. But why bring Merris into it? What kind of a father was he?

I intended to say a few sharp words to him when I got home. Unfortunately, it looked as if I wouldn't be getting home soon. The car was listing and there was an ominous repetitive flapping sound coming from underneath. Climbing out of the car in high heels, I surveyed the damage. The tire was so flat the wheel was practically resting on its rim. I looked up and down the pine tree-lined road. No gas station or telephone in sight, naturally.

I don't like to think of myself as one of those helpless types who can't cope with the internal combustion engine, so I had once made it a point to learn how to pump my own gas and check my oil and water. I could also change a tire—in theory. That is, I knew exactly how to do it, but I hadn't actually done it yet. The skies were black with rain clouds, and a fresh breeze augured ill for those planning outdoor car repairs.

I looked inside the trunk. Spare tire—check. Tire iron—check. Funny little thing to hook the tire iron into thus turning it into a jack—check. I pulled out the tire iron and pried off the hubcap. It popped off easily, making it suddenly plain to me why hubcaps are always getting stolen. With the hubcap off, I could see the lugs that held the wheel onto the axle. Now came the sticky part. I was going to have to jack up the car. I wished I hadn't read any of those gory newspaper accounts of what happened when jacks slip out squashing hapless owners under the car.

I looked up and down the road again. I was on a stretch of blissfully picturesque and undeveloped road. Hell.

A tan Mercedes appeared on the horizon. This was reassuring—I felt that the average kidnapper-murderer-rapist stalking the highways does not drive a Mercedes. Abandoning my feminist principles, I leaned limply against the bumper and did my best to look like a damsel in distress.

The car pulled up at once and James Brannigan got out. "Car trouble?"

I stiffened. I was not quite as willing to act the damsel in distress for Brannigan's benefit. Also, being rescued by him would put me in a bad position for saying the sharp things I planned to say. "I was just about to change my tire." I made a grand gesture with the tire iron.

He smiled and folded his arms. "Can I watch?"

I threw the tire iron into my backseat. "No. You can give me a ride to the nearest gas station."

"I'll give you a ride home. You can call the gas station from there."

He got back into his car, and I slid in next to him. The leather on the seat was still so new, it gave off that lovely smell that I associate with well-kept tack rooms. Brannigan had obviously just come from swimming. A towel slung around his neck was soaking up the water dripping from his hair, and his thin shirt was sticking to him. His wet hair curled slightly, and in the shadowy interior of the car, his head looked like one of those darkly beautiful heads by Caravaggio that seem to be forever gazing at things bloody and decapitated.

He felt my gaze. "This Feininger asked me over to his place," he explained, "and I no sooner hit his pool than this pack of neighbors showed up." His lips twisted wryly. "I didn't wait to dry off before I got out of there."

"Next thing they'll be camping on your lawn."

"Maybe so." He shook his head. "You can't trust anybody anymore."

I couldn't get over how chummy Brannigan seemed to be with the people at Feininger's. You would think they'd be shaking in their shoes for fear he would sue after what had happened to his wife. Of course, maybe they were trying to keep him from baring litigious teeth by softening him up with hospitality. It was possible.

"Do you know Dr. Feininger pretty well?"

He smiled. "Obviously not."

Face it, the man had a smile that would melt iron ore. But that was neither here nor there. I had decided to let neither his indisputable beauty or my gratitude for his rescuing me stand in the way of the necessary confrontation about Merris. In slightly different circumstances, I might have assumed I had here a simple case of a father projecting his own fear and depression onto his child. Or that since the death of his wife, Brannigan was being morbidly overprotective of his only daughter. These were logical theories but they just didn't square with what I sensed about him. In the course of my training, I had seen a lot of upset and worried parents, and Brannigan was not like any of them.

"As you know, I saw Merris today," I began. "I was just wondering—what did Feininger's say about her?"

"Why don't you ask them?"

"Okay, I will. Will you sign a medical release form?"

"Nope." He smiled amiably.

"Nothing's wrong with Merris, is there? Why are you bringing her around to Feininger's and having a complete workup? Why the testing by Miller? Why the therapy with me?"

"I'm concerned."

"I don't believe it."

He looked at me with amusement.

"You aren't worried about Merris. You aren't even worried that all this testing is going to give her the idea that something's wrong with her. You think she's too solid to start thinking that."

"I like the way you charge off half-cocked," he said slowly. "You know, with no evidence or anything."

"I'm cute when I act like an idiot?"

"Something like that."

He was right, I thought suddenly. I was getting out of line. For all I knew he was worried sick about Merris and was simply too self-possessed to show it. I didn't have any right to sit there accusing him. Raindrops began to splat on the windshield, and a flash of lightning briefly illuminated the woodland landscape around us. We were now past the unspoiled stretch of road and were going along a thoroughly spoiled bit. Though the rain was coming down heavily, I could make out the gaudy colors of a pizza parlor, a quick oil-change place, a dry cleaner, and a grocery store near a neighborhood shopping center. Brannigan did not slacken his speed.

"Guess who's hanging out at our house these days?" he said. "Your Dr. Miller's kid, Tim. He came over with some car keys he thought belonged to us, and he's hardly been out of the place since. Kid eats like a horse."

"Not much like his father, is he?" I said.

Brannigan frowned. "No. No, he's not."

"Red light," I commented as we ran it.

Brannigan quickly returned his attention to the road, looking as near to embarrassed as I had ever seen him.

"They shouldn't put those red lights right out in the middle of the road like that," I said sympathetically.

"Well, it is practically out in the country, for crying out loud."

I couldn't quite fathom Brannigan's attitude toward Tim. He seemed pleased that Tim had shown up at his house and yet under that I sensed in him a certain restlessness about the idea. Not that it necessarily meant anything. Mixed feelings are pretty common in fathers when their daughters begin taking an interest in other males.

The car turned again, and the small businesses gave way to broad lawns and hedges. A minute later we pulled up in front of my house.

Even though I knew I was being silly, I couldn't bring myself to thank him for the ride. I quickly opened the car door and stepped out into a puddle. With my feet squishing in my delicate Italian shoes, I strode in the direction of my door. Water streamed in runnels down either side of my nose, and my hair was pasted to my cheeks and neck. I stood at the door fumbling for my key while rivulets ran down my neck and trickled in warm drops down my back.

Finally inside the house, I stepped out of my shoes and left them drooping on the tile floor of the foyer. In the bathroom, I stripped and draped my clothes over the shower rod to dry. Wrapping a robe around myself, I toweled my hair to passable dryness on my way to the phone. I called a service station and arranged for them to retrieve my car. Then I decided to talk to Avise MacBride. I had a few questions for her. I needed to put my suspicions about Brannigan to rest for good. Or else confirm them.

It would probably have made more sense for me to ask my questions of Brack Prideaux, but I was afraid he would wonder what I was up to. Avise, on the other hand, had too many of her own worries to have much curiosity left about what I was doing. At least that was what I figured.

I dialed her number. When I reached her, I was careful to lay it on about how I wanted to get familiar with the local inpatient units. Then I asked who would know about the workings of things at Feininger's. A few minutes later, when I hung up, I had scribbled on my notepad the name of a nurse who worked on the floor at the adult unit. I gave a small, satisfied sigh. If everything went according to plan, I would soon be a whole lot better informed about the circumstances of Jessica Brannigan's death.

On Monday, I had an appointment to meet the nurse, ostensibly to learn more about the inpatient offerings at Feininger's. We met at the Primrose Inn, which was famous for its chess pie. The inn's decor was Colonial Williamsburg as interpreted by the plate-glass industry. Broad sheets of smoked glass looked out onto boxwood bushes nestled in beds of pine bark nuggets. The interior featured cream-colored wainscoting, Wedgwood blue-patterned wallpaper, brass sconces, and an impressively efficient air-conditioning system. Outside were prim Colonial eaves and, atop it all, a brass weathervane for those who cared to see which way the wind was blowing.

My nurse, Eunice Caruthers, turned out to be a plump woman whose large features looked kindly. More important, she immediately revealed a weakness for gossip, which was fine with me. I didn't want a responsible, conscientious type. I wanted the loose lips that sink ships.

To maintain my cover I began by asking intelligent questions about the facilities at Feininger's. Along the way, I also dished out a liberal dose of sympathy about Eunice's feet, which bothered her incredibly, being on them all day the way she was. In no time we were fast friends and I judged it safe to bring the conversation around to what I really wanted to know.

"Since you've been at Feininger's so long," I said, "you must have known Dr. Miller when he was clinical director at the unit."

"Oh, yes. He was at the clinic ten years, dear, but it seemed like a hundred, believe me. Picky, picky he was. He was a perfect maniac about people being on time. If you had a sick child or car trouble, did he care?" She sniffed.

"How was it that Dr. Miller happened to leave Feininger's? Wasn't he happy there?"

"My dear, *he* was happy. It was the rest of us who were miserable." She paused a moment as she spread three balls of whipped butter on her roll. "Not

that Feininger's asked for his resignation, you under-
stand. They backed him all the way. Of course, Dr.
Miller is very close to Dr. Jim—not old Dr. Charles
Feininger but the young Dr. Jim Feininger."

I presumed it was young Dr. Feininger whose
pool Brannigan had been swimming in the other
day. I was already wondering what he was like.
Eunice, it developed, had some opinions on that.

"Dr. Jim thinks he's God," she confided, "and Dr.
Miller agrees with him, so the two of them get along
like a house on fire." She patted her plump lips with
a napkin. "I think Dr. Miller's conscience bothered
him, if you want to know the truth. I think that's why
he resigned. Why, that poor girl would be alive
today if it weren't for him."

"You mean he was responsible for someone's
death?" I said in shocked tones.

"Oh, my dear, it was horrible." She shivered. "I'll
never forget it to my dying day. The screams. And
she was the most beautiful girl, too. But she was
awful depressed. Could hardly even dress herself,
poor thing. Couldn't sleep, couldn't eat. She was just
skin and bones. When she came in, she was put in a
semiprivate room at first because we were having
the second and third floors painted and we were
kinda crowded. She insisted on talking to the medical
director about it personally—that was Dr. Miller, of
course—and she told him she had to have a private
room on the top floor. She was used to a view, she
said. She felt hemmed in. Well, I ask you, a sick girl
like that—don't you think a person would stop and
think? Of course hindsight is twenty-twenty, but Dr.

Miller just bowed and scraped and moved her right up to the eighth floor without so much as a by your leave. He didn't even check with her therapist, Dr. Carmichael. She hadn't been in the room an hour before she jumped out the window."

"Horrible!"

"Oh, my dear, such a waste! I don't even like to think about it—it still gives me chills. I wouldn't be in Dr. Miller's shoes for anything. To have that on my conscience! I know we all make mistakes, but praise God I haven't made one yet that's killed somebody, knock on wood." She tapped formally on the polished table.

"Was it Jessica Brannigan?" I prompted her. "The girl who killed herself, I mean."

"I see you've read about it." She gave me a meaningful look. "It was in all the papers. To tell you the truth, I think Dr. Jim was absolutely petrified that we were going to be sued."

"I wonder why the husband didn't sue?"

"I don't know. Somehow it all blew over. I'll tell you, it's my belief that he just wanted to put all the unhappiness behind him. When you think about it, if they'd taken it to court they'd have to go all over it again, and it's not like anything could bring her back."

"True. I see what you mean."

"But this is the sad thing." She lowered her voice. "Do you know that the girl's daughter was over at Feininger's this very week? I guess she's breaking her heart about her poor mother. As they say in the Good Book, the parents eat sour grapes and the children's teeth are set on edge. In our business we see it again and again, don't we?" She picked up a fork and handily finished off the last of her ham with raisin sauce.

By then my fingers were numb from our sitting directly under the air-conditioning vent and I was surfeited with soft rolls and butter, but it had been worth it. I had found out what I wanted to know. Not only had Miller been medical director at Feininger's when Jessica Brannigan fell to her death, but—if Eunice was to be believed—he had been personally responsible.

The chess pie proved a desiccated-looking affair that reminded me forcibly of the custard pie found in flyspecked bus terminals. Eunice assured me it was a great delicacy, but with open cowardice, I ordered the fruit cup.

Over dessert I cradled my coffee cup in my hand. "You know, Eunice, I'd like to come over to the unit sometime and look around. Get a feel for the place. Should I ask for you?"

"I'd love to take you around, dear, but you'd do better to call the main office. I'm always tied up on the floor. Dr. Jim is the one who usually does the honors." She gave me a conspiratorial look. "I think that taking people around makes him feel as if the place actually belongs to him instead of to his dad, if you want to know the truth."

"So old Dr. Feininger still runs the place?"

"In a manner of speaking. He hardly ever comes in these days. He's getting pretty feeble. But when Dr. Jim told him he wanted to build a new wing on the substance abuse unit, you could have heard the roar from here to New York, and that was the end of that. Dr. Charles is still the one who calls the tune."

I was certainly getting plenty of information. The problem was, I wasn't sure what it meant. Was it actually possible that James Brannigan had come back here to enact some terrible vengeance on Miller? That might make a convincing plot for a Jacobean play, but it was hard to imagine it happening in modern-day Bailey City.

That afternoon when I got home from work, I decided to take Brannigan up on his invitation to use his pool, then casually mention what I had found out and watch his expression. Unfortunately, the only swimsuit I owned had been bought before I became a responsible professional woman. There was little to it in back and almost nothing to it on the sides. I resolved to check the stores as soon as possible for a replacement more suitable for a serious psychologist. Meanwhile, I threw an old shirt over the suit I had and headed next door. Right at the moment I was less concerned with modesty than with clearing up a few things.

Along the tall hedge that separated our properties, the grass gave way to a stand of thyme, its vaguely purplish blossoms bent under the weight of bees busy collecting pollen. I raised my hands to shield my face from the branches of the hedge and squeezed through, giving the thyme a wide berth. As I stepped into the next yard, I saw Brannigan at the far side of the pool. He dived off the diving board, his body arching white in the sunlight for a moment. There was a spatter of glittering water and then the translucent blue closed over him.

Merris was sitting under a pool umbrella with a tall, frosty drink. The white shirt that covered her swimsuit fluttered in the warm breeze, and she anchored her floppy hat with a firm tug before flashing me a smile. No sun-worshiper, she.

Tim Miller, in white shorts, sat at her feet with his sketchbook. His pen moved quickly over the paper.

"Hello, Merris, Tim."

Tim awkwardly struggled to his feet.

"Don't get up. I don't want to interrupt you."

"Show her what you're doing, Tim," said Merris. "He's really good. You should see some of his stuff, Dr. Fellowes."

"I already have."

Tim flushed. It struck me that the two of them were remarkably alike with their angelic blond coloring and that indefinable air of assurance in the way they held themselves. They were like echoes of each other. Tim, however, was not as cautious as Merris about the sun. The bridge of his nose was already red and peeling.

Brannigan's head came to the surface, sleek and dark as an otter, at the side of the pool. He pulled himself up and grabbed a towel.

Suddenly I realized that I could hardly cross-examine him in front of Tim and Merris. It was not as if there were any secluded corners around the pool where we could talk privately. And even if I got him to go inside the house with me under the pretext of getting a drink, the bodyguard and the secretary were presumably in there.

"Glad you came over. Want a drink?" Brannigan looked me up and down with a connoisseur's eye.

"Okay," I said weakly.

I hated to admit it, but my coming over to his place was another instance of my going off half-cocked. In a moment of insane optimism I had envisioned a scene in which he would look steadily into my eyes and tell me the truth. What a hope! Othello and Desdemona seeing a marriage counselor, Hugh Hefner confessing he's gay, Barbie dolls taking up nudism—all were more likely scenarios than Brannigan telling me the truth. I jumped in and swam twenty-four laps in sheer frustration.

Concluding this insane burst of activity, I hung clinging to the side of the pool, panting heavily. Brannigan was sitting near me on the edge dangling his feet in the water. He glanced down at the two drinks at his side. "Looks like yours got sort of melted. I'll get somebody to bring out another one."

"No, no," I gasped. "Don't bother." I hoisted myself out of the pool and caught the towel Brannigan threw at me. Merris and Tim had vanished.

Brannigan arranged himself languidly in a lawn chair and picked up the phone. "Could we have another gin and tonic out here?" he said into the receiver.

The staff must have had gin and tonics on tap because by the time I had dried myself off, a trim, graying woman, her face carefully blank, was placing a frosted glass on the table by Brannigan's lawn chair. She went back to the house at once and I realized this was the moment to begin drawing Brannigan out, but it was hard to summon the will for it. I couldn't make up my mind whether I was being ridiculous about my suspicions or not.

I stretched my tired arms and legs out on a lawn chair and took a long swig of the cold gin and tonic. I noticed that the thyme had crept through the grass on its way to the swimming pool, and in places the emerald grass had a slight purple haze. I listened to the buzzing of the bees on the thyme and saw through half-closed eyes that the sky was that absurd baby blue you see in Renaissance paintings. My skin felt tight as it dried, and I was conscious of that sense of well-being that comes from excessive exercise and a good stiff drink.

Brannigan's voice startled me. "So, aren't you going to jump on my case again?" he asked. "This looks like a good time for it. Nobody around."

I shifted my position so my hip wasn't grinding against the frame of the chair. "Not now. Don't bother me. I'm feeling good." I took another sip of my drink and it occurred to me that playing it coy might be the most cunning approach of all. Direct questions had got me nowhere with Brannigan. Perhaps it was better to lie here in the sunshine, inspiring confidence with my honest, trusting face. Maybe if I didn't ask him anything, he would suddenly have an impulse to tell all. I closed my eyes. I wanted to know what Brannigan was really doing in Bailey City. But somehow right at the moment, I was in no hurry. All in good time. I covered my mouth with my hand and yawned.

"Ouch, dammit," yelled Brannigan.

I sat up, clutching my towel to my chest. "What's wrong?" I cried.

He looked at his hand ruefully. "What do you do for a bee sting?"

"Meat tenderizer. You don't see a stinger in there or anything, do you? If there's a stinger in it, you're supposed to take it out with tweezers."

"Nah." He winced. "I don't see anything in it. Jesus, it hurts."

I scrambled up from my chair and slipped on my shoes. "Come on. I've got some meat tenderizer in my kitchen."

Brannigan followed me back to my house, holding his hand awkwardly in a cupped position. I am a great believer in the efficacy of meat tenderizer for all assaults of the animal kingdom short of elephant stampede. The papaya juice seems to be the magic ingredient. I don't know what it does, but it seems to work. Nevertheless, I was careful to sidestep the bees in the thyme on my way back through the hedge.

I pulled meat tenderizer out of my spice rack, dampened some on my finger, and dabbed it on Brannigan's hand. We were so close I could feel his breath on my hair. There was something oddly affecting about the way he held his hand stiffly, wincing a little. It almost persuaded me that he was an ordinary human being whom I could trust.

"How did it happen?" I asked. I know I may have dozed a bit beside the pool but I was sure I would have noticed it if he had gotten down on his hands and knees and started crawling through the thyme, which was about the only way his hand could have landed on a bee.

"Oh, I saw a big bee on those funny little purple flowers. I was just watching it, and then—I grabbed it."

"You grabbed a bumblebee?" I looked at him in astonishment.

"You don't have to act like I'm a raving lunatic," he said irritably.

"What on earth made you do such a thing?"

He shrugged.

"You grabbed the bee?" I repeated. "That wasn't very kind. I think they die after they sting somebody."

"I'm not exactly worried about the bee right now, okay? Do you mind?" He blew on his hand.

"You could try taking an antihistamine," I said. "That might help." I favored antihistamine as my second line of defense against the world of nature.

"I don't want antihistamine," he said, aggrieved. "I want sympathy."

"I'm sorry. Really, I am."

"Why don't you take a look at it and see if you can make out any stinger."

I took his hand in mine, carefully turning it to the light so I could see better. Then with his good hand he lifted my chin and kissed me. I could feel my toes warming and my breasts straining against the thin spandex of my swimsuit. He pressed his hand against my back, pulling me closer. My blood hummed in my ears, and my breath began to come quickly.

He smiled and brushed his fingertips lightly

against my cheek. It was a small, intimate sign of possession and somehow it hit me like a blast of cold air. I had a sudden bleak vision of hearts and flowers, *Modern Bride*, his and her matchbooks and other revoltingly commercial symbols of attachment. With an effort, I pulled myself away from him.

I licked my lips. "How does it feel now?" I asked. "The bee sting, I mean."

He looked at me, slightly puzzled. "It hurts more than I thought it would, to tell you the truth."

His eyes searched mine and he reached for my hand. "I think your meat tenderizer saved my life. Maybe I could stay a while?"

I backed away from him. "You'd better not."

"No?"

"No," I said firmly.

"You sure? Is everything okay? You aren't mad or anything, are you?"

Obviously he was having trouble making sense of my behavior—melting passion followed by deep freeze. Whereas to me, a trained clinical psychologist, figuring it out was the merest child's play. I was not fully recovered from the disaster with Jason yet. Some primitive part of me still associated passion with domestic slavery. I hesitated, wondering how much of this I should confess.

"It's just—too soon," I said finally. "I know this sounds dumb, but I just broke up with this man and sometimes it's as if he's in my head blocking out everything else."

"No, I don't think it's dumb," he said quietly. "I have that trouble a little bit myself sometimes."

I felt a sudden pain like nausea. I had been so intent on my own problems I had forgotten about Brannigan's wife. A fine, sensitive listener I had been.

Suddenly I was uncomfortably conscious that we were wearing only a few inches of spandex and I felt in need of a large fig leaf.

"So, your hand is okay, now?"

"Forget it," he said. "It's already feeling a lot better. Look, you want to go back and finish your drink?"

Maybe I should have gone back to the pool and made civilized chitchat to smooth over this absurd episode. But I reflected that my drink had probably melted again. I didn't know if I could face having that very organized-looking lady replace my drink a second time. She probably had contempt for people who let two perfectly good drinks sit in the sun and melt. "I've got a lot of stuff to do here, actually," I said.

"Sure." He ran both his hands over his wet hair and smiled at me a little wryly.

In spite of all my mature understanding of what had happened, after Brannigan left I felt pretty shaken. Nothing is so unnerving as when sexual attraction somehow misfires. I wondered if some important part of myself was broken. Permanently out of order. I felt as if Jason were looking out of my eyes, continually pushing other men away, as fatally possessive as when I was living with him.

A vague feeling of sadness clung to me for hours after that. I counted over all the mistakes I had ever made and then moved on to tabulate all my personal flaws one by one. From that I went to thinking how unlikely it was that my character could improve at this point in my life. It was some time until I got around to considering Brannigan.

He had seemed so human, nursing his bee sting in my kitchen. But at the same time, I had the sense that there was something about him that I did not understand.

I went out the kitchen door and knelt beside the thyme and watched the bees. Their legs showed plugs of thyme pollen, yellow as butter, stowed there for the return flight home. The bee nearest me was plump, black and yellow, vibrating with a mysterious energy. It was fascinating to watch him defying the laws of thermodynamics, and I can certainly understand people who want to get close to nature. But it was beyond me to fathom what impulse had made Brannigan close his hand around a bumblebee.

six ///

The next afternoon I visited Feininger's. I told myself that I did need to get familiar with the mental health facilities in the area. It wasn't as if I were actually investigating Brannigan. Not really.

A beautiful wrought-iron gate, fifteen feet tall and obviously bought from some impecunious English lord, adorned the entrance to the hospital grounds. Only a double row of plumed horsemen parading through would have done the gate justice. For me to go through it, dressed for the heat in simple lime-green espadrilles and a matching cotton skirt, seemed not just unpoetic but ridiculous. I was relieved when the gatekeeper let me in through a wooden door next to the gatehouse.

Inside, what met my eye was a collection of square brick buildings with Victorian porticos. They sat on an expensive, golf course-style lawn that extended over rolling hills and back to a modest pine forest. A powerful sprinkler spewed a slowly moving arc of water onto the grass, while a few oak trees conveniently indicated the middle ground of the scene. Two uniformed nurses walked into the tallest of the buildings, and a trio of dark young men passed by me speaking Spanish. I knew that the luster of the Feininger name drew students from all over the hemisphere, and I deduced that these young men were either taking postdocs or were training to become analysts. I did not envy them. Although my internship in the teeming wards of St. Luke's had been no sinecure, I had the feeling that even St. Luke's would be preferable to coming to this oppressively ordered place every morning. As far as I was concerned, an internship at this place would have been like living and working on a Monopoly board.

"The administration building is over thataway," said the gatekeeper.

I obediently moved along the sidewalk in the direction he had indicated, but my eyes lingered on the eight-story building to my left, the one I had seen the two nurses enter. It stood a hundred yards from the entrance, bounded by sidewalks, with matching hollies on either side of the portico. There were no bars on the windows of the upper stories, perhaps because bars would have spoiled the country club atmosphere. I saw at a glance that it would be amazingly easy for a woman to fall from one of those high windows to her death on the sidewalk below.

Inside the administration building, the secretary told me that if I would just take a seat, Dr. Jim would be with me in a minute. I perched on a chair close to the entrance of his office and tried to decide whether to wile away the moments with *Field and Stream* or with *Hypnosis Quarterly*, when suddenly I realized that not only could I see Dr. Jim through the cracked door but could hear every word he was saying.

"Fine. Come about seven. I was beginning to think we were never going to get together. Don't you do anything but work these days? Evie was just saying that it seems like forever since we've seen you. No, no, don't bring a thing. You know Evie. She's got the damned dinner mapped out like the invasion of Normandy. See you. Oh, wait a minute there, Aubrey, I got hold of that name you wanted. Let me give it to you now while I'm thinking of it. Macon Sherwood. That's M-a-c-o-n, Macon. His number is 555-9292. Same area code. He's one of the best in the field. I've done some asking around. Sure, glad to help out. See you tomorrow."

I hastily jotted the phone number on a deposit slip in my checkbook. Maybe the world was full of men named Aubrey, but it seemed unlikely. Dr. Jim had surely been talking to our own Dr. Aubrey Miller. My own experience of Miller made me feel it best to keep a sharp eye on what he might be up to. Sherwood was one of the best men in what field? Did this, by any chance, have something to do with Miller's plan to make a bid to Continental Health?

Dr. Jim came out of his office extending his hand. I shook it. Even though I suspected him of colluding to destroy my livelihood, my careful upbringing enabled me to practice social deceit with perfect confidence. I smiled cordially.

He was no taller than I, about five feet five, with

thick chestnut hair and the unconvincingly matey manner of the heir to the throne traveling under the name Lancaster.

"My dear Dr. Fellowes. How kind of you to come and see what we have to offer. I gather you're new to Bailey City."

"That's right. I've moved into the suite of offices that Dr. Miller owns. Dr. Aubrey Miller. I believe you know him?" I threw in another charming smile for good measure.

"Yes. Yes, indeed. A close personal friend of mine. I have the greatest respect for Aubrey."

"He used to be director of the adult unit here, didn't he?"

"Ah, yes. A very able man, Aubrey," he said smoothly. "We were sorry to lose him, but he wanted to get away from administrative duties and spend more time on testing—where, as you no doubt know, he is something of an authority. Now, would you like the overview of the hospital, or is there something in particular you would like to see?"

"I'm interested in the drug-abuse program," I said firmly. "That's really the main thing I'd like to see." I had decided to avoid the adult unit, where Eunice worked. I was afraid she might say something that would let Jim Feininger know that I had more than a casual interest in his hospital.

He beamed at me. "Ah, we are particularly proud of our substance-abuse program. A model of its kind. We are one of the few programs that offer in-depth treatment of the addictive personality. Each patient is assigned both to an individual therapist and to a group. One of our social workers, of course, meets with the family." We walked out into the sunshine and moved in the direction of a two-story brick building flanked by azalea bushes. The conviction began to grow on me that the buildings had been given cute names like "The Hollies" and "Azalea Lane."

"With the tremendous increase in cocaine use, we have hopes of building a new wing in the near future." Feininger rubbed his hands together at the thought.

Recalling old Dr. Feininger's vehement opposition to the wing, I deduced that in the near future meant after Dr. Charles had left this world for that great hospital in the sky.

"What's your success rate?" I asked, unable to resist the temptation to annoy him. I knew that success rates for treating alcohol and drug abuse tend to be dismal.

"Some aspects of our program are relatively new," he hedged, "but Dr. Simpson, who coordinates the program, hopes eventually to publish a paper on the uses of traditional therapy in dealing with addiction, which will help answer that question for us. All we can say now is that we are very encouraged by our short-term results. Of course, there is much we have yet to learn. It's a vast subject. You haven't by any chance read my book *Name Your Poison*? In that I tried to define some of the central issues of treating addiction."

I admitted that I hadn't but I did my best to look as if I were panting to get my hands on a copy. He opened the door to the addiction unit for me. The shiny brass plate on the door, I noticed with satisfaction, was engraved Azalea Haven.

From what I could see as we toured the building, the substance-abuse program served chiefly well-coiffed women of uncertain age. It gave me perverse pleasure to imagine my ex-patient, the budding Hell's Angel, reducing the place to rubble in less time than it took Feininger to finish his elegant peroration. But perhaps I wasn't being fair. Some of the attendants in their crisp white uniforms looked quite muscular. Feininger offered me the chance to go on to the adult unit, but I politely declined.

"Before you go," he said as my guided tour came to a close, "you might care to visit our dining hall. We are justifiably, I think, proud of our fresh seafood, and chocolate desserts are something of a specialty with us."

I was visited by a vision of an ex-inmate recalling her hospitalization: "The people were impossible, Cissy darling, but oh, my dear, the *pot au chocolat*!"

"Let's stop by the kitchen together," suggested Feininger. "Our chef usually can come up with some samples of our famous meringues for guests."

I can only take so much oily charm before I begin longing to say "Aw, come off it," so I pleaded a pressing engagement and made my escape. In fact, my only engagement was a dinner date with Brack Prideaux and that was not for hours.

After I left Feininger's I had plenty of time to go home, stretch out on my bed where the air-conditioning could wash over me, and brood black thoughts. I recognized that I had developed prejudices during my internship at St. Luke's and during the time I had worked at a community mental health center. For me, there was something distasteful about the country club atmosphere of Feininger's. It was like those funeral homes with drive-in windows that do weddings on off days, so intent are they on pretending they have nothing to do with death. But trying to be fair-minded, I acknowledged that all that surface gloss might be comforting to people who are seriously disoriented or depressed. And for all I knew the therapy there was first-rate. It probably was.

Still, my visit left a bad taste in my mouth, and it had only sharpened my interest in the questions about what Miller was up to and what had brought Brannigan to Bailey City.

That evening, Brack picked me up at eight. He had invited me out with the obvious intention of exploring our common tastes and displaying his warmth and charm. Had he known how preoccupied I was with figuring out the machinations of Miller and Brannigan, he might have saved himself the effort. I was ready to see conspiracy and deceit everywhere—not the best mind-set for a maiden going a-wooing.

"Pretty area you're in out here," he said as we walked out to his car. He glanced over his shoulder at my house. "What do you do with all that space?"

"Enjoy it," I said with feeling. I had been visited by a sudden vivid memory of the cozy squalor I had recently escaped.

"Pretty expensive, though, isn't it?" Brack opened the car door for me.

"A relative left me a legacy," I explained a little awkwardly. "I thought this would be a good way to invest it."

"You're probably right about that." After a glance at my broad emerald lawn, and the imposing bit of pseudo-Colonial architecture smack in the middle of it, Brack climbed into the car.

Great, I thought. I would have to look guilty when he asked me about the house. Probably now he thinks I'm paying for it by dealing drugs or something.

My family's money had been embarrassing me for years. I remembered my first date. It had been rather a long time coming. I was too much my father's daughter and didn't find it easy to adopt the kittenish manner that seemed to draw adolescent boys. At last, however, when I was fifteen, a boy I knew from the youth group at church had asked me to the movies. "Okay," I had said. I had given him my address, and he arrived at the front door Friday evening. Sweat was streaming down his face and his top shirt button had come undone. He had evidently gone first to the gardener's cottage and had gotten redirected down the tree-lined avenue that led to our front door. By the time he confronted my father at the front door, he was completely unnerved. He never asked me out again, which wasn't really surprising, I suppose.

My feelings about my family's money were so complicated it was hard to sort them all out. On the one hand, money was taboo. The unspoken assumption was that nice people didn't think about it and if anyone like my unfortunate date was knocked back on his heels by the sight of our house, it was a sign of a weakness of character.

Growing up I don't believe I ever saw money in my parents' hands. When we went into the village on the weekends to pick up knickknacks for the house or to get sodas, we signed chits. I presume bills were sent around to the house later. My parents' philosophy was that children should fix their thoughts on nicer things than money. Rabbits. Flower gardens. And, when sufficiently mature in years, art museums.

I remember once in the seventh grade writing a paper about my plans to go to college and then graduate school, with possible trips down the Amazon or to the Far East during summer breaks. When my teacher handed the paper back she smiled at me and said, "Are you sure you'll have enough money for all this?"

I went home in a panic and asked my father if I would have enough money for college. It wasn't as unreasonable a question as it sounds. I had never seen any money around the house. I had no idea what made the sprinklers come on and made the flowers in the garden bloom, what straightened my teeth and kept fresh melons on the table all seasons.

My father was furious with the teacher's little joke. As a member of the school's board of directors he was in a position to make things very uncomfortable for her. I have the impression that my mother's steadier temper prevailed in the end. I heard sibilant whispers from the study, and then, after an eternity, my parents emerged and assured me in stately voices that my "dreams would all be possible," that I needn't trouble myself any longer. And that was as close as we came in those days to discussing money.

Then when I was sixteen my father had a heart attack. Suddenly the curtain of silence about money lifted, and I was given a bewildering crash course in the family business.

I had known even as a child that hotels were important to us. It was legend in our family that on my parents' Paris honeymoon they had changed hotels five times because the service didn't meet my father's standards.

So I drank up information about the hotel business and about stocks and bonds and partnerships as well. I believe my father had distinctly mixed feelings when it turned out I took to the business so quickly. What he couldn't realize was that all those years of steady avoidance of the subject had given it mystic importance. Money seemed to me like sex— terrifically private but with a powerful influence. I read the *Wall Street Journal* the way some kids read *Lady Chatterly's Lover.* Money was the secret that adults had among themselves. I was clear about that much.

It was only when I went away to college that I became fully conscious of the most sinister angle on the subject. Money didn't just scare away the odd, insecure date. It could separate me from people I really cared about. I never had the courage to ask my roommate to come home with me. I had grown ashamed of my family's palatial pile, and I was afraid of what she might think.

There was another drawback. The money in the family seemed to undermine my accomplishments in my own eyes. I was accepted at the college of my choice. I had never doubted that I would be. But sometimes as I lay staring at the dorm ceiling at 2 A.M., I wondered if the reason I had been accepted was because the college's music building was named after my grandfather.

The issue simply wouldn't go away. It nagged at me. Years later, when I heard that a kid I grew up with had given away his money and was working at repairing lawn mowers in Des Moines, I felt the shameful sort of thrill you get when you find out someone you know has a kinky sex life. I had tried all my adult life to be matter-of-fact about money, but I never quite managed to pull it off.

Mostly I coped by avoiding the subject. I reasoned that nobody needed to know about the family loot unless I told them. I drove a modest car. When it came to money, I went incognito. It was years before I noticed that I was echoing my family's approach to money. I felt no more comfortable talking about it than they did.

After my father died, the hotels went public. It didn't seem practical any longer to keep the company privately held. My mother and I, and miscellaneous other relatives, were left with large blocks of stock. We were no longer entitled to have a proprietor's hot interest in the business. It was devastating in a way. Our identity had been so tied up in the hotels. The newspapers always called my father "hotelier Sanford Fellowes" and I had been referred to as the "hotel heiress." Yet as sad as I felt about the change, I felt free for the first time. It would be easier to get distance on my family background now, I told myself. I would be a regular person who just happened to have a trust fund. I would make a break with the past.

Yet here I was living in a palatial pile that was strongly reminiscent of others owned by my clan—the same sort of place I had despised when I was in college. What did it mean? I had the uncomfortable suspicion that I was reverting to type.

Brack's voice broke into my thoughts. "Who's got the Mercedes at the house next door to you?"

"James Brannigan. You remember he's bringing his daughter in to see Miller? I told you about that."

"Right." He paused a moment as he negotiated the sharp curve on Baker Street. "Do you see much of them?"

"Oh, I've seen them now and then," I said a bit self-consciously. "I've been over there, swam in the pool."

He shot me a look that I answered with a bland smile. I could feel myself mentally digging in my heels. This is none of his business, I thought. I don't owe it to him to tell him about my background or about my relationship with Brannigan. Not that I could have summed up my thoughts about either of them neatly even if I had wanted to.

Either Brack sensed my resistance or he had suddenly lost interest in my house and my movie star neighbor because he didn't ask any more questions. As we drove, darkness crept into the suburban streets and the dove-gray sky shaded toward regulation black.

We had already discovered over lunch that we shared a passion for Chinese food, so we tooled off in the direction of Ho Nan's Chinese Garden. When we passed the electric scoreboard thermometer at the Farmer's Bank, it flashed 87 degrees. I have a poor opinion of a twilight that can't do better than that at cooling things off. A man in a track suit with a German shepherd on a lead jogged past us. I figured if he was jogging at 87 degrees, he must be schizophrenic.

"Brack, do you happen to know why Miller left Feininger's?"

He pursed his lips. "I've wondered about that, myself. Feininger's is such a big name I would have thought that somebody with a frail ego like Miller would cling to it for all he was worth. You know what I mean—you've heard him talk about having lunch with 'the senator' and treating the 'opera star' and conferring with 'the monsignor.' Hopes some of the glow will rub off on him, poor guy. Can't get enough of that reflected glory."

Brack pulled up in the parking lot of Ho Nan's and, with old-fashioned courtesy, got out and came around to open the car door for me. Putting his arm at my waist, he guided me up to the door as if I were tottering on bound feet.

"I don't want to seem overcontrolling or anything," he said, "but I think we've talked enough about Miller. We're supposed to be off from work tonight, remember?"

I could see that Brack might think I was getting a little obsessive about Miller. And maybe he wasn't far wrong. Whenever I thought about Miller, he seemed like a fat spider sitting at the center of a web, a sort of evil presence. Maybe if I had had enough work of my own to do I'd have been too busy to worry about what other people were up to. But I wasn't busy. Far from it. I had lots of time to look around me and think.

A gratifyingly cold blast of air hit us as we entered the restaurant and as my pores contracted to meet the challenge of that arctic air, I felt my mental balance returning. I resolved to forget my ailing practice, forget Brannigan, forget Miller, and concentrate on having a good time. It was something I had never been much good at.

"How did you happen to specialize in child psych?" I asked when our order arrived. "Weakness for checkers?"

"Weakness for kids."

"Do you have any of your own?"

"My wife left me before we got started on kids. It was probably for the best," he said, looking sad.

"Do you ever hear from her anymore? Have any idea what she's doing now?"

"The lady with all the questions," he said lightly. "Too bad I don't have any answers. Last I heard she was still living with that scuba diver in Atlanta. 'You never wanted me to go scuba diving.' That's what she said when she was packing. This is grounds for divorce? I was floored. Jeez, I said, if it's that important to you, go scuba diving. Get bitten by a shark, get the bends if it'll make you happy. "'It's over,' she said. 'I don't love you any more.'" He slapped a hand to his heart and winced comically. "Ouch. She had me there."

I shot him a sympathetic look. "Should I not have brought it up? You don't want to talk about it?"

"Nah, don't worry. It was a long time ago." He prodded his bok choy aimlessly with his fork. "Of course, when it happened, I went crazy. Followed her down to Atlanta. Actually went to work for a VA hospital down there for a couple of years." He made a face. "I guess I kept thinking she was going to come to her senses. Hell, I don't know what I was thinking. I didn't want to be working at any VA hospital, that's for sure. Finally, I just came back here and picked up the pieces. Everybody was tactful. No questions asked about whether I was currently back among the sane or not. Miller offered me a pretty good deal on the office so I took it and moved my stuff in. Nowadays I just see my patients and keep my life real simple. When I think about being married, it's almost like it happened to somebody else." A wistful smile crinkled his eyes. "To somebody who was younger and maybe more optimistic."

I was beginning to feel like a social disaster. Brack takes me out and buys me dinner with egg roll, and I cross-examine him and remind him of his marital failures.

"Mrs. Smythe tells me you've picked up a

patient," he said, promptly changing the subject.

"I guess she mentioned that it was Merris Brannigan."

"She did happen to mention that. Not too discreet when it comes to movie stars, Mrs. Smythe."

"I don't think it's going to be a long-term case," I said glumly.

"Don't let it get to you, Fran. It's slow for everybody starting out. A year from now, you'll look back on these first months and laugh."

I doubted it. I was the type who tends to look back and cringe.

We led the conversation purposefully into non-painful areas and kept it there while we attacked our food. This, of course, ruled out personal accounts of old romances entirely, which suited me fine.

Our fortune cookies had stupid fortunes. "A smile is worth a million tears," said mine. Brack's "Your hard work will be rewarded" was actually punctuated with a happy face. "I do think there ought to be some sort of quality control on these things," I said. "What's wrong with 'A handsome dark stranger will come and take you away from all this'?"

"Or 'You will come into a large sum of money,'" suggested Brack.

My stomach churned uncomfortably. It hit me that I had both the large sum of money and the handsome dark stranger—Brannigan—and I was not a bit the happier for it.

"I've got it," I said. "It should predict success in your chosen career!"

"At least." Brack stood up and helped me out of

my chair. He had a most pleasant way of making me feel like a fragile porcelain doll. It was embarrassing to realize that I was so unliberated as to enjoy that. In small doses.

When we got back to my house, I invited him in for a drink. It was the least I could do, I figured, after dragging up all that stuff about his ex-wife.

I pulled a bottle of white wine out of the fridge and opened it. When I flung open the cabinet to get wineglasses, my hand hovered uncertainly a moment next to Grandmother's crystal, then grabbed a couple of jelly glasses. I was a mess of neurotic conflicts.

I took the wine in to Prideaux on the couch and sat down next to him.

"Thanks for the dinner," I said. "It was lovely."

"You, too."

"What?"

"Are lovely." He put his arm around me.

I was thinking fast. How far did I want to go with this? What if I encouraged him only to have my nerve give out, humiliatingly, as it had with Brannigan? In this case it would not be so easy to walk away from my mistakes. We were going to be working in the same building. Yet I had an overwhelming impulse to nibble at his ear if for no other reason than to prove to myself that my sexual impulses were still in sound working condition. Brack nuzzled my ear and I snuggled up a little closer to him, deciding to work out all the messy details later. Life was, unfortunately, not as neat as a fortune cookie.

The jangle of the phone rent the air. I leapt for

it and was able to answer it before the third bone-shattering ring. "Hullo?"

"Fran, I miss you in the most god-awful way." The voice was sickeningly familiar. Jason had somehow gotten my number. My insides went all hollow and my blood temperature sank to reptilian levels.

"Go a-way," I said distinctly. "Do not call me again. I mean this. Good-bye." When I hung up the phone, I was managing only a little shallow breathing. Slowly I became conscious of Brack's gaze.

"Want to talk about it?" he asked.

I shook my head.

He sighed. "Something tells me that it's time for me to shove off."

I took the phone off the hook. "You don't have to go," I said. But my voice sounded thin and unnatural even to my own ears.

Brack had stood up, but he was smiling. "It's okay."

"I feel like I've been such bad company," I said remorsefully.

He patted my shoulder. "Don't be stupid. It's okay. Look, I'll see you tomorrow."

I watched him leave, my mind on Jason. I couldn't help it. I wished I could honestly say that all my feeling for him was gone. But obviously I could not have been so intensely afraid of him and of anyone remotely like him, if he had not still had some kind of hold on my heart. It seemed to me that our relationship was like a swing after a child has jumped out of it. It had no life in it anymore, but still it swung up and down and even jerked dangerously once or twice before finally coming to a stop. I simply needed time, I told myself. Someday my relationships with men would be simple and sweet once more. It wasn't as if there was anything really, basically wrong with me. Not really.

I realized then that I was showing three of the eight signs of clinical depression. I had worked myself into that paranoid state of mind in which I felt I was walking in a hall of mirrors. If I took a single wrong turn, a macabre special effect like those favored in old horror movies would be sprung on me—a jack-in-the-box laughing insanely, a knife in a shower—something along those lines. I was forced to admit that in many ways, it had not been a very fun evening.

seven ///

The offices of Psychological Associates were open on Saturdays. In compensation, they closed Wednesdays. Miller, who was a workaholic, used the quiet time when no phones were ringing to catch up on paperwork. Prideaux invariably played golf. Finch taped his television program. Mrs. Smythe visited with her grandchildren. Avise played tennis. I was the only one for whom Wednesday had no special meaning. Since I was new to the practice, it had not yet become a distinctive day for me. I spent the morning out in the community diligently trying to drum up business, and at noon I went on into the office.

When I stepped into the waiting room, sunlight was streaming in through the sheer polyester curtains. There in the eerie silence I saw Miller on the floor. He was lying in the sunshine, next to the coffee table, which was piled with current magazines. He was facedown, but I recognized him at once from the argyle socks—an inch or two of their pattern was visible above his brown shoes. His wispy reddish hair was matted with blood, and I saw, without really comprehending, that his head was mis-shapen. It seems odd that I didn't immediately realize that he was dead.

The first instinct of someone trained in one of the helping professions is to try to help. I knelt at once beside Miller, frantically trying to remember what I had been taught in CPR class. Checking his mouth and nose for breathing obstructions was the first step, I recalled. As I reached for his shoulder and started to turn him over, my hand brushed against his. It was cold. And it was not just cold, it had the flat, inert quality that only a dead hand can have.

I rocked back onto my heels, feeling sick. I shakily rose and went into Mrs. Smythe's office, fear flutter-ing like a bird in my throat. I didn't see how Miller's death could have been an accident, and I think I dimly realized that the murderer might still be in the offices somewhere. I closed the door to Mrs. Smythe's office behind me and locked it. Then I dialed 911.

"Can you send an ambulance at once? It's a head injury. I think—I think he's dead."

I gave the dispatcher the office address. "Will it take you long to get here?" I asked anxiously.

"We ought to be there in less than five minutes, sweetie," she said. "You just hang on."

Then I called the police. After I hung up the phone, I became aware of how really alone I was. The silence in the office seemed to pound against my ears like an alarm. A dead body is no company.

I should notify someone about what has hap-pened, I thought, fighting a wave of fear so strong it was like nausea. I should notify someone from the office. I tested the door to the office to reassure myself that it was still locked. I had some difficulty steadying my finger long enough to dial the phone. First, I dialed Brack and listened to his phone ring. It was hard to give up the hope of pouring out my fears to Brack, but I finally had to face it that he wasn't at home. My hand still shaking, I pulled over Mrs. Smythe's appointment book and found her list of the staff's home phone numbers. I swiftly dialed Finch, thinking how I would love to hear that reassuring voice; its very timbre implied that everything would be all right. But Finch wasn't at home, either.

I told myself that there was no reason to feel afraid just because the first two numbers I tried hadn't answered. I hesitated. I wasn't keen to talk to Avise, but she was, after all, practically Miller's next of kin, so I dialed her next. No answer. Then I tried Mrs. Smythe. The entire world was out somewhere and I was alone with this dead body, I thought blankly. I slammed down the receiver. The only other numbers on the list were the Evergreen Cleaning Service and Shorty's Vending Machines. Had I been on the job long enough to be chummy with the maintenance people, I would have called them. I was that anxious to hear a human voice. Instead, in desperation, I found myself dialing James Brannigan. At least someone at his house would answer the phone, if only his secretary.

When the phone was picked up on the third ring, relief washed over me. I had begun to feel like the last sentient being in the world. "Is Mr. Brannigan in?" I asked. "This is Dr. Fellowes."

"I am not sure he's available, Dr. Fellowes," said the secretary. "Would you care to leave a number where you can be reached?"

"No. I'm at the office. Just tell him that Dr. Miller has been murdered. I've called the police."

"Excuse me—would you repeat that, please?"

"You heard me. Murdered. Dead . . . tell him." I heard the scream of a siren. "I've got to go," I said abruptly. "I hear the ambulance." I hung up and bolted out of the office.

I went out and closed the front door behind me, leaning against it to steady myself. A van marked "Rescue Squad" pulled into the parking lot, its red lights blinking urgently. Four young men jumped out and ran toward me.

"He's inside," I said. "I'm afraid he's dead." Suddenly the sidewalk seemed to heave and buckle, and overcome with nausea, I sat down on the curb.

Two young men trotted past me carrying oxygen tanks. It wasn't long before they came out of the building again. "Are you okay, ma'am?" one asked me. "Here, put your head down between your legs. Don't breathe too fast."

I did as they said. I felt fine as long as I didn't allow myself to think of Miller's head, the awful flatness and stickiness of it, and the dead feel of his hand. A police car pulled into the parking lot next to the ambulance, and a man in chinos got out on the passenger side. The boys on the Rescue Squad threw all their equipment back into their vehicle, hopped in after it, and fired up the engine.

A polite young man in uniform knelt beside me.

"Lieutenant Pittman here would like to ask you a few questions."

Lieutenant Pittman, the man dressed in chinos, with his shirtsleeves rolled up, sat down on the curb next to me. "Can you identify the deceased, ma'am?"

I nodded. But for a second I couldn't speak. I did a lot of swallowing. "I'm sorry," I said. "But it's been such a shock. It's Dr. Miller. I think he must have come in to do paperwork. The office is actually closed, you see, on Wednesdays. I forgot."

Footsteps passed behind me. Men were carrying cameras and tripods into the office. I did my best to answer Lieutenant Pittman's questions, and his interest in what I had to say couldn't have been more flattering. He hung on my every word.

"So you came into the office by accident," he said finally. "No one was due here until tomorrow morning, right?"

"That's right." I stopped myself. "No, wait, that's not right. I think someone told me that the cleaning service comes in Wednesdays. I'm not sure when. Mrs. Smythe would know." I covered my eyes with my hand. The world was beginning to spin around and I had a very real fear that I might throw up.

"You'd better let us drive you home," said the lieutenant. "Give me your keys, and we'll bring your car around to your place later."

"Really, I'm all right."

"I insist. Sommers? Give this lady a ride back to her house."

Only as I was being driven home did it occur to me that Lieutenant Pittman probably wanted to search my car for a telltale bloody blunt instrument. Instead of alarming me the idea only made my arms and my feet feel heavier, as if I were suffering from some sort of desperate fatigue.

After the police car let me out at my place, I went to the kitchen and mixed myself a stiff drink. I was squeezing a lime with intense concentration and trying not to think of dead bodies when the doorbell rang.

"What's this junk about Miller being murdered?" Brannigan said when I opened the door.

"Want a drink?" I offered, moving back toward the kitchen. "I need one. A lot."

I poured out another gin and tonic and handed it to him. I had already begun on mine in the hope it would add stiffening to my knees. "I found the body," I explained, taking another healthy gulp. I went into the living room and fell onto the sofa. I looked idly around the room, taking comfort in it—the familiar oriental rug, the thriving plants, the fireplace with the spray of dried flowers on the hearth. The living room reassured me that some simple homey things were still securely the same.

"What happened?" asked Brannigan.

"It looked to me as if someone had bludgeoned him to death. I hope you won't mind if I don't go into details." My fingers were cold and didn't seem to have much strength. I put the drink down on the table and took a few deep breaths until the wave of nausea went away.

"He must have left the office door unlocked."

"What makes you think that?" I asked, looking up suddenly.

"Stands to reason. Some crazed addict or somebody probably came by and did him in. What was Miller doing in the office today, anyway? I thought you people were closed on Wednesday. That's what they told me when I was making those appointments for Merris."

"I suppose he was doing paperwork. The other day he was bragging about how much work he got done on Wednesdays when everyone else is goofing off. I think he always came in on Wednesdays." I was finding the liquor a comfort. I fingered the glass affectionately and took another swallow. I decided I had been wise to put in two jiggers of gin. I remembered that some sage had once said that practically any neurosis could be cured in the short term by a stiff drink. How true. How very, very true. I took another swig.

"Did you talk to the police?" asked Brannigan. "What do they think?"

"Of course I talked to the police," I said a trifle indignantly. "They are probably even now searching my impounded car. I found the body, remember?"

"Oh, come on. They don't think you did it."

"I have no idea what they think." I looked at him with wide eyes. "Where were *you* this morning?"

He gently took the drink from my hand.

"Hey, wait a minute, I'm not finished with that."

"Have you had any lunch?"

"I'm not drunk."

"Then how come you're sitting there accusing me of murder, huh?"

"Well, did you kill him?"

"No, I didn't kill him and if you thought I did you'd be pretty dumb to ask."

"You really hated Miller, didn't you?" My head felt hot and slightly disassociated from my body, but at least for the moment the vision of Miller's body, which had persistently hovered behind my eyes, was fading.

Brannigan started toward the kitchen. "Got any crackers and cheese? Great for soaking up alcohol, crackers and cheese."

"You blamed him for Jessica's death, didn't you?" I called.

He stuck his head back into the living room. "He killed Jessica, and he did it to get to me. He was a bastard and I'm glad he's dead, but I hadn't got around to killing him yet. Where do you keep the crackers?"

After I ate them, I was surprised to find I was feeling less sick. Now I only felt cold.

"You'd better go upstairs and go to bed," ordered Brannigan. "You're starting to shake. And do me a favor. Don't go telling the police that I killed Miller, okay? Some of them aren't too bright, and they might just believe you."

"Tell me, just satisfy my curiosity on this point— where were you this morning?"

"I borrowed a horse and went riding. I was out all morning."

"The horse will testify to that, of course."

"Sure. Go to bed."

After he left, I did go upstairs and crawled into bed. It was as if I had some draining illness like the flu. I was cold all over and didn't feel that I could trust the sturdiness of my legs or my arms anymore. I think some primitive voice inside me was whispering "It could have been you." The fact that Miller had died so suddenly made me feel my own mortality breathing close behind me, making the tiny hairs on the back of my neck stand on end. I hugged my quilt close and shuddered. My capacity to reason was mostly gone, and no detective instincts surged to the fore. Right now, I only wanted safety and security. Suddenly the phone beside the bed rang and I jumped just about out of my skin. It was Brack.

"Fran? I just talked to the police. Jeez, I can't believe it about Miller."

"It's true, all right." I gulped. "I found him."

"I'm coming right over."

He hung up before I could protest. Heaving a sigh, I got dressed again and went downstairs. Brack arrived in only a few minutes looking white and shaken. "Do you have a drink or something?" he asked. "It's unbelievable. Murdered!"

I fixed a gin and tonic for him and a milk for me. On mature reflection, I had decided it was of the utmost importance that I keep my head clear while deciding how much I should tell the police.

Brack stared into his drink. "Look, I didn't want to talk about this over the phone, but I think it would be better if you didn't mention to the police that business about Miller hitting Tim the other day."

I looked at him in surprise. "You don't think Tim took your advice and did hit his father back, do you? He's just a kid."

"The family are always the first people they suspect. I don't think for a minute that Avise and Tim
had anything to do with it. But that's why we've got
to be careful about what we say to the police." Brack
put his drink down on the coffee table and shook his
head. "You'd think that having Miller for a father
would be enough bad luck to last a kid a lifetime, but
now he's got to go and land in this."

I was not as convinced as Brack that Tim could
not have killed his father. I agreed that it seemed
unlikely, but then I recalled reading that some had
found Lizzie Borden a quiet, well-behaved young
lady. "What do you think was the problem between
Tim and his father, anyway?"

He waved away my question. "What difference
does it make? Miller had gone completely round the
bend."

"You think he was actually psychotic?"

"Let's just say his grip on reality wasn't the tight-
est," said Brack wearily. "He got this crazy idea that
Tim wasn't his son. He was flipping out. Abusing the
kid. It started before Avise and Miller split up. That
might even have been the reason for the split for all I
know. My guess is that Avise was willing to let him
walk all over her, but she wasn't having any of it
with Tim."

"You say Miller was 'abusing him.' Abusing him
how?"

"Oh, verbally, emotionally. That's what's worrying me. If the police find out about it, I'm afraid
they'll jump to the wrong conclusion—the abused
kid turning on the parent. What the police aren't

going to see is that Tim isn't a desperate kid. He's got his mother, he's got his talent. He's really sort of cocky. Tim didn't need to beat up on his dad. In fact, I think he probably felt superior to him."

I had to admit that what Brack said made sense. I remembered the way Tim had talked about his father in tones of easy contempt. He had been upset, that day in the office, but he hadn't seemed desperate. The boy was thinking lawsuit, not murder. "What did you make of this idea that Tim wasn't his?" I asked.

Brack smiled a little. "Maybe when Tim turned out to be a tall, good-looking, talented kid, Miller jumped to the conclusion that they couldn't possibly be related." He shrugged. "Nah, I think it was just a classic case of projection. Miller didn't like himself much. So, he didn't like his kid much. That simple."

"You never thought there was anything to it?"

"The idea is absurd," said Brack. "Believe me, until the marriage started to fall apart, Avise was devoted to that pathetic little man. He sold her on the idea that he was a saint in the service of humanity. She gave up her acting career so she could help dear Aubrey in his work."

"Look, Brack, I understand what you're telling me about Tim and I agree that we really ought to consider very carefully what we say to the police. We don't want them to get the wrong idea. The best thing is probably just to be offhand about it. If they ask, we can say something like 'Oh, sure. Typical case of adolescent rebellion.'"

Brack shot me a grateful look. "Right. God knows I don't want to obstruct justice, Fran, but I've known all these people for years. Why, I've known Tim since he was five or six. I'm sure he didn't kill his father." He got up. "I've got to go to the office. The police want me to look over the place and see if anything's missing."

"Were you the only one from the office they were able to reach?"

"I guess. You know what Wednesdays are like. Everybody heads for the hills. I'd probably still be out on the golf course myself, but I was shooting such a lousy game, I decided to hang it up."

"Who were you playing with?" I asked.

Brack looked sharply at me. "What are you getting at? I was out by myself. The pediatrician canceled out on me." He turned to leave.

"The police didn't say anything to you about whether they had any leads, did they?" I asked.

"No, and I don't see how they could at this point. It was probably some addict. A lot of street people have the idea that we keep drugs in the office. We had a break-in last winter, as a matter of fact."

The drug-crazed addict was going to be a popular choice for the murderer. But as I walked Brack to the door, I couldn't help thinking that it would be odd for a man who had as many enemies as Miller to be killed by a stranger. Very odd. Life was hardly ever that convenient.

After Brack left, a shiny police car pulled up in front of the house. I had to say the picture-book line "the policeman is our friend" several times out loud before I found the courage to answer the doorbell. I threw open the door half expecting to have handcuffs clipped on me.

A wholesome-looking young police officer whose cheeks were downy and impossibly pink said, "Lieutenant Pittman would like you to come back to your office with me, Dr. Fellowes, if you're up to it. He has some questions he'd like to ask you." The young police officer's eyes were pale blue and incurious. He had that vaguely inhuman quality men so often take on when in uniform. I followed him meekly to the squad car.

When we arrived at the office, an ambulance was just leaving, presumably with Miller's body. At least I wouldn't find him still sprawled on the floor. I wasn't sure my nerves could have stood that.

The officer took me in through the back door and led me down the hall to Miller's office. Brack and Lieutenant Pittman were standing beside the desk.

"If you don't mind, Dr. Fellowes," said the lieutenant, "please don't touch anything. The fingerprint boys aren't finished in here. Dr. Prideaux suggested I have you come in and give me an opinion about the work Miller was doing this morning. We're trying to more or less reconstruct what happened."

"I looked it over, Fran," said Brack apologetically, "but it's been years since I've seen most of this stuff, and I know you studied under Weinbaum."

"Sure, I'll take a look. What do you want to know?"

The lieutenant indicated the papers spread out on Miller's desk near a large manila envelope. "What do we have here? Does it look to you like he was scoring these tests when he was interrupted?"

"Good Lord." I leafed through the papers. "This is

a full neuropsych battery, along with all the patient's records. Looks like the man has a long history of hospitalization." It was an unusually fat file. At St. Luke's we had had a rule of thumb, the thicker the file, the worse the patient. By those standards, this guy was a crock. "Here you've got the hospital records, Feininger's admission assessment, CT scan. Then he's got the testing protocols here—the Reitan, the Wechsler. Here's where Miller converted the raw scores into scale scores. He'd finished the scoring. Here are his notes on the interview, and here's where he scored the Rorschach, popularly known as the ink blot test."

"Is that a neurological test?" asked Lieutenant Pittman.

"Not strictly speaking, but it's often given as a part of a neuropsych battery to help settle the question of whether the patient is just crazy or something is wrong with his brain."

"Was this patient crazy, would you say?" asked Pittman.

I glanced at the printer of Miller's computer, where the first paragraph of his report had been printed out. "Evidently not. Miller has already started his report. Left hemisphere dysfunction."

"You think somebody with that kind of brain damage might turn violent?" asked Pittman.

I looked at him in surprise. "Are you thinking that the patient was here this morning?" I asked.

"That's not the way it works, Lieutenant," Brack explained. "Miller would have seen the patient when he interviewed him, asked him about his symptoms and so on. He would have seen him when he administered the tests, if he did administer them. In this case it looks as if the technician over at Feininger's did most of the actual testing."

"He probably gave the Rorschach himself," I added.

"Yeah," agreed Brack. "But after that initial contact, Miller normally wouldn't see the patient at all. Feininger's would send him the records, and Miller would pull them all together with his own testing, make the diagnosis, and send his report to the patient's therapist."

"And that's what he was doing this morning," said Lieutenant Pittman.

"Evidently." I darted a look at Lieutenant Pittman. "Have you found the weapon?"

"We are continuing our investigation," he said coldly. "Dr. Fellowes, what I'd like to know from you is, in your opinion, approximately how long would it have taken Dr. Miller to get as far as he did on this report?"

"Oh. You're trying to establish the time of death. Do you know what time he got to the office?"

"You don't have to worry about that part of it. Just give us an estimate on the time it would have taken to start this report."

I leafed through the papers. "It would have taken *me* hours. You see, you'd have to translate the scores, then read all these records, interpret the test scores, pull everything together, and make a diagnosis before you can even write the first line of the report."

"Do you think it would have taken Dr. Miller hours?"

"Well, Miller was an expert, of course. This kind of report is what he did all the time. He wouldn't have to pull reference books off the shelf and keep referring to them the way I would. But yes, I would say it would take him a minimum of two hours, assuming he was starting from scratch with the raw test data."

"Thank you," said Pittman. "Just as a matter of routine, Dr. Fellowes, we're searching the houses of some of Dr. Miller's co-workers. Do you have any objection if we begin with yours?"

I looked at him in astonishment. "N-no," I stuttered. "Of course not." No one knew better than I that the police would find nothing incriminating at my house. But all the same there was something unsettling about the idea of a squad of policemen leafing through my underclothes, checking my medicine cabinet, and taking note of my unpaid bills. For a split second, I thought of withdrawing my consent and demanding that Pittman produce a warrant. Only the conviction that his eyes would glitter with delight if I did prevented me. Besides, I thought dolefully, he probably wouldn't have any trouble getting a warrant. I had been the one to discover the body, after all.

Pittman looked down at Miller's papers. "If you'll just hand your house key over to Officer Bailey, we'll get on that. You might want to do some shopping while we take care of this little matter."

Pittman nodded to the young police officer waiting at the door to Miller's office, and I found myself being ushered out. Shopping? The man was acting as if I were a Barbie doll—large wardrobe, small cranial capacity. I cast a resentful glance behind me as we got into the squad car. Lieutenant Pittman needed someone to lead him gently into the modern world.

I wondered what Pittman was saying to Brack back in the office. Probably asking him for the name of an expert who could confirm what I had said. They could hardly take my unsupported word if I were a suspect.

I noticed, as I was riding away in the police car, that three policemen were approaching the dumpster in the back of the parking lot with an air of purpose. Maybe everybody really was being searched as a matter of routine. I wondered if all the other suspects found this as embarrassing as I did. It gave me some satisfaction to imagine the police plowing through the desks of all my office mates. I could imagine what they would find in Finch's drawers—a cache of candy bars. Brack would have that hoard of giant cookies he gave to the kids. As for Avise, I wouldn't venture to guess. Valium? Not a murder weapon, that was for sure. One of my co-workers might just conceivably be a murderer, but none of them was stupid.

Though I knew nothing about normal methods of police investigation, from what I had seen so far, it didn't seem to me that Lieutenant Pittman was a leading proponent of the theory that the murderer was a drug-crazed addict.

eight / / /

The first thing I did when I got home was call Mrs. Smythe. In the office she was the one I always turned to when I was short of paper clips or when I wanted to know the time the mail was picked up. I cherished the crazy hope that in this case, too, she would know more about what was going on than I did.

"Oh, my dear, isn't it horrible!" she gasped. "I just heard. Right in the office! And I always thought the office was so safe. Not like those nasty old places uptown with no decent lights in the parking lots. But it seems like you aren't safe anywhere anymore. The police want me to go right over there and check my office to make sure nothing is missing. I don't see how I'll be able to make myself go in that door. Of course, the police will be right there and nothing else could possibly happen, but still—you know what I mean."

"I know. I just got back from there. I was the one who found the body."

"Oh, my dear, how awful! Was there"—she hesitated—"a lot of blood? Not that it makes any difference really, I suppose. But it would seem more awful, somehow."

"Not a lot. The blows fractured the skull. He must have died almost instantly. I think the police are trying to establish what time it happened. Do you know when he normally came in on Wednesdays?"

"Eight o'clock," she said promptly. "I told the police that. You can be sure, I said, that he was in there at eight o'clock this morning because he always was. You could have set your watch by him. Many's the time he'd call me up wanting to know where I'd put this or that, never mind that it was supposed to be my day off—he'd want to know why something or other wasn't on his desk. He would get me up right out of bed. So after he left work yesterday, I was real careful to put that folder from Feininger's on his desk as soon as it came in the mail because I knew he would want to start work on it bright and early this morning and I'd be sure to hear about it if he couldn't find it. Oh, dear, it just doesn't seem possible that he's dead."

"He left work yesterday before you did?" I asked. That didn't sound like Miller the workaholic.

"Yes, he had a cocktail party and banquet to go to, and I remember he had to go pick up his clothes at the cleaners first."

"So he didn't come back that evening and work on the report?"

"Oh, no, dear. How could he? He was going to give a speech at the banquet and everything. He always loved that kind of thing because it got his picture in the paper. I just hope the police catch whoever did it soon. Just knowing that somebody violent like that is out running around—none of us is safe." I heard her breathing unevenly, her distress evident. "Oh, it's terrible!"

My doorbell rang. "That must be the police at my door, Mrs. Smythe. I'd better go."

A couple of men in uniform were standing at my front door with sour expressions that seemed to announce their contempt for the Fourth Amendment. "We're here to look around the house," one of them said.

"That's all right," I said, grabbing my pocketbook. "Help yourself. I was just going out."

I couldn't think of anyplace to go. Though I had bitter feelings about following Lieutenant Pittman's suggestion, I ended up doing some shopping after all. Since Bailey City wasn't exactly thick with midday amusements, it turned out I had little choice but to cruise the mall with the dedication of a Valley Girl. I certainly didn't want to watch the police search my house. When I arrived at the mall, I noticed that The Art of Bailey City Schools had been removed and that the bulletin boards were now adorned with a display of Good Nutrition, featuring large illustrations of bread loaves, leafy green vegetables, and gallons of generic milk.

I gave it my best—two gruesome hours of trying on shoes and considering such weighty questions as whether I could possibly use a sequined fuchsia silk blouse—a real bargain at fifty dollars except that it made me look as if I were about to elope to Acapulco with a rock musician. The entire time I was regarding my image skeptically in a three-way mirror, I thought of Miller and how unlikely it was that anyone would miss him. I thought of the police and wondered if they had any leads yet. Also, I thought about how my situation could be worse—my ex-love Jason could still be hanging around with his snaggle-toothed grin, his freckles, and his everlasting passion for jazz at midnight. Reminding myself of that made my present situation seem less grim. Whatever happened, at least I wasn't in for another year of Jason. My spirits were substantially improved by this train of thought. I took a deep breath of the ozone and carbon monoxide air of the shopping center parking lot and it smelled like freedom.

On my way home, I stopped at a convenience store to get the local paper. Miller's murder had not been reported in time to make the evening edition, but the paper did contain an account of his speech the previous night. "Psychologist Speaks to Rotary Club," the headline read. It was obviously his own press release. I wondered if it would have given Miller any satisfaction to know that he had died in a way guaranteed to make the front page.

I had folded the paper to toss in the backseat when Brannigan's name caught my eye. I unfolded it and scanned the inside page. It wouldn't have surprised me if I had imagined it. My mind, not to mention my nerves, was not in the best of shape. But incongruously, there it was in a little column called "Town Talk," next to a photograph of the middle-aged lady columnist that looked like a mug shot.

"Visitors at Dr. Manning Carmichael's Timberline

Stables were surprised to see movie star James Brannigan riding Wings of Wind, affectionately known in the Carmichael family as Wendy. Movie fans who remember that James Brannigan was his own stunt man in *Pride of Lions* will not be surprised to learn that Dr. Carmichael was willing to trust his prize horse to the actor. Mr. Brannigan declined to give an interview to this reporter, explaining that he was in town visiting friends, but I was fortunate enough to join the Carmichaels for lunch and I can report that Mr. Brannigan does not watch his calories. He had quiche Lorraine and polished it off with a very healthy portion of Melissa Carmichael's wonderful baked Alaska."

Brannigan's alibi, I thought sourly. Not only the horse but Dr. Carmichael and a nosy reporter. Everybody's got an alibi but me. I presumed this was the Dr. Carmichael who had been Jessica's therapist. Brannigan had stayed awfully friendly with that bunch. Of course, maybe he didn't blame Carmichael for what had happened. I remembered the nurse had said Miller had moved Jessica without checking with her therapist.

When I got back to my house, there was no sign of the police. I went around rattling the doors and windows to make sure they had locked up the place before they left. After all, there was a murderer running loose out there. I hadn't forgotten that. Then I leafed through the stack of mail on the small table by the front door. As far as I could tell, they had steamed no envelopes open. I went across the room to move the antique candlesticks on the mantel a quarter of an inch to each side, straightened the print over the bookshelves, and fluffed up the couch cushions. It took an effort to force myself to quit fidgeting and sit down. Knowing the police had searched the house made me feel hot and ashamed, as if they had frisked me on a public street.

The doorbell rang. For an awful second my palpitating stomach convinced me it was the police with an arrest warrant, but it turned out to be Brack Prideaux. His hair was sticking damply to his forehead and his shirt was rumpled, as if he had spent the afternoon beating his breast.

"How long were you with the police?" I asked sympathetically.

"Hours. It seemed like hours, anyway. When I left, Mrs. Smythe was on the phone trying to reschedule everybody's appointments. What a mess." He winced. "I was the one who had to break it to Avise and Tim."

"How are they taking it?" I led him into the living room.

"Stunned, like the rest of us." He sat down on the couch next to the newspaper, and I watched him grow rigid as he spotted Miller's picture and the headline. Then his head suddenly jerked up. "Have you thought about talking to a lawyer?"

"No," I said calmly. "Have you?"

"I mean since Pittman seems determined to give you a hard time about being the one to find the body, you might think about getting some legal advice."

In the past I had found silence an excellent way

to get people to come across with what was on their mind and this was no exception. It took less than a minute for Brack to blurt out, "I didn't tell Pittman what you said about hitting Miller with the planter."

"Wait a minute!" I was alarmed. "I never said I hit Miller with my planter!"

He avoided my eyes. "No, but don't you remember that you told me you picked up your planter and if he'd taken another step you'd have killed him?"

"Well, I didn't."

"You don't have to look at me like that, Fran. Nobody would blame you for defending yourself. I wouldn't blame you."

"Thank you. But your sympathy is unnecessary. The occasion didn't arise."

With some discomfort, I remembered that I had weighted the planter to make it a more effective missile. Being a suspect in a murder case had a kind of hideous fascination—like looking at gorgeously colored plates of diseased organs in medical books—but I couldn't say I was enjoying it. "You didn't tell anybody else about what I said, did you?" I asked. But as soon as I caught the look on Brack's face, I regretted I had spoken.

I jumped up and walked over to the fireplace. Absently, I moved the left one a quarter inch closer to the center, then moved it back a smidgen. It was as if I needed the candlesticks to be symmetrical in order to counterbalance the confusion inside me. "I just don't want the police to get the wrong idea." I glanced over my shoulder at him. "You can't really think I would murder Miller just because he jumped me, can you? I mean, the idea's ridiculous on the face of it." I was glad to hear the note of conviction in my voice. But I noticed Brack's hands were clenching and unclenching and his face looked taut. "I thought Tim was the one you were worried about," I said. "What made you suddenly decide I'm the number one suspect?"

He shook his head. "It's just that when I saw the body there—his head—it suddenly came to me about how he attacked you. But that's ridiculous. No, it must have been some drug addict. It's got to have been."

The doorbell rang again. Brack followed me to the foyer, evidently to offer his protection should the visitor be carrying a bludgeon.

I flung open the door.

"Lyman!" exclaimed Brack. "Where the hell have you been? Have you heard about Miller?" Finch, his bulk effectively filling the doorway, bounced expectantly on the balls of his feet, looking full of vitamins and good cheer. His cheeks were rosy and his bright eyes seemed to say Merry Christmas.

"Edith Smythe called me over at CCE and told me," he said, moving forward to hold my hands in his. "My poor child. Edith tells me you found the body. What a terrible experience!"

"It was horrible," I agreed. "To top it off, I seem to be the prime suspect."

"How can that be?" Finch's jolly features settled into a look of disapproval. "You should get yourself a lawyer! You can't allow them to treat you that way."

"I was just telling her that," said Brack.

"But I'm innocent," I insisted. "I don't need a lawyer. There's no evidence against me. There can't be, since I didn't have anything to do with it."

Wondering, with a sense of unreality, what sort of hospitality was appropriate for an après-murder party, I headed for the kitchen and reappeared with cheese, Pepperidge Farm cookies, crackers, and a pot of Sleepytime herb tea. It said on the label that the tea was good for jangled nerves. I could hope.

I plopped the tray down on the coffee table and was not surprised to see Lyman Finch reaching at once for a cookie. With the infallible instinct of an addict, he zeroed in on a bittersweet-chocolate Orleans cookie. I had a weakness for those myself.

"So do you have any idea how the police investigation is proceeding?" asked Finch. He bit into the cookie and delicate little crumbs tumbled down his chin.

"As I said, it seems to be proceeding toward me," I pointed out.

"Surely not!" he exclaimed. "What motive could you possibly have?"

"Unbridled lust."

Finch looked from me to Brack, confused.

"His, not hers," explained Brack. "Self-defense, Fran means."

"Ah, yes. Well, that makes more sense. A capable man, Aubrey Miller, admirable in many ways—but not the sort, I would think, to attract feverish advances from the opposite sex." Finch's eyes twinkled at me, and I at once began to feel better. I decided Finch must appeal to my deep and suppressed desire for an all-understanding father.

"Besides," he went on, "don't you have a—what-doyoucall it—an alibi?"

I perked up a bit at that. An alibi. Maybe I did have one. But after a moment's thought, I was forced to shake my head. "I don't think so. I called on school counselors all morning, but I was driving all over town. I had time to swing back by the office and do Miller in if I had the urge. But I didn't."

"Do they have the time of the murder pinned down, then?" said Finch.

"It looks to me as if it happened sometime between ten and noon. I don't know if they've pinned it down any more closely than that."

"If you're right about that, it's a great weight lifted off me." Finch sighed. "Don't you see, Brack? Tim's got an unshakable alibi for that time."

"He does?" said Brack.

"He was on the teen panel of my talk show this week. 'Peer Pressure and You.' I'll be able to swear that he was in the station from nine until almost lunchtime. After that I piled all the young people into my car and treated them to lunch at the steak house. Fortunately, I'm not the only witness." He waved his cookie in the air. "Cameramen, the station manager, secretaries, and all the other teenagers on the panel will be able to swear that Tim never left our sight."

"You're sure it happened between ten and noon?" Brack asked me.

"I don't see any way around it," I replied. "Mrs. Smythe said Miller always started work at eight on Wednesdays. If he reviewed all those records, interpreted the test scores, analyzed the data, and began his report in less than two hours, then I'm Sigmund Freud. He couldn't have started on them before this morning because he was tied up all yesterday evening at that Rotary Club banquet, the one that's in the paper."

"It does sound as if Tim's in the clear," said Brack slowly. "That's good news."

"Indeed," agreed Finch. He crossed his legs—not without difficulty—and beamed at both of us.

"If you've got any spare alibis lying around," I said sourly, "I could use one."

At this delicate juncture, James Brannigan strolled in from the kitchen.

"How did you get in?" exploded Brack. His eyes narrowed in suspicion. I gathered that Brannigan's undoubted appeal did not extend to the members of his own sex.

"I guess the cops left the kitchen door unlocked. Careless sons of bitches."

I looked at him, wondering if it had been a penchant for grand entrances or need to eavesdrop that drove him to jimmy open my kitchen door. I would have to get a locksmith to put on a dead bolt.

Finch stared at Brannigan, trying to figure out what was familiar about him. Brannigan, his shoulders hunched, his hands in his pockets, moved across the room, generating enough electricity in his progress to make cash registers a quarter mile away ring up million-dollar totals. He perched on the corner of the piano stool, where sun from the tall west window skated across the beautiful bones of his face and cast a shadow under his lower lip. I reluctantly tore my eyes from him.

"Lyman, I don't think you've met my neighbor, James Brannigan," I said. "James, Dr. Lyman Finch and Dr. Bracken Prideaux."

"Brannigan," said Finch, the light dawning. "You're an—uh—actor, aren't you?"

Brannigan waited a fraction of a second, probably debating whether what he did could legitimately be called acting, then inclined his head slightly in agreement. "So what have you been able to find out?" he asked me. "Who are the police after?"

"Me," I said bleakly.

"You? Why do they think you would want to kill Miller?"

"The idea seems to be that I acted in self-defense."

"How did you know Miller was dead, Brannigan?" Brack interrupted. "The story hasn't broken yet. It hasn't even been on the radio."

Brannigan smiled a Mona Lisa smile. "Fran called me while the body was still warm at her feet."

"You could have phrased that better," I said. "Besides, he wasn't warm. He was cold. Well, anyway, cool. That means he'd been dead for a while, doesn't it? Can't the police tell how long he's been dead?"

"Only within fairly broad limits," Brack answered. He was looking at Brannigan with something approaching loathing. I could see how it would not be pleasant for Brack, all hot and rumpled from a police interrogation, to meet up with gorgeous

Brannigan in a loose-weave natural silk shirt that must have cost as much as the gross national product of some underdeveloped countries. Add to that Brannigan's go-to-the-devil manner that would make even a mild-mannered person want to shove his teeth down his throat, and you had a foolproof recipe for dislike.

"I wonder when the police will let us know anything?" said Finch.

"Probably never," I said. "At first I thought detectives would be chatty, like reporters. I imagined we'd have nice cozy talks about the murder over coffee, and that the police would take us into their confidence and welcome our clever insights. All I can say is that I've met Lieutenant Pittman. Forget it!"

"I think you're taking too pessimistic a view of the matter," said Finch. He poised his hand over the cookie tray, letting it hover indecisively between a gingersnap and a sugar cookie. "I believe we can tell something about the progress of their investigation by comparing notes among ourselves about what questions they asked us. For example, you, Fran, told us that they are trying to establish the time of death. That's the sort of thing I mean. If we exchange our impressions as we go along, we should be able to get an idea of where their thinking is heading. Then maybe we can correct any misapprehensions they've developed and help them with their investigation."

I could just imagine how Lieutenant Pittman would welcome Lyman Finch's help.

"After all," Finch went on, "our goal has to be to get the office back to normal as quickly as possible.

Life must go on even though, of course, we will certainly miss Aubrey."

Brannigan clasped his hands around one knee. "We will?" The amusement in his eyes made it impossible not to regard the question as a taunt, but Finch seemed oblivious to the malice. He looked up vaguely in the direction of the piano; obviously he had forgotten about Brannigan as soon as he pegged him as an actor.

"Well, yes," said Finch. "None of us would pretend, I suppose, to have been personally close to poor Aubrey, but his business acumen was undeniable." He carefully fixed a slice of cheese between two crackers. "I daresay this Preferred Provider scheme of his will have to be shelved now. I certainly don't have the time or the interest to see it through. I'm strictly a clinician, not a businessman."

"You know," I said, clearing my throat, "I'd just as soon you didn't mention that to the police, Lyman. They might get the idea that that gave me another motive." When I saw the look on Brack's face, I wished I had held my tongue.

"Motive?" said Finch, his cracker hesitating in midair. "How could that be a motive? Why, from what Aubrey told me, it would have brought pots of money into the office."

"Well, it might have brought pots of money to you and Aubrey, but I wasn't very keen on the idea myself."

"You could have just not joined, then," said Finch briskly. "You mustn't let this police investigation make you paranoid, Fran. Why should the police have any interest in the business workings of the office? That's not the sort of thing people commit murder over. Mark my words, I'm sure we'll find that this terrible crime was committed by some very, very disturbed young man—probably one of the unemployed."

"A drug-crazed addict," I suggested.

"That's the sort of person," said Finch, looking at me as if I had said something terribly original. He patted my knee briskly. "You're looking awfully tired. You must try not to brood about this unfortunate tragedy. It will all work itself out in time."

I hoped he was right. I realized my head was throbbing and I pressed my fingers to my eyes.

Finch stood up. "I think we'd better let Fran get some rest. This has been an awful strain on her, worse than for any of us."

I couldn't deny it. I managed a wan smile as Finch began shooing everyone out but I certainly didn't try to persuade them to stay. I only wanted to find an aspirin and a restaurant that delivered egg rolls so I could curl up in front of the television.

"Get some sleep!" Finch said as he left.

I promised I would.

Brannigan smiled and quietly disappeared. I suppose he went out the kitchen door, the way he came.

Brack didn't even mutter "good-bye" as he stepped outside. It was only after I closed the door on his disgruntled back that an uncomfortable explanation for his bad temper occurred to me. Did he imagine that I had given Brannigan a key to my place?

nine ///

"**I**t has to have been someone looking for drugs," said Avise shrilly.

I eyed her uneasily. "Yes, I'm sure you're right."

I was sitting on Avise's couch, which was upholstered with a design of carnivorous-looking chartreuse and yellow flowers. Tim sat in the corner under a spider plant in a hanging basket. His eyes were blank, and his mouth twitched at unpredictable intervals. Merris Brannigan was next to him, her blue eyes moist with sympathy. At the telephone table near the door of the apartment, James Brannigan was determinedly doodling on the cover of a telephone book.

"If they would just settle it." Taut lines stood out on Avise's neck. "To have it hanging over us like this! How can we be expected to function? I'm sure it was someone looking for drugs. That's what it was."

"Yes," I agreed faintly.

She sniffled. "He was such a bad father. And a bad husband. I can't be a hypocrite about it. Everyone knew what he was like. No one would believe me if I said I'm sorry he's dead. Threatening to cut off Tim's support payments—as if he didn't already pay little enough. I was afraid to take him to court, he knew that. He was so vindictive, so petty!"

Tim seemed oblivious to what his mother was saying. I thought I had an idea of what he was going through. I'd been along that road myself. A parent you've been fighting with can be the hardest to lose. Death suddenly puts an end to the whole absorbing battle, leaving the surviving combatant feeling oddly rudderless. I remembered being very angry at my father for so abruptly bowing out of our quarrel. It seemed unfair of him to die before I had a chance to make peace.

"He was pathological about money," Avise said, turning her feverish eyes toward me as she gripped the back of the chair with a rigid hand. "He would save up little bits of soap in jars. He washed and folded tiny pieces of tin foil. We had to take the icicles off the Christmas tree, wind them around cardboard rolls, and use them again the next year. Icicles! At seventy-five cents for five hundred! He figured out what each kitchen paper towel cost and wanted us to use dishcloths to save the money.

"And his jealousy! It was like a disease. When I married him, he seemed so good, so kind. But then after Tim was born I started to see what he was underneath. It was like poking around in an old shed, turning up sticky spiderwebs and bits of insects and grubs—all these awful, grimy little corners of him. I kept thinking it was my fault, that if I had loved him more . . ." She trailed off.

"Then even after the divorce, he wouldn't let go

of me. He seemed to think he owned me. I think he hated me for leaving him. I was afraid of him." She choked back a little sob. "It would have made more sense if it had been my body you found in the waiting room."

"I don't think I would tell the police all this," I said uncomfortably.

"Oh, no. Of course not. I'd never say this to them. They've already been over here asking questions. They wanted to know if Aubrey had any enemies. They wanted to know when I last saw him! They asked me where Tim was yesterday. It was terrible. The only way I got through the whole thing was by acting like Eleanor Roosevelt." She laughed shortly. "I think it went over pretty well—stodgy patrician dignity. I was in a college production once of *Sunrise at Campobello*." Her eyes moved irresistibly over to the telephone table where Brannigan was sitting. "You know, I used to be an actress." She abruptly looked away.

The doorbell rang. As Avise passed Brannigan to get to the door, she drew away from him, as if his very presence threatened to singe her flesh. Brannigan didn't seem to notice. He kept moving his pen monotonously in squares and circles. He was dressed in faded jeans and a beige T-shirt. Nondescript, with his head down, intent on his doodles, he might have been a plumber's assistant. I had not realized that the erotic force that burned from him like a flame could be turned off at will.

The man Avise let in did not even glance in Brannigan's direction. So perfect was Brannigan's self-effacement that I don't believe the man even saw him. The new arrival was bald and was dressed as if for a funeral in a somber summer-weight suit and a gray silk tie dotted with discreet green fleurs-de-lis. His mouth was broad, his eyes were shrewd slits, and his voice was slow and careful. I guessed at once that he was the family lawyer, though the casserole dish he carried struck an incongruous note below his lawyerlike face. After introducing him to us all, Avise took the dish from him with disjointed thanks and went into the kitchen to park it next to the roast beef that I had brought.

"Such a tragedy," the lawyer murmured to no one in particular. "Terrible." He walked over and rested his hand on Tim's shoulder. "I'm so sorry, Timothy. A terrible thing. I knew your father for years. I know no one can replace him." Tim only looked more bewildered, rather as if he thought the man had confused his father with someone else.

I was relieved when Avise returned from the kitchen. She managed to look a facsimile of her usual stately self.

"It's so kind of you to come by, Frank." She lowered herself in one fluid motion onto the tufted chair opposite the couch.

"Not at all. Not at all," he said, coloring slightly. I thought I understood why his arrival was such a tonic for Avise. He was an admirer. He showed all the signs—flushed face, warm glances, heightened behavior when she reentered the room.

"This is a terrible thing. Terrible," he repeated. "Emily thought you wouldn't feel up to cooking. I said I'd bring the casserole over because I wanted to offer my personal condolences to Timothy. And I thought it might be a comfort for you to know just where you stand with the will and so forth." There was a delicate pause as the lawyer glanced uncomfortably in my direction. Brannigan gave a look to Merris across the room, and as one we all rose to make ourselves scarce.

Brannigan and Merris went out back where a scrap of patio and a wall decorated with a few pots justified calling Avise's place a "garden apartment." I, however, chose my retreat more cunningly. I moved into the kitchen and busied myself with tea bags and hot water. I had technically absented myself and even, with some ostentation, closed the door. But thanks to the bar that was cut through the kitchen wall to the living-dining area, I could not only hear perfectly but see as well.

The lawyer sat on the ugly couch and folded his hands over his paunch. "Aubrey had told me he was going to bring the will up-to-date, Avise, but Fate intervened before he could do so. I have every reason to believe that the will in my files is his most recent one. Yes, I believe I can say that with a reasonable degree of confidence since I spoke to him only last week."

I could almost feel the words *how much?* trembling on Avise's lips, but instead of speaking, she licked her lips and carefully folded her hands in her lap in an unconscious echo of the lawyer's posture.

"It's a simple will," he went on. "Everything will go to Tim, of course, as the only issue of Aubrey's marriage. I should warn you that it may take a year or more to wind everything up properly, but I don't expect to find any outstanding liens against the estate. Aubrey was careful by nature. I've suggested to Mel Lewis, Aubrey's broker, that he call and tell you exactly where the estate stands, since I know you will want to be able to plan for Timothy's future. And you, of course, must feel free to call on me at any time if there's any way you feel I can help."

He leaned over to press her hand in his and looked into her eyes. Avise produced a brave smile that reminded me unaccountably of Ingrid Bergman in *The Inn of the Sixth Happiness*.

At length, after many expressions of esteem and assurances of his deep desire to be helpful, the attorney ceremoniously took his leave, and the rest of us returned to the living room. I was beginning to think it was time for me to leave as well. It wasn't, after all, as if I were a close friend who would be expected to stand by and assist with funeral arrangements.

But just as I was groping for my purse, the doorbell rang again. When Avise opened the door Brack and Finch stepped inside, their expressions plainly indicating that they were full of news. My pulse quickened. What could they have come to tell us? Unfortunately, entering the apartment right behind them was a man who turned out to be Mel Lewis, Miller's broker. He was a pink-faced blond man whose somewhat overweight form was squeezed tightly into a three-piece suit. It was obvious that his presence had an inhibiting effect on the other two because once they were in the living room, Brack and Finch kept casting impatient glances at Mel Lewis, obviously anxious for him to say his piece and be gone so they could tell their news. The broker seemed quite unaware of their pointed looks.

Noting this, I distributed my belongings around me on the couch once more and settled down to wait. I didn't want to leave until I heard what was going on.

"Avise, sweetheart, what can I say?" said the broker. He put his arm around her. "I just want you to know that you don't have to worry about the money end of it. Good sound bonds and mutual funds, solid business property—Tim should be sitting pretty. He may want to unload the property, unless he's interested in business like his father was. If selling the real estate is the route he wants to go, I can recommend some very good growth stocks he could get into instead." He winked at Tim. "And maybe a sports car, huh? I was young once." He squeezed Avise again. "Listen, Avise, girl, I know how you're feeling. Two divorces I've got under my belt. You hate their guts, but still there's something there, you know what I mean? This is a rotten time for you. I hope they get the bastard who did it."

Brack, sitting next to me on the couch, rolled his eyes skyward.

"You don't think the estate has any outstanding debts?" Avise asked timidly.

"Chicken feed. Hell, not to speak ill of the dead, but we all know Aubrey had every penny he ever made, right? If we don't clear a half million after taxes, call me a fruitcake. He had a knack for making money. There it is." Another squeeze. "I know it can't bring 'em back, but money never hurts is what I say. Life goes on, right?"

Taking a quick count of all the men swarming about Avise eager to offer their advice and protection, I wondered, in passing, if possibly Miller might have had grounds for his pathological jealousy.

The broker at last departed. The door had not even closed behind him before Brack growled audibly, "I thought he'd never leave." He directed a hostile look toward the telephone table as well, but it was wasted on Brannigan. Brannigan's doodle must have attained the complexity of the ceiling of the Sistine Chapel by now, but he kept at it.

"Brack and I have done a little asking around, my dear," Finch said to Avise, coming to the point at once. "And I have talked to the police. I must say I feel very reassured."

I looked at him in surprise. Had he talked to the same police I had?

"They've pinned down the time of death as sometime between ten and twelve," Finch went on. "The medical examiner's wife is in my wife's literary book club, and I gather he is loathe to fix the time of death very precisely, so they are dependent largely on external evidence. They phoned a Greensboro neuropsychologist, who confirmed Fran's estimate of the amount of time it would have taken poor Aubrey to work up the sort of report he was doing, and we can say with confidence now that Tim is in the clear. The police questioned me very closely, and the station manager at WTTG told me the police had a man at the station checking their time logs—the tape and so forth—and that he left satisfied."

"It's so lucky that Tim was at the television station all morning," Avise said.

"It does seem providential," agreed Finch. "Absolutely providential."

"And they still don't have any leads?" asked Avise. "None at all?"

"I don't know. Officially, 'The investigation is continuing,'" said Brack, imitating Lieutenant Pittman's doleful tones.

"I hope they catch the murderer soon." Avise sprang to her feet. "I don't have to pretend with you two. You knew how it was. Tim coming into Aubrey's money is going to make all the difference. If they will just make an arrest, we can put all this behind us and our troubles will be over. I'll still be able to send the usual amount to Mother, and Tim's education will be taken care of."

"I don't want the money," Tim said thickly. He got up suddenly and rushed down the hall to his room. Merris darted an anxious glance after him, as if wondering if she should follow. The spider plant in the corner swung silently where Tim had brushed against it.

"He's upset," said Finch. "It's natural."

"Maybe it won't be long before they clear this up," said Brack. "Lyman and I think they may have found the murder weapon."

"The murder weapon?" I said. "They've found it?"

"Mrs. Smythe saw two policemen walking away from the dumpster in the parking lot," Brack said.

"That's what we came over here to tell you. She saw them carrying a tire iron and looking pretty pleased with themselves. I guess we can draw our own conclusions."

A tire iron? The weapon had been a *tire iron*? The news hit me hard somewhere just below my ribs and left me gasping.

ten ///

"**W**ait up," Brack called as I hurried to my car. I had barely managed to utter a few civilities before rushing out of Avise's apartment. Brack jogged to catch up with me. "Can you give me a lift home? I rode over with Lyman."

"Sure," I said shortly. I threw open the back door of my car and regarded the bare carpeting of the floor with stark disbelief. No tire iron. Yet I distinctly remembered seeing it in the backseat when the mechanics delivered the car to me that day I had the flat tire. I remembered thinking that they must have used their own tire iron because mine didn't look as if it had been moved.

"Looking for something?" asked Brack.

"No. I was trying to remember whether I picked up a loaf of bread or not. All those emotional scenes in the apartment blew everything else out of my mind." I got into the car but in my agitation dropped my keys and had to fish them out from under the hand brake. The tire iron is in the trunk, I told myself. Obviously I put it back there and forgot about it.

"Just a minute," I said, jumping out of the car suddenly. "Just need to check something."

I dashed back and opened the trunk. The spare tire sat in splendid isolation. I even felt around under the flap. No tire iron. Slowly, I returned to the driver's seat. I, too, had seen the police going to search the dumpster. If only I had, like Mrs. Smythe, watched to see what they had found there, this news would not have hit me with such a blow.

"No bread in the trunk either, huh?" asked Brack.

"Nope," I said curtly. I didn't see any reason to confide in Brack. I fished a tissue out of my purse to wipe the grit off my fingers, and a slip of paper fell into my lap, a deposit slip with a phone number written on it. I remembered jotting down the number the day I visited Feininger's. I hastily thrust the paper and the tissue back into my pocketbook and backed out of the parking place. My body was so stoked with adrenaline, I probably could have pulled the car out of the parking place with my teeth. "Where was it you said you lived?" I asked.

"Greenwood Terrace Drive. Head out Montjoy and I'll tell you where to turn." I was conscious of Brack's eyes on me as I drove. "You haven't come up missing a tire iron, have you?"

"I don't think so. It's not the sort of thing I usually keep track of. Why?"

"Oh, come off it, Fran. This isn't Drop the Handkerchief. This is murder. When are you going to go see a lawyer?"

I wondered why it is that even the nicest men turn overbearing eventually. I hadn't given Brack the slightest encouragement to imagine he could tell me what to do, but that wasn't stopping him.

"Do you know what even the suspicion that you were involved in a murder could do to you?" he persisted. "Can't you see that people are already asking who is this Dr. Fran Fellowes who discovered the body? It's not the kind of publicity you need. The next step is to have it go around the bridge clubs and the PTA circuit that it looked very bad for you but they didn't have a strong enough case to press charges."

He had hit a nerve. The fact was, I could not imagine being arraigned for a murder I didn't commit. That sort of thing happened only to illiterate people who had the misfortune to be "known to the police," not to people like me. But a nasty rumor could happen to anybody.

I felt for the first time the painful delicacy of my position. If James Brannigan were mixed up in a murder, it would probably not damage his reputation much. Movie people are notoriously open-minded. If I could believe the newspapers, statutory rape, drug possession, and assault are practically perquisites of their profession. But with psychotherapists, a single misstep can ruin a career. With a sick feeling I recognized that Brack was right. Even the suggestion that I had been involved in a murder might be enough to destroy my hope of building a practice in Bailey City, or anywhere else for that matter. The world of any profession is effectively quite small. At the regular gatherings of the tribe—professional conventions, workshops, and seminars—an extraordinary amount of gossip is exchanged.

"Turn right here," said Brack. "What if they never pin it on anybody, Fran? What then? Keep in mind that's a very likely scenario if the murderer is a nut case."

"Okay," I said. "I'm thinking of calling a lawyer. Happy?"

"Do that. I'll sleep a lot better. It's too bad you didn't have the foresight to play in a bridge tournament this morning like Avise."

So Avise had an alibi. I was conscious of a pang of disappointment and promptly felt ashamed of myself.

We drove up to Willowbranch Townhouses where Brack lived. It was a sprawling complex of black-and-white Tudor-style townhouses with hanging baskets of flowers decorating most of the second-floor balconies. The ground-floor entrances seemed to run rather to six-speed bicycles, temporarily abandoned soccer balls, and towels spread out to dry. It was the sort of place I could imagine Brack living in; it was teeming with life. Beyond tall chain-link fences were some impressive-looking tennis courts and next to them, with a lower fence, a large aquamarine swimming pool where teenagers were splashing. The midday sun painted a trail of brightness on the pool's surface.

I stopped the car, and Brack reached to open the door. "Why is this Brannigan guy always hanging around?" he asked, aggrieved. "What was he doing over at Avise's just now?"

"His daughter Merris has been seeing a lot of

Tim. I suppose he brought her over so she could offer her condolences."

"Every time I turn around, there he is," said Brack. "You can't get away from the guy. What's he doing in Bailey City, anyway?"

"Don't you remember? He brought Merris to Feininger's. Grief reaction. Her mother died about a year ago."

His eyes narrowed. "There's something about that guy that I don't like. I wonder how that wife of his died."

"Suicide. Jumped out of a window at Feininger's. He didn't have anything to do with it."

"He's awfully good-looking," said Brack, getting down at last to what it was about Brannigan that he didn't like.

"Yes." My voice sounded subdued to my own ears.

He got out and slammed the door, then bent over to look in the open window. "He probably drove her to it."

I managed a smile since I perceived that the remark was intended as a witticism.

"Don't forget," he cautioned me.

"See a lawyer," I repeated.

I stepped on the gas pedal so quickly, he had to jump clear of the car. I did plan to call Owen Windersley, a lawyer and an old family friend, that night to get his point of view. But I had no intention of employing some officious local idiot who would insist on telling me what to do every step of the way. I knew lawyers. Whatever you had in mind was "ill-advised" or "unwise." They were not above telling you how to comb your hair and warning you to appear publicly only in sober, conservative suits. I didn't want a lawyer. At least not until I had done some of the other things I had in mind. What I needed to do was make sure that the police solved the murder. That was crucial. There must be some way to shed a little light on the crime. The phone number I had scribbled on the scrap of paper in my purse, for example.

But unfortunately there was something else I had to do first. I had to tell the police about my missing tire iron.

Later that afternoon when I was at the station having my fingerprints taken I was finding it harder and harder to maintain my conviction that the police don't arrest my sort of people.

"We're taking the prints of all the people who work at Psychological Associates," said Lieutenant Pittman smoothly. "That way we can tell if any of the ones we lifted from the waiting room don't belong there."

"Did you get any prints off the tire iron?" I asked.

"Our investigation is continuing." Lieutenant Pittman was a large man with a long, tombstone-shaped face and pale eyes. In an attempt to make him seem less intimidating, I tried to imagine him as a sniffling child consumed with a burning ambition to be a cop. My attempt failed miserably when I uneasily realized that what had prompted the image in the first place was my impression that Pittman was a person of unusual determination. Under the circumstances, that was hardly encouraging.

He sighed. "So you say you left your car unlocked."

"Sometimes I lock it," I said, squirming in my seat, "but when I'm in a hurry . . ."

"A bad habit, Dr. Fellowes. You should always lock your car. When did you last see the tire iron?"

"The day I had the flat tire. The mechanics who changed my tire might have noticed. But I don't think they used my tire iron. I noticed it was still in the backseat when they brought my car to me. That must have been last Thursday." I suddenly remembered that one person knew where I had put the tire iron—Brannigan. He had watched me toss it into the backseat.

"Can you think of anybody else who might have known that the tire iron was in your backseat?" asked Lieutenant Pittman, as if he had been reading my thoughts.

"Well, I haven't given a ride to anyone that I remember," I said, feeling my face grow warm. "But when I was parked out in front of the office, anybody could have looked inside the car and seen it."

Pittman looked at me a moment as if inviting me to come clean. I folded my hands in my lap and looked back at him. I had used that ploy myself too often to succumb to it.

"But on Wednesday, you say, you didn't go to the office until lunchtime."

"That's right. I was seeing school counselors all

morning." I saw what he was getting at. If my tire iron had been the weapon, it ruled out the drug-crazed addict. Either I had used that tire iron myself, or someone had lifted it from my car with the idea of using it to kill Miller. Either way, the murder had to have been premeditated.

"Tell me, Dr. Fellowes. Dr. Miller ever give you any, uh, trouble?"

It was heartening to see that Lieutenant Pittman was capable of embarrassment.

"Lieutenant Pittman, I am a grown woman, perfectly capable of rejecting a man's advances without killing him."

"Then he did, uh—"

"He did behave extremely inappropriately once at the office," I admitted. "I was just sitting in my office minding my own business and he jumped on top of me. I had to throw him off. It was really embarrassing. After that I wouldn't have wanted to be left alone with him. I tried hard to keep my distance. I admit that being around him made me pretty uncomfortable."

Lieutenant Pittman favored me with a thin smile. "Uncomfortable enough that you felt the need to provide yourself with a weapon for your own protection?"

I stared at him blankly. "You mean a gun? I don't own a gun."

"I mean a brass planter weighted with buckshot."

I felt the blood drain out of my face. There was a long pause while I considered whether I could claim I had bought that buckshot only to keep the planter from tipping over. My claim would have been more credible, I realized, if I hadn't been white as a sheet. I decided I had better come clean.

"Okay, I guess after he jumped me that time, I was pretty shaken. It made me feel so helpless, you know? So I thought, well, maybe I'll just reinforce my planter a little bit, and if he gives me any trouble again, I'll, well, uh, have it."

"Is that what happened?" he asked softly.

"No! He never gave me any trouble after that."

"If you have something to tell me, Dr. Fellowes, it would be better to tell me now. I can understand you might have panicked and hit him too hard. But if you were only defending yourself—"

Everything in the room suddenly seemed washed in a cold, crisp light in which I could plainly see what Lieutenant Pittman was getting at. My brain cleared. This was a trap, obviously. Pittman's phony sympathy was designed to lure me into making damaging admissions. Whoever had killed Miller had not been acting in self-defense. The murder had premeditation written all over it. Nobody casually waltzes into an office carrying a tire iron. Even I could see that.

"I didn't need to defend myself," I said steadily. "I thought I explained that. He never gave me a bit of trouble after that one incident."

"Funny thing." Pittman shot me a curious look. "You run into a fair number of hoods with rolls of nickels in their pockets and pretty often young hoodlums have a fistful of heavy rings or nails in their belts, but I never have come on a lethal planter before. Officer Henderson was pretty shocked when he figured out what was going on. He tells me, by the way, that you're giving that philodendron too much water."

"Okay. I overreacted." I cleared my throat. "Naturally, I feel pretty silly about it, now. In fact, looking back on what happened, I've about decided Miller never really intended to try to rape me or anything. He just had no idea how normal male-female relationships work. However, he obviously got the message when I threw him back against the desk. Even Miller could tell that meant no. And that was all there was to it. He never tried anything again."

Lieutenant Pittman studied a sheaf of papers on his desk. "He never made, uh, lewd remarks to you?"

I looked at him in surprise.

"Edith Smythe, the secretary at the office, tells us that he once made a lewd remark about you in her presence."

"Good grief!"

"So, you and Dr. Miller were never, uh, intimate?"

I forgot my dignity and stuck out my tongue. "Yuck."

"What did you say?"

"No. I said no. Be real! I just told you, he came on real strong and I threw him off and that was the end of it."

"Have you ever seen this before?" Pittman pushed across the desk a sheet of paper that had been crumpled and then smoothed out. I leaned over and looked at it curiously. It was typed and began, "My dear Franny." Embarrassingly, it appeared to go on at length about what the writer would like to do to and with the said Franny. After I got the drift, I drew away from it and sat back.

"Miller had a richer fantasy life than I gave him credit for," I said.

"You aren't disturbed by this letter, Dr. Fellowes?"

"Lieutenant Pittman, I'm a psychologist. I've seen it all. You wouldn't believe how bizarre people's fantasies can get. When I worked with psychotics at St. Luke's—"

"Would you say that Dr. Miller was psychotic?" he asked.

"Well, no. But I'm beginning to think he was more than a tad loopy, if you want to know the truth."

"Loopy. Is that a technical term?"

"Not exactly. Contrary to popular belief, we psychologists speak English. So were there any fingerprints on the tire iron?"

He ignored my question. "That's all for now, Dr. Fellowes. We may have some more questions for you later."

My only comfort was that Miller had not actually been killed with my buckshot-weighted planter. That would have been a very sticky situation indeed. With me so tenderly overwatering my plant, the brass probably had my fingerprints all over it. I was well aware that my situation could have been far worse. Nevertheless, things as they stood were not good. Until the police came up with someone better, it seemed I was slated to be the prime suspect.

When I thought of those absurd letters of Miller's implying that he and I had had some sort of relationship, I was so angry I got hot all over. Miller had not only attacked me, he had fixed it so I looked like the chief suspect in his murder. I could have thought he had done it on purpose if it hadn't seemed that dying was a rather extreme length to go to in order to get revenge on me.

When I left Pittman's office, I was not whistling a happy tune. I knew it was in my best interest that the real murderer be apprehended as soon as possible. There was a great deal more to this murder than a line of evidence that led to me. It was my job to turn it up. The first thing I needed to do was find out more about Macon Sherwood, the guy Miller had planned to consult.

When I got home, I called the number I had scribbled on the deposit slip.

"Dr. Sherwood's office," said a woman's voice.

So Sherwood was a physician—or possibly a Ph.D., or even a dentist. I thought fast. I didn't want to be put through to Sherwood until I had figured out what tack to take with him. I took a stab in the least likely direction. "Does Dr. Sherwood take on maternity cases?" I asked, doing my best to sound not very bright.

"Dr. Sherwood does consult with prospective parents. Were you referred by your obstetrician?"

"No—that is to say, not exactly." I quickly shifted my ground. Maternity cases had turned out to be the wrong tack. "I heard that Dr. Sherwood might be able to help me. I'm looking for someone who does hypnosis. You see, I'm sort of the nervous type. I worry a lot and all that, and I figured hypnosis might be a help."

A smile crept into the woman's voice. "I'm afraid you have the wrong Dr. Sherwood. This is the Genetic Research Center of Duke Medical Center. Dr. Sherwood is a geneticist."

"Oh," I said, feigning disappointment. "He doesn't hypnotize people, then?"

"I'm afraid not."

I hung up, chewing on my lip thoughtfully. Sherwood didn't have anything to do with HMOs after all. He was a geneticist. Miller must have been following up on his obsession about Tim not being his son. I couldn't think of any other reason for his consulting a geneticist.

But why now? Why would Miller wait until Tim was sixteen to set about proving such a thing? Even as the question came to my mind, the answer seemed to present itself. According to Brack, Avise was dating again, taking a serious interest in other men. And I had Brack's word for it that Miller had found this turn of events disturbing. If he in some crazy way still thought of himself and Avise as married, it must have stirred in him a deep anger. No wonder, then, that he might be prompted to act on the suspicion that Tim was not his child. What did he have in mind, though? A court case to disprove paternity so he could withdraw support payments? It would hardly seem worth the trouble. If Avise was to be believed, he didn't pay much support and in any event Tim would be eighteen in another year or so

and his support payments would end. Maybe the
threat of disproving Tim's paternity was just another
screw to tighten on Avise to make her uncomfortable. I knew Miller had a taste for that kind of thing.
He had tried it on me.

eleven ///

"**F**rances, what you tell me is extremely alarming." Owen Windersley's dry, elderly voice came to me clearly over the line from New York. "I implore you not to talk to the police again except in the presence of your attorney. If you leave me your number, I will get back to you tomorrow with the name of a local man I could recommend."

"But you would just get his name out of some book, wouldn't you?"

"Perhaps. But I'll ask around. I seem to remember a classmate of Jack's who went south a few years ago. University of Virginia Law School, Law Review. Very sound fellow, though of course quite inexperienced."

"I'd rather not have Jack's friends practice on me, thank you. Wouldn't you say it's a good sign that the police haven't advised me of my rights?"

"No, Frances, I cannot take comfort in that. If every policeman—or every attorney, for that matter—knew his job and did it properly, frankly, this would be a world I would scarcely recognize. The incompetence at every level is appalling. You admit yourself that you know virtually nothing about the way the investigation is proceeding. For all you know the police could at this very moment be making out a warrant for your arrest. But what is rather more important, you yourself may have already made statements that will prove to be sadly damaging. I wish you had seen fit to call me sooner," he grumbled. I envisioned him taking off his glasses and polishing them the way he always did when he was thinking hard. "I think perhaps the best thing for me to do," he said at last, "is to fly down there at once and take a look at the situation. It is unfortunate that I am unfamiliar with local conditions, but I trust I can at least persuade you to keep quiet. I'll have Miss Pinkney advise you of the time of my arrival as soon as my flight is confirmed."

"No, don't come down here," I said. "I'm coming up there. I'll see you sometime tomorrow."

"Frances—"

"Talk to you later. Good-bye." I hung up abruptly. When Owen Windersley had mentioned sadly damaging statements, something clicked in my mind. I had heard it through a mild alcoholic haze, and I had been in a state of shock at the time, but now, as clearly as if it were a tape inside my mind, I could hear James Brannigan saying, "He killed Jessica, and he did it to get to me." Why would Miller want to "get to" Brannigan? Was it because he suspected Brannigan was Tim's father? Was this why Avise had been afraid of taking Miller to court? Was she afraid of the notoriety that would result if Miller made that charge stick in court? I doubted that she would relish having the question of Tim's paternity splashed all over the tabloids.

I got the next afternoon's flight to Kennedy Airport and took a taxi into the city. New York was baking in the heat, and a dome of pollution hung over it. As soon as I checked into my hotel, I splashed cold water onto my face, told myself I felt completely refreshed, and set off for the public library.

The lions in front welcomed me with their usual supercilious look, but when I got inside, I discovered that things had changed since my last visit. The card catalog had vanished and been replaced by a computer system.

In spite of my difficulties with this new and supposedly superior method of obtaining materials, at length I did find myself sitting at a microfilm machine flipping through facsimile pages of old issues of *Theatre Week*. I really needed to check through only two years, 1973 and 1974, but that involved a good bit of microfilm.

At last I emitted a hiss of satisfaction. In the April 1973 issue I found what I was looking for—a production that listed James Brannigan among the players. One Avise MacBride had also appeared in the cast on that occasion. I had never heard of the play or of the Dolphin Theater; maybe the place had since been torn down or turned into a warehouse. But one thing was certain—at roughly the time when Tim had been conceived, James and Avise had been working in the same production. The crucial question was, what was Tim's birthday? For the first time I regretted that I was not one of those tiresome people who go about continually asking people what their sign is. That at least would have given me something to go on.

When I got back to my hotel, I hoisted the phone book onto my bed and leafed through it without much hope. To my surprise, the Dolphin Theater was listed. The address seemed improbable, but the theater did still exist, and quite irrationally I felt I would like to see it. It was as if the theater itself held a piece of the puzzle I was trying to put together.

The idea of looking at the Dolphin Theater, I had to confess, didn't make a lot of sense. And for the moment I had to push it out of my mind because I needed to get to Owen Windersley's office. I knew that if he didn't hear from me soon, he would become uneasy, and I didn't want that. Back when I was small and my loyalties were easily bought, he used to bring red pinwheel peppermints for me when he came to see my father, and I had a certain fondness for him.

At his law offices, I made it past Miss Pinkney and the bleakly elegant interior decoration in the outer office and settled into a leather armchair opposite Windersley's desk.

He got up and, with pointed discretion, closed the door. "Do the police know you've left town?"

"I think you're enjoying all this."

"Far from it, Frances. Far from it. I am deeply concerned. The appearance of committing a crime can be almost as damaging as actually committing the crime. Well, no, perhaps not that, but all the same, very damaging." He creakily settled himself into his chair. "Even remote involvement in a police investigation can do considerable damage to a professional person. Who now remembers from the Watergate affair which were the criminals, which the informants, and which the prosecutors? An unsavory smell hangs around everyone involved. I will put it to you plainly. A young professional cannot afford a contretemps with the police of the sort you have described to me."

Windersley's dire predictions had occasionally made me giggle, but right then I couldn't have giggled to save myself.

"Now, now," he said, catching a glimpse of my face. "It's not as bad as all that. We'll muddle through this thing." He fished a handkerchief from his pocket and began polishing his glasses with energy. "I called Jack's friend in, uh, Winston-Salem and I've obtained the name of a sound man with some experience in criminal law. In fact, I have already spoken to him about your situation. What we need now is less a brilliant trial lawyer than someone who has dealt with the local police, someone who can guide you through this preliminary investigation, and, above all, someone who can impress upon the police the need for the utmost discretion. I feel reasonably confident I am putting you into good hands with this"—he checked his notes—"Robert Lenoir."

"I hate lawyers," I said.

Owen raised his eyebrows a fraction.

"Present company excepted, of course," I added hastily.

He pressed his fingertips together and pursed his lips slightly. "You're upset, Frances. That's perfectly understandable. But get in touch with this man, Lenoir, and follow his instructions to the letter. Believe me, that's the thing to do."

I folded the slip of paper he handed me and stowed it in my pocketbook. "I know you're right," I said. "I appreciate your going to all this trouble for me."

"Not at all, not at all." He closed his notebook. "You're not the first to complain about lawyers to me, my dear. But when you're in trouble who else are you going to call?" He permitted himself a wintry smile. "Ghostbusters?"

I made my way out of the office feeling a good bit more depressed than I had before. In Windersley's office the Victorian past seemed as close as a pea-soup fog. I felt that Windersley still lived in a world where *bankrupt* was still a dirty word and where ladies never dealt with the coarse-minded police. He had made me feel that I had hopelessly compromised myself. I had half expected him to suggest I ship out and start life over on a sheep farm in Australia. I knew my position was difficult, but I had hoped he would fasten on some bright spot I had overlooked. I should have realized that no lawyer built a career by looking at the bright side. I spent a restless night at the hotel.

The next morning I hailed a taxi and gave the driver the address of the Dolphin Theater. Flying obstinately in the face of Windersley's expert opinion, I felt an absurd optimism rising within me. Examined closely, my optimism could probably be traced to nothing more than a feeling that I was due for a break. I resolved not to examine it that closely.

"Here?" said the cabbie. "You sure this is the place, lady?"

I checked the address, then glanced out the cab's window. In faded letters The Dolphin could be seen arched over the door. The legend was flanked by a couple of awkwardly sporting bottlenose dolphins depicted in flaking gray paint. To my surprise, the door to the theater was open.

"I guess this is it," I said. "You'd better wait."

When I got out of the cab, the heat rose off the sidewalk and hit me in the face. In the glaring light I momentarily felt a little confused. The theater in front of me looked so derelict that when I made out something moving just inside the door, I thought of ghosts. But I was able to sort out from the roar of the street sounds around me a faint swishing sound within, and such elements of my reason as were unaffected by the heat told me someone was sweeping the floor. I turned back to the cab driver. "I may be a while."

As I hesitated in front of the door of the theater, I realized that the swishing sounds had faded. Suddenly a dollop of cold water hit the crown of my head. I touched the wet spot on my hair ruefully and cast an anxious look upward at an air conditioner sticking out a window high overhead. Quickly I stepped inside. I looked around and was relieved that the house lights were on, though they seemed grossly inadequate and merely lightened the gloom. In spite of the rows of seats, the place had the dimly lit ambience of a barn. I found myself unconsciously looking down at my feet, expecting mice. With hesitant steps I moved down one aisle toward the stage, where a huge, white-haired man was pushing a broom. His pear-shaped frame was draped in a loose T-shirt, and as pants he was wearing striped pajama bottoms. The shadowy interior emphasized his deep-set eyes and his loose, heavy bottom lip. My steps echoed in the emptiness.

"Theater's closed," he said.

"I know. But I thought maybe I could look around anyway. You see, I know somebody who used to work here. It must have been almost twenty years ago." My voice seemed thin in the vastness of the empty theater.

He leaned on his broom and looked at me.

"I had a few minutes to spare," I went on, fingering my purse, "so I asked my cab driver to wait outside while I looked around." The man did not look like a homicidal maniac, but the place was so spooky, I thought it best to let him know I would be missed if he should take it in his head to strangle me.

"It's your funeral," he said in a deep voice.

I cleared my throat. "Could I just take a peek at the dressing rooms?"

"Dunno. Insurance and all, you know."

I ignored him and mounted the steps to the backstage area on the theory that it is easier to obtain forgiveness than permission. After a moment I heard his footsteps trailing after me.

Once I had walked through the stage door, I at once felt braver, maybe because I had taken a decisive step. In the narrow hallway of the backstage area, I picked my way through wadded-up bits of paper and fallen plaster. A heap of rope lay in the shadowy corner ahead where the hallway turned. The dimly lit passageway was lined with photographs of old productions, all of them shot with the lurid, dramatic lighting of the stage. The penciled eyebrows of the actors stood out in sharp relief against their clownlike white faces.

"Nothing back here," said the man with the broom, catching up with me. "They're closing down this place for good. Going to turn it into a restaurant supply business I hear." He snorted. "Who is this girl that used to work here? Maybe I know her, huh?"

"Not a girl. A guy." I scanned the row of photographs. "James Brannigan. He's a neighbor of mine."

"How about that! A neighbor? You must live in a pretty classy neighborhood. I guess he's rolling in it these days. Yeah, he went on to be a big star, but he got his start right here at the Dolphin. Maybe it wasn't his first part, but it was way before he hit the big time, anyway. Here he is, right over here."

I turned and incredibly saw James's face looking so smoothly round as to be almost pudgy. It was enveloped in an Elizabethan ruff.

"And here's the whole cast to that play," said the man. "I wouldn't forget that lot. Not on your life. Back then, of course, I had more of what you call a managerial-type position. That was before I retired. And was that bunch a handful! Scenes?" he said, seeming younger in his animation. "Man, you wouldn't believe the scenes and I'm not talking about scenes on stage either, I can tell you. See this girl here? The brunette? I was standing right over there when James Brannigan knocked her flat. I'm not kidding you. Laid her out like a flounder."

"You mean he knocked her out?"

"Well, not to say he actually knocked her out, no," he admitted regretfully. "But I heard this crash. Like I said, I was standing right here and I heard this sound like maybe some makeup mirrors going down or something, and then I took off running, and that's how I found them. He was standing over her." He hesitated. "Hey, you aren't a newspaper reporter, are you? I don't want to get into one of those libel suits or anything."

"Oh, no. I'm not a reporter." I looked closely at a small image of Avise's face in a group photograph. Her hair had been a good bit darker then. Now, although still dark, it was shot through with silver. In the same photograph, Brannigan stood in the row behind her, his hands resting on the shoulders of a pretty, fair young woman directly in front of him. There was something familiar about the woman, yet I couldn't quite place it. But my guide had begun speaking again, and I turned to face him.

"I tell you, back in those days it was something or other every minute. It made me old before my time. How old would you say I was? Take a guess."

From experience, I had learned this was a no-win question, but I decided to err safely on the side of youth. "Sixty?" I hazarded.

His belly shook with laughter. "Lordy, wouldn't I love to see sixty again. Nope, I'm every bit of seventy-five. Outlived two wives, God rest their souls."

I couldn't help but remember the ticking of the taxi meter outside. I turned the conversation back to Brannigan and Avise. "So he actually knocked her down? Did you ever find out what it was about?"

"You can bet your britches I did. All these actor types will talk your ear off. I heard fifty different versions of it and more. Cat fight, that was the pure and simple of it." He extended a dusty index finger to point at Avise. "This one got her claws into this one—" He moved the finger down at the pretty girl on whose shoulders Brannigan was resting his hands. "Somebody said she actually pulled her hair, but I don't know if that was right or not. The long and the short of it was, Brannigan got the idea of sticking up for the little one here—that's the one who was to become Mrs. Brannigan, you see—and whop, he belted the other one. He's got a temper. But they were all like that. I couldn't tell you half the things I saw—the jealousy, the yelling, the carrying on." He smiled in pleasurable reminiscence.

Now that I looked at the photograph again I realized who the pretty girl reminded me of. Merris, of course. Once I knew that I was looking at Jessica Brannigan, the resemblance was plain.

"Did you ever find out what the two women were fighting about?"

He shook with laughter again. "Brannigan, naturally. Ain't that a pip? Women. But I tell you, it could've been anything. I saw a girl stick a pin right in another girl's behind over a matter of billing. Top billing and sex—between the two of them, I'd say that it was billing that caused the most trouble."

I heard a scuffling noise out front. "Lady?" called the cabbie, his voice thin in the empty theater.

I hurriedly pressed a twenty-dollar bill in the old man's hand and scurried back out to meet the cabdriver. "I'm sorry," I said breathlessly. "I didn't expect to be so long."

The driver looked at me resentfully and wiped his dripping brow with the palm of his hand. "You had me worried for a minute there, lady. You can't be too careful these days."

"I know," I said, chastened. I slumped into the backseat and breathed in the smell of stale cigarette smoke that permeated the seat cushions. A big tip was going to be in order.

twelve ///

Thanks to the speed of air travel, I was back in Bailey City by the next afternoon. The Sunday comics strewn around the couch were garish in the sunshine that streamed in my tall west windows. I sat on the floor sifting slowly through the newspaper and thinking of what I had learned at the Dolphin Theater. I no longer doubted that Brannigan was capable of violence. But that was not what was troubling me most—it was this inchoate feeling I had that actors were not real people. What was it Avise had said about Miller? Dark corners, pale grubs that stirred when you poked around in dark corners. That was what it felt like.

The spookiness of the all-but-abandoned Dolphin Theater lingered around me in my sunny living room. I had been unable to kick the mood of the place. But wasn't there a rational basis for my feeling as well? I had seen the masks slip both on Avise and on Brannigan, after all. Avise was not the stately Eleanor Roosevelt type she tried to appear, but a frantic, desperate woman trying to protect her only son. Listening to her talk about her marriage, watching the way men crowded around to support her, I sensed a fragile personality, someone who might not ever be fully capable of standing on her own. Ironically, in Miller she had found a partner even weaker than herself, a demanding, angry, dangerous man.

With Brannigan, as with Avise, I was conscious of a mask, but Brannigan, thanks to his greater resources both psychological and material, had been more successful in maintaining a convincing facade. Still, more than once I had had the sensation that I had been allowed to see only what he wanted me to see.

I remembered how Brannigan had hesitated before owning to Lyman that he was an actor. Maybe that was because he had lately played only himself, in motion pictures starring Brannigan playing the devastatingly attractive Brannigan, whatever the character was called in the script. Playing oneself had to be the most insidious sort of acting. Wouldn't the public persona begin to intrude on the private personality? Where did the actor end and his self begin? What was the strange relationship between the actor and his vision of himself? Was there any "real" person in the case of a man like Brannigan?

A supervisor of mine had said once that play therapy with kids is easy because even if you don't catch on right away to what kids are saying in their play they keep doing it over and over again until you do catch on. His point was that the child really wants to be understood. I once thought that everyone is like that, that everyone is groping to communicate, that everyone, fundamentally, wants to be understood. Now I knew that wasn't true. People can have good reasons for hiding what they are really like. Particularly in a murder investigation.

Considering that, my conviction that Brannigan hadn't killed Miller was absurd. I couldn't possibly be sure. The thing to do was to go to Lieutenant Pittman and point out that Brannigan had a motive, the opportunity, and access to the murder weapon. Pittman should know that not only was I not the only suspect, I wasn't even the most plausible suspect.

So why didn't I do it? Sex, I thought glumly. When you scrape away all the education, the intuition, and the carefully framed logical reasons that people give for the things they do, it generally boils down to either sex or money. The unpalatable fact was that if Brannigan had looked like Finch, I probably wouldn't have been nearly as confident that he was innocent. If I imagined myself standing on the moon viewing my attraction to Brannigan from a vast Olympian distance, it was almost funny—the psychologist as groupie.

But I couldn't seem to believe that he could be the murderer. When I accused him of killing Miller, I had actually only wanted to hear him deny it. I remembered he hadn't been at all bothered by my accusation. That might mean he was innocent, but it could also mean that he was pretty sure I wouldn't turn him in. Maybe that wasn't surprising. I had a feeling Brannigan was pretty knowledgeable about women's reactions to him.

Accepting for the moment that I didn't seem

capable of siccing Lieutenant Pittman on Brannigan, the question remained of what I should do next? I had the name of a reliable lawyer. I supposed my next step was to call the man up and throw myself on his mercy. I doubted he'd be happy about having the careless sort of client who tends to discover bodies and mislay tire irons, but there was no help for that. Owen Windersley seemed to have it all set up. I had to call the man. First thing on Monday, I promised myself.

I went to the fridge, spooned some frozen pink lemonade out of a can, and stirred it smartly into cold water. After that it took a minute for me to locate the TV schedule in the midst of the heap of Sunday papers. I flipped through it, hoping I would be lucky enough to find one of the old movies that are among the few things that make Sunday afternoons worthwhile. I moved my finger down the listings until I came to the four o'clock time slot. **"Psychology and the Family"** read the bold type. "Peer Pressure and You. A teen panel examines the issue of peer pressure and discusses ways to cope with it."

I sat up suddenly. That was the tape that Lyman and Tim had made on the day of the murder. And holy moley, it was time for the show. I ran upstairs, sloshing pink lemonade onto the carpet in my headlong gallop, threw myself down onto my bed and switched on the television. The set gave a brief sputter, and Lyman's broad face appeared on the screen looking green. I adjusted the color until he looked less like one of the Munsters and turned up the sound.

"The teen years are a time of great turmoil," Lyman was saying, "both physically and emotionally. A group identity can be a comforting fixed point on which a young person may anchor his or her own identity."

I felt myself falling under the hypnotic spell of his soothing voice. No wonder the guy was raking in patients by the score. I should try to practice his technique.

"Today," he went on, "we will examine some of the benefits and dangers of peer pressure as viewed from the eyes of young people themselves."

I noted that his lines had been taken practically verbatim out of Berg and Evans. It seemed unfair that Finch had such a sweet setup for getting himself all this free advertising when I was sure I could have done a better job of that show.

The kids on Finch's teen panel sat behind name plates—a blond girl with an uncertain smile called Mindy; a tense boy in glasses called Anthony; a short, very brunette girl with an intelligent face called Eloise; and our own Tim Miller, looking surprisingly cool and sure of himself. Of course, I reminded myself with a start, the show had been filmed before he learned of his father's murder. That was why Tim looked so composed. There was that faintly cocky air about him that I remembered noticing the first time I had met him. The other kids looked unbearably self-conscious. I watched them sympathetically. Not for thousands would I go through being sixteen again.

"Have you, Mindy, ever done something or seen

someone else do something solely because of peer pressure?" intoned Lyman.

Mindy, the blonde, looked as if she wished she had volunteered to give her body to be burned instead of rashly agreeing to serve on a teen panel. "Well, sort of," she admitted. "Like, in a way."

"Sure," Tim put in. "Like with Ray•Bans. In the ninth grade, seemed like everybody had to have Ray•Bans."

There was general laughter at the ridiculous insecurities of the ninth grade.

"Ray•Bans," said Lyman thoughtfully, touching his steepled fingertips to his lips.

"That's a kind of sunglasses," Tim explained.

"Ah, yes. Sunglasses. There is a protective coloration, is there not, in looking like one of the crowd. Sunglasses might be almost symbolic of the anonymity we hope to achieve by being part of a group. But does the pressure to be one of the group, the pressure to be like everyone else, ever extend to things more serious than sunglasses?" Lyman beamed at them. "Sex, for example?"

A dead silence greeted this infelicitous remark.

Perceiving that he had laid an egg, Lyman quickly shifted his ground. "Or grades. Is there ever any pressure against making good grades?"

"I know some kids who feel like that," Mindy said virtuously. "But they're only hurting themselves."

I thought I heard the microphone pick up the muttered comment "nitwit" from the brunette, but I couldn't be sure that it wasn't a spot of static.

"Did you say something, Eloise?" asked Finch.

"I think the problem of peer pressure is overrated," said Eloise in a flat voice. "Berg and Evans state that for most teenagers the primary influence is still the family."

The camera panned to Finch, who cringed visibly at this revelation that Eloise had read his source book.

I turned the sound off so I wouldn't be distracted by the chatter and studied Tim's face. Did he look like Brannigan? His nose was not aquiline, I noticed, but then, neither was Merris's. In fact, although Tim did not particularly look like Brannigan, he looked as much like him as Merris did. What was even more noticeable was that he didn't look like Miller. In fact, he was so much more attractive than Miller that he looked as if he had come not only from another family, but from another species. Where Miller had been flabby, Tim was taut. Where Miller had been blotched and discolored, Tim was smooth and golden. Could youth, health, and exercise really make that much difference?

The problem was, I realized, that family resemblance can be elusive. Among fifty members of the same family at a reunion, a ghostly likeness, an indefinable cast of feature can link them together, but with two of them side by side, the chances are the resemblance will not be as clear. The infinite variety of human features makes it certain that most people look purely and simply like themselves.

Suddenly the phone by my bed rang. I snatched at it.

"Dr. Fellowes? This is Lieutenant Pittman. I've been trying to get hold of you since yesterday morning."

"Sorry. I've been out of town."

There was a meaningful silence. "Out of town?" he said at last.

"I flew up to New York for the weekend."

"I wish you would keep me notified of your movements. Until I let you know otherwise, Dr. Fellowes, I would prefer that you not leave town."

I had an insane impulse to yell, "Then charge me! Lock me up!" Luckily, instincts of self-preservation prevailed.

"Of course," I said meekly.

"Would it be convenient for you to come to the station tomorrow at nine?"

"What for?"

I fully expected him to recite his formula, "The investigation is continuing," but instead he reluctantly parted with a morsel of fact. "We want to see if you can identify the murder weapon as your tire iron."

"I don't think I can, Lieutenant," I said nervously. "Tire irons look pretty much alike to me."

"You know yours wasn't pink, don't you?" he snapped. "Nine o'clock."

That little communication from on high cast me into gloom. It was hard to avoid feeling that the police were closing in on me. I peered out the bedroom window. I could easily see over the hedge into Brannigan's backyard. Merris and Tim were sitting out on the flagstone patio in swim clothes watching a portable TV. Of course, they would be catching Tim's performance on *Psychology and the Family*. I turned back to my set and switched the sound back on. Finch appeared to be doing his wrap-up. Eloise was looking smug and Finch rather worn down, but I figured it served him right. That should teach him to research his subject a little better.

As soon as the show was over, I clicked off my set and took my glass downstairs. It would be useful, I thought, to know Tim's birthday. Probably the best way to find out was to ask. Tactfully and obliquely, of course. It seemed to me that it would be quite natural for me to stroll over and compliment him on his television performance, and I could ad lib from there.

I poured fresh lemonade and took it with me to give my visit that casual, spontaneous look.

I pushed my way through the gap in the hedge. "Hi, Merris, Tim," I said brightly. "I just saw the television show. You really have remarkable stage presence, Tim. Congratulations."

"He was great, wasn't he?" said Merris.

Tim uneasily stroked his peeling nose. He was sprawled in a deck chair wearing white shorts and a blue knit shirt. With his bony knees sticking up in the air, he looked very young.

"Virgos are good performers," I said. "Very balanced, very cool. I'll bet you're a Virgo."

Tim blinked. "No," he said hoarsely. "I'm Leo."

"You'd make an awful detective, Dr. Fellowes," said Merris scornfully, turning the full force of her periwinkle eyes on me. "You're so obvious. You might as well ask right out when Tim was born. I guess you're wondering whether Dad is Tim's father. I can save you the trouble. Tim and I worked it all out, and it's too close to call. Tim's mom got married right after she broke up with Dad—sort of a marriage on the rebound, I guess you'd say. So it's anybody's guess."

It seemed to me that Tim was less comfortable than Merris with this frank outline of the circumstances of his birth. The monotonous hum of the bees in the thyme sounded in the uncomfortable silence that followed.

Merris studied the perfect ovals of her nails. "It's no big deal. I figure, who cares? Incest worked out okay for the ancient Egyptians, didn't it? Tutankhamen and that bunch were always making it with their sisters, keeping the pharaoh business in the family."

Too late, she perceived that Tim was looking as if someone had socked him in the stomach. "It's really nobody's business anyway," she ended lamely.

"I expect Tim is sort of interested in the question," I said. "But what you mean is that it's none of my business, don't you? And you're right. I'm sorry I was nosy, and I apologize."

Anger flashed in Merris's eyes. "People don't seem to understand that all this stuff is getting to Tim enough as it is without anybody laying anything else on him. Lots of people around town don't even know that Tim has an alibi for the time of the murder, and when he goes to the drugstore or anything, people look at him funny."

"I sympathize," I said ruefully. "People look at me funny, too."

"You?" said Tim. "Why would they think you killed Dad? What reason would you have had?"

I felt I had already done enough damage without going into Miller's lewd remarks, and I doubted if it would comfort Tim, either, if I alluded to my tire iron having been used to clobber his father. I shrugged my shoulders helplessly. Glancing at Tim, I judged he had already had about all he could take. I made some polite noises and got out of there.

It was clear that Tim's attitude toward his parentage was not as casual as Merris thought, pharaohs or no. I couldn't help feeling that it would be better for all concerned if this mystery were sorted out. The puzzle had obviously been very much on Miller's mind when he died. Wasn't it reasonable to think the answer to it might provide a key to the murder?

Maybe I was, as Merris had said, not much of a detective, but I did have Macon Sherwood's name, which gave me a lead that the police apparently did not have. What's more, I knew a guy who had done a postdoc at Duke. The odds were good that he was still on the staff there. I had a feeling that my old friend Myron might be able to put me in the way of finding out what, if anything, had passed between Miller and the genetics expert.

thirteen ///

The next morning I forgot to set my alarm and was awakened by the ringing of the phone. I put out a leaden paw and knocked the phone off the hook. Eventually my fingers managed to find the receiver and convey it to my mouth. I sounded like a hung-over frog, and my face was numb where it had been pressed against the pillow. The seventh cranial nerve controls that part of the face, I remembered muzzily. "On old Olympus's towering top a fat-armed girl vends snowy hops"—that was the way to remember the names of the cranial nerves.

"Dr. Fellowes, are you planning to come into the office this morning?" It was Mrs. Smythe.

I kneaded my brow with my fingers, suppressing a groan. "I guess so. I have to go see the police the first thing, but after that I'll check in at work. I haven't had any new referrals, have I?"

"No," she admitted, but added kindly, "Dr. Prideaux's and Dr. Finch's appointments are way off, too. I think a lot of people think the office is closed. The police have strung a paper tape across the front

door that says Crime Scene. Do Not Cross. If you ask
me, that's bound to put people off. The patients can
come in the back door, and that's how we're managing things, but there's no denying it's a mess." She
paused briefly. "I'm not calling just to tell you all that,
though. It's about something else. I know it seems
awful to think about it, but do you remember that
report Dr. Miller was working on when it happened?
Feininger's wants it. They need to know what's
going on with that man he tested. The police kept
the original report, but they gave me the photo-
copies back. The only trouble is, it's just a bunch of
numbers and one measly paragraph. I can't send it
to Feininger's that way. They called me Friday and I
said I'd see what I could do, and I've been trying to
get hold of you ever since."

"I've been out of town," I admitted. I felt ridicu-
lously guilty. Maybe it was being a murder suspect
that was getting to me.

"Dr. Prideaux said I should call you because you
were the best one to pull together a neuropsych
report."

I felt an absurd glow of pleasure mixed with
quivering insecurity. "Maybe Dr. Finch should do it,"
I said, hating myself as soon as the words were out.
I realized I was beginning to show the lack of self-
confidence characteristic of the chronically unemployed. I was going to have to shake myself out of
this state of mind. But that would be easier if the
police would quit breathing down my neck.

"I thought of Dr. Finch. I forgot just for a minute
that you were with us, dear. But when I said that,

Dr. Prideaux just laughed. I guess now that I think of it, Dr. Finch is awfully busy."

"Well, I'm certainly not too busy," I said lightly. "I'll come by the office and pick up the file as soon as I finish with the police."

"That's a load off my mind." She exhaled audibly. "I can check that off my list now. You wouldn't believe the details there are to take care of with all this mess. And it all falls on me."

After I hung up, I dragged myself out of bed and forced myself to go downstairs and get breakfast. The idea of food was repellent so I broke an egg into the blender with some orange juice and drank it. No sooner had I downed it than I remembered all those newspaper articles I had read about how raw eggs were contaminated with salmonella and I immediately began to feel queasy. My survival skills seemed to be in poor shape. Uneasily, I realized that I hadn't even craved chocolate lately. I was sure this was a bad sign. No doubt my will to live would be the next thing to snap.

After breakfast, I went to the police station and was ushered into Lieutenant Pittman's office. For once I scarcely noticed his long pale face. My attention was fixed on the tire iron lying on his desk, a tag attached to it with twisted wire. When I noticed discolorations on it that could have been blood, I had to sit down suddenly. I held on tight to the sides of the polished wooden chair as if I were afraid it was going to buck.

"Is that it? The weapon?" I croaked.

"Yup. Is it yours?" He looked at me.

"It's hard to say."

"You would say, though," he said wryly, "that it could be your tire iron."

"I guess so."

"You don't remember whether yours had any distinguishing marks? Any chips, anything like that that would help you identify it?"

"No. You might ask the guys who changed my tire."

"I did. They used their own tire iron."

"I had the oil changed at the dealer's as soon as I got to town," I said helpfully.

"It may surprise you to learn this, Dr. Fellowes, but they don't normally use tire irons to change the oil." He gave me a look that would have eradicated crabgrass.

"Are you making much progress with the investigation yet?" I inquired timidly.

"Well," he said, "we've got the murder weapon and we're pretty sure who it belongs to." He stared at me grimly.

After that, I couldn't bring myself to ask if they had any hot suspects. My Nancy Drew instincts seemed to wither under the lieutenant's basilisk gaze.

"Can I go now?"

He shuffled some papers. "Sure. Go. Just—"

"Don't leave town," I finished. "I know."

As I left the station, I realized that I felt insensibly comforted. If Lieutenant Pittman were about to arrest me, I was certain he would have been in a more cheerful frame of mind.

I drove to the office and picked up the file from Mrs. Smythe, intending to get right down to it. But the problem was, I couldn't quit thinking about the murder. If only the murder were solved, I told myself, I could get back to building up a therapy practice instead of sitting here staring helplessly at this half-done report. However, my problems weren't going to solve themselves. If I didn't make a push to find out who had murdered Miller, what did I have to look forward to but more and more police interrogations? Maybe even jail. After some thinking along these lines, I picked up my phone. In only a quarter of an hour, I tracked down my old classmate Myron Stone at Duke Medical Center.

"Fran Fellowes!" he cried. "What a surprise! Are you here in Durham?"

"Not exactly, but close enough. The reason I'm calling, Myron, is I need a favor."

"Anything, you know that. After that business with Sylvia, I owe you one."

I had once spent an entire night filling his ex-fiancée with black coffee, walking her around the block, and persuading her that it wasn't such a good idea to get on the phone and pour the whole story of Myron's perfidy into the elderly and easily shocked ears of his dissertation director.

"I want to have lunch with Macon Sherwood," I said.

"Macon Sherwood?" He sounded amused. "Is this some kind of crush or what? The man is happily married."

"Very funny. No, I need some off-the-record information about a patient. Maybe not exactly a patient, but someone who probably consulted Sherwood."

"I don't know. That could be a problem. Confidentiality and all that."

"Sylvia," I said simply.

"I'll see what I can do," he said hastily. "All I can promise is to vouch for you to Sherwood. You have to put your case to him yourself. Okay?"

"Is he a stickler?"

"Nah. Real nice guy. My guess is, if you've got a legitimate reason, he'll listen to you. Strictly off the record, you understand, one professional to another. I'll try. Let me get back to you."

After we hung up, I picked up the thick folder Mrs. Smythe had given me, but I couldn't concentrate on it. When I told the police it would mean hours and hours of work, I hadn't been kidding. It wasn't the sort of thing I could do when most of my mind was engaged in wondering what I would find out from Sherwood.

The phone rang, and I hurriedly grabbed at it. It was Myron. "Ran into Sherwood in the hall," he explained. "He's free for lunch today. Can you make it?"

I glanced at my watch and tried to estimate the driving time to Durham. "I can be there by twelve-thirty."

As I drove along, my mind churned continually. I kept going over the same names—Tim, Avise, Brannigan—but the idea of any of them as a murderer seemed ridiculous. I tried to imagine them bludgeoning Miller to death but the picture just wouldn't come into focus.

I met Macon Sherwood in the hospital cafeteria. Trays clattered around us, and nurses moved past us with their plates full of healthful fruit and cottage cheese. I was not hungry but picked up a salad in the line anyway. I didn't want to look conspicuous. Sherwood turned out to be a square-built man with stubbled gray hair and a military-looking mustache. But there was nothing military in his manner, which was quiet and affable, like a college professor.

"So you're in Bailey City, Myron tells me," he said, deftly cutting his chicken off the bone. "Feininger's, by any chance?"

"No, I'm in private practice." Considering my embarrassing lack of patients, I felt as if I were uttering a bald-faced lie. I only hoped I wasn't actually blushing.

"You must have known that poor fellow Miller. I saw it in the newspaper. He was killed right in his office, you know. Murdered by some burglar."

"Yes, we worked in the same office. As a matter of fact, I was the one who discovered the body."

"Goodness! How awful!" His fork paused in midair.

It was refreshing to be talking to someone who did not immediately leap to the conclusion that I was the chief suspect.

"It's hard to believe he's dead," mused Sherwood. "Not two weeks ago, I had lunch with him right here in this cafeteria."

I blinked. I hadn't expected it would be this easy to introduce the subject of Miller. "Yes, I knew he had been to talk to you, and I was hoping you could tell me what you talked about. I presume he was consulting you on some genetic matter. I'm wondering exactly what you told him."

"Nothing, really. I could tell something was bothering him, but he was a prickly sort of man. You know what I mean. Part hedgehog. And, I should add, secretive. He put to me the hypothetical question of how parenthood can be determined. I guessed at once that his interest in the question was personal. Oh, we talked about genetic markers, blood types, and some obviously inherited defects, ranging from color blindness to Tay-Sachs disease. But he was obviously dancing around his real intent, which as far as I could make out was to get the goods on someone." Sherwood's eyes twinkled. "Is that making sense?"

"Perfectly," I said.

"Of course, most people know that these days far more can be done to prove parentage than was ever possible before. A DNA match gives you a fairly definite answer to a question that used to be pretty murky. Not long ago the most you could do was prove that a particular man could *not* have fathered a particular child and you couldn't always do that. Now it's a different story. We can prove parenthood. I think that's what brought Dr. Miller in to talk to me. What he couldn't seem to grasp was the human dimension of the problem. There isn't any way that you can force someone to have a DNA analysis. It requires the full cooperation of all parties." He took a mouthful of his salad and regarded me with amusement. "Thus, it's a medical procedure not very well suited to blackmail."

"You think blackmail was what Miller had in mind?"

"It certainly didn't sound to me as if he expected to be able to get the cooperation of the other parties. To tell you the truth, I felt sorry for the poor man. I couldn't escape the feeling that he had doubts about his wife. It sounded to me as if he needed a lawyer, not a geneticist." He shot me a shrewd glance. "You don't imagine this had anything to do with his death, do you?"

"I don't know whether it does or not," I said. "It's just that the police don't seem to be getting anywhere . . ." My voice trailed off.

Dr. Sherwood skewered a morsel of chicken. "His wife doesn't happen to be a suspect in the murder by any chance, does she?"

"If she is, she's only one of several. The police seem to be suspicious of everyone who knew him. That's why we all want to get this whole thing cleared up."

He shook his head regretfully. "I expect the culprit will turn out to be some pathetic unemployed young man. The worst thing about these affairs, it seems to me, is that when the police finally nab the culprit, it usually turns out to be some sad specimen of humanity who one can't even work up any satisfying anger against." He made a helpless gesture. "Poverty, drugs, racism—those are the real crimes to my way of looking at it. As a matter of fact, I have to admit my wife and I are rather looking forward to our return home, in that one respect, though the winters will take some getting used to after we've become so spoiled. We have safer cities, and not so many that are hopelessly poor."

"You're not an American," I said. "Of course. I can't put my finger on it, but there's something different in the way you say *about*."

"You picked up on that, eh? Yes, I'm a Canadian. Of course, a Canadian with a good ear can pick out another Canadian immediately, but down here I usually pass for an American." He raised an eyebrow. "I'm not sure whether I should be pleased about that or not. There are so many different varieties of Americans, you see, that no one makes anything of another unfamiliar accent."

"Lyman Finch, a psychologist who works in my building, is a Canadian, but he doesn't have your accent."

"Well, the accent depends on where you come from, and Canada is a big country. But as it happens you are mistaken about Lyman being a Canadian. He is a native of the Bahamas, although he was educated in Canada."

"He's awfully nice, isn't he?" I rested my chin on my hand in resignation. It looked as if my investigation had come to another dead end. "He's really different from Miller."

"Oh, very. I haven't seen him in many years, but I don't think people change fundamentally, do you?" His eyes twinkled at me. "Of course, you haven't had quite the opportunity of judging that I have. In another twenty years you may agree with me. Lyman stood out on the campus, of course, but he didn't mind that. A star athlete. Quite extraordinary at tennis and swimming. In those days, with the shorter warm season, there perhaps wasn't quite the opportunity for Canadians to develop in those sports that there was in regions farther south, and he was outstanding. He was a runner, too. If I remember right, he ran the four-minute mile."

"Lyman Finch! I can't believe it."

Sherwood patted his stomach. "Well, time leaves its mark on all of us. I suppose I was wrong about people not changing. Of course, we're all changing, all the time. Oh, I see a beautiful unity when I look back, but it may be mostly an illusion."

"It's hard to reconstruct the past." I was thinking morosely of my foray into the Dolphin Theater.

"Exactly." He warmed to the subject. "You see what I'm getting at. The mind looks for order. Maybe we force some kind of unity on the past the way an artist imposes unity on his raw materials. Have you ever heard divorced people talk about their ex-spouses?" He laughed. "You'd think the ex-spouse never did a decent thing in his life. But when you think about it, at one time those two people loved each other. They've blotted all that out in the interest of simplicity."

I winced as I thought of Jason, once the love of my life, now cast as arch villain. "You're a philosopher, Dr. Sherwood."

"It comes with middle age, I'm afraid." He pushed away his plate. "I'm sorry I wasn't able to help you more with your inquiries. Myron told me he was most anxious to repay a favor that you did for him once."

"It's been a nice lunch, anyway."

"I enjoyed it, too." He smiled. "Listening to me run on like that—you must be a good therapist."

I smiled wanly.

"Give my regards to Lyman," he said. "I saw his name on the roster of a workshop last summer, but I never did run into him there. One of these days we'll have to get together and talk about old times."

On the drive home, I did my best to overcome my disappointment. Like Miller, I had had a touching faith in Macon Sherwood's being able to solve my problem. Now I was no nearer finding out who Tim's father was than I had been before. It didn't sound to me as if Miller had learned anything from Sherwood that would have given him grounds to take decisive action either to disinherit Tim, to cut off his support, or even to confront and humiliate him or Avise. Was I on the wrong track? Was the question of Tim's parentage irrelevant to the murder?

Or perhaps I was looking for something so subtle that it could not be found. Perhaps what I needed to know was not what Sherwood had actually told Miller, but what the murderer thought he might have told him.

fourteen / / /

Tired as I was, as soon as I got back from Durham I went to the office, determined finally to at least make a start on that report for Feininger's.

"Fran?" Finch called through his open doorway.

I halted and turned, dismally certain that he would ask about the report. For once my instincts were on target.

"Edith tells me Feininger's has been calling again about that report Aubrey was working on."

"I was just about to get down to it."

"You poor child. After the shock of finding—"

I felt myself growing cold as the image of Miller's body coalesced before my eyes. Finch seemed to sense my distress because he stopped short of finishing his sentence.

"Look," he said kindly, "don't push yourself. I'll take the thing off your hands. Maybe you'd better give me that file and go home and lie down."

"I was just about to get down to it, honestly."

"You don't look as if you're sleeping too well." He frowned. "When's the last time you had a decent meal?"

I sank into the leather chair by his desk and let his solicitude wash over me, but I couldn't help feeling guilty about getting all that sympathy under false pretenses. Far from brooding about the tragedy of Miller's death, as he seemed to think, I was actually preoccupied with the doom of my own professional prospects and frustrated by my inability to make any headway solving the murder. If I looked drawn and tired, it was because I had spent most of the previous evening and the entire morning in a futile effort to track down an old chum who might have access to the Red Cross's records of donors' blood types.

"I think you might be taking on too much," Finch said

"Really, I'm fine," I protested. I noted that everything in Finch's office was thin. On the chaste raw silk walls hung a delicate brush picture of an anorexic heron framed in thin bamboo reeds. The desk and the chairs had spindly legs; the briefcase on the floor was the trimline model. Even the bonsai plant on his desk was a spare, twiggy specimen. It was as if he had put his office furniture on a diet. I supposed he was expressing a yearning for the days when his thighs were svelte and he was running the four-minute mile.

"I saw an old classmate of yours yesterday," I remarked as I got up. "Macon Sherwood. He sends his regards."

"Eh, yes. As I remember, Macon's area of interest was genetics."

"That's right. He's at Duke. He said he must have just missed seeing you at a workshop last year."

Finch shot me a sharp look. "What were you consulting Macon about?"

I began to wish I had never mentioned it. "Oh, I just got together with an old friend of mine, Myron Stone," I said fluently, "and Macon ate lunch with us."

"I've got to catch up with him one of these days. Good old Macon," said Finch.

I hastily backed out of the office, glad to evade any further questions. I preferred that no one find out how much I was nosing around about the murder. For one thing, I was sure Lieutenant Pittman wouldn't like it. For another, I was afraid that the murderer wouldn't like it.

Back in my own office, I was prey to a number of uncomfortable feelings. Not only had I let out more than I intended to Finch, but after I had analyzed the hidden yearnings evident in his office, my own office suddenly appeared nakedly revealing. The wall of diplomas of which I had been so proud now seemed to demonstrate insecurity about my competence. The desk my mother gave me clearly revealed a powerful unconscious wish to cling to home. Even the fact that I had a philodendron on my desk seemed ominous. Was I afraid I was not here to stay? Was it a symbol of my fear that I couldn't put down roots? Had I sensed from the beginning that I wouldn't make it in private practice?

This way lies craziness, I told myself firmly. I stuffed the file and some standard neuropsych texts into my briefcase. I needed to get out of this place. If a mob of patients appeared unexpectedly demanding my services, Mrs. Smythe could always call me at home.

I staggered out of my office tilting to the right from the weight of the briefcase. I noticed Brack's door was open and stuck my head in. "I'm going home for the day, Brack. If anybody needs me they can reach me there. I don't know, I can't seem to concentrate."

"I've got the same trouble," he admitted. "I can't even go up to the front office to get a pencil without going over and over this murder business obsessively. I'm starting to wonder if the police are ever going to catch the guy. I hear you were in talking to them yesterday. Were you able to find out anything?"

"They asked me to identify the tire iron. That's all."

"So we were right. The tire iron was the weapon."

"Looks like it." Over Brack's desk was a vast array of diplomas. I hadn't noticed them before amid all the general clutter. "You've got your diplomas up." I smiled idiotically.

He glanced over his shoulder at them. "Yeah. I always have this awful feeling that people come in and think, 'Who is this clown? He probably doesn't know from beans.'"

It made me feel better that someone as blatantly full of mental health as Brack suffered from the same problems I did. "Insecurity, thy name is humankind," I murmured.

Brack gave me an absentminded smile. "Seen that lawyer yet?"

"No, but I'm going to do it really soon. Honest."

I hurried off before he could give me any more unwanted advice. Brack's protective instincts were really very sweet and did him credit, but right at the moment I didn't need to hear his incessant litany, "See a lawyer." It made me feel as if I were helpless and inadequate, an uncomfortable state of mind even if it happened to be true.

I did my best to avoid going home and getting down to work on Miller's report. First, I remembered that I could use some groceries. I stopped off at the A & P, assuring myself that grocery shopping was not an avoidance activity but a necessity. A girl has to eat.

I wheeled a grocery cart into the produce section and considered a brightly lit, inclined tray of strawberries and blueberries. Suspiciously, I lifted the cellophane top of a pint of blueberries to make sure they were fresh.

"Hullo, there." The voice sent a chill down my back, reminding me as it did forcefully of the clamgray walls of the police station. I dropped the blueberries and wheeled around to see Lieutenant Pittman wearing Levi's and a knit shirt.

I placed my hand over my pounding heart. "Jeez, you scared me."

"It must have been the way I said 'hullo.'"

"That must be it. I'll bet you have suspects confessing all over the place when you really get warmed up and start threatening them."

"We aren't allowed to threaten suspects."

I regarded him doubtfully. No sign of a gun or

even handcuffs, so it did seem unlikely he had come to arrest me, and I was relieved to note that he seemed significantly less intimidating while standing next to a bin of cantaloupes. His long face looked almost comically prosaic in this setting. I turned away from him and pretended to be intent on inspecting the bags of carrots. I noticed out of the corner of my eye that he wheeled his cart past me and put a five-pound bag of potatoes in his cart. No surprise there. Pittman was a meat-and-potatoes man if ever I'd seen one.

I lagged behind in the produce section, hoping to lose him, but I ended up catching up with him at the bread. We exchanged uncomfortable smiles. On the toilet paper aisle, I spotted him again. I pretended to be so engrossed in a price comparison that I didn't see him. It was no use. A moment later his cart collided with mine in front of diet drinks.

"Small world," I said.

He leaned on his cart. "We can't go on meeting like this."

I was shaken. Lieutenant Pittman was cracking a joke?

"Do you always shop here?" I asked. If he did, I promised myself, I would switch my shopping to Piggly Wiggly at the first opportunity.

"Yeah," he said, "I do. I like this place. You'd be surprised how many single women I meet over by the deli."

Chalk up another wrong deduction for me. I had figured Pittman for a wife and three kids at least.

"Little League games are good, too," he added.

"You go to Little League games to pick up women?"

"Nah, I go to see my kids play. The women just happen to be there. I'm divorced."

"Oh." I pushed my cart over to the deli section. I purchased a half pound of lox and a quarter pound of thin-sliced pastrami. Pittman wheeled his cart up right behind mine and ordered a half pound of honey-cured ham.

"That stuff is death to your cholesterol count," I said with some satisfaction.

"Don't you worry, Dr. Fellowes. I'm going to live long enough to finish your murder investigation."

I recoiled. "Look, Lieutenant, it's not 'my' murder investigation."

Quickly I wheeled my cart to the magazines. I stood there staring at house and garden magazines, too frozen with self-consciousness to pick one up. Looking at Pittman out of the corner of my eye, I noticed he was leafing through a motorcycle magazine.

He glanced at me. "Want to go somewhere and have a drink?"

"What did you say?"

"You want to go somewhere and have a drink?"

That's what I thought he had said. "I don't drink," I said firmly. The last thing I wanted was for my inhibitions to be lifted by a drink while Pittman took notes on everything I said.

"How about a bite to eat, then?"

I regarded him suspiciously. "Is this a chance to soften me up and worm the truth out of me or what?"

"I don't know." He returned my gaze blandly. "Are you hiding anything?"

I mentally shook myself. What was wrong with me? Pittman was literally shoving under my nose a chance to pump him about the investigation. How could I pass up the chance? The only real issue here was did I want to know what the police were up to or not? I did.

"I'd love to get a bite to eat," I said quickly.

"Good." He did not smile. I doubted that he was capable of it. But his face looked momentarily slightly less cold. "Just let me get my stuff in the car first."

We collected our groceries at the checkout. "My car's the blue Chevy," he said.

"I'll follow you," I said.

"Waffle House okay?"

I nodded.

As I followed Pittman's blue Chevy down the highway, I congratulated myself on thinking fast and keeping my own car at hand. I wanted to have a ready way to get away if he had brought along thumb screws.

The waitress at the restaurant was a bony, blond woman with nervous, thin nostrils. She obviously knew Pittman. "The usual?" she asked. She pulled a pencil from behind her ear and poised it over her pad.

"Nah, give me a waffle." He glanced at me. "I gotta start watching my cholesterol count."

She looked at him for a second in surprise. "A waffle?" She pronounced it "wawful." Pittman nodded.

"Do you have any herb tea?" I asked.

"No, honey. But we got decaf. How about that?"

"That'll be fine. And"—I scanned the menu—"scrambled eggs and bacon."

She twitched her white apron and swept off.

"Now," said Pittman, "let's get back to what you're hiding."

"I'm not hiding anything. Honest. I mean, I told you about the tire iron as soon as I noticed it was gone, didn't I?" It had occurred to me that the thaw in his attitude toward me might mean that a better suspect had come into the picture. I hoped so, anyway. On the other hand, I had to consider the very real possibility that he had just noticed my excellent legs. Stranger things had happened. I leaned toward him. "Are you making a lot of progress with the investigation yet?"

"We are baffled." His cold eyes met mine. "You can quote me."

"Your work must be very interesting." Looking down, I realized I had unconsciously begun shredding a napkin with my fingers, which somewhat undercut the image of cool self-possession I wished to project. I let the napkin drop to the floor and carefully folded my hands.

The waitress plopped the plate of eggs and bacon down before me with a clatter. "One waffle." She laid a matching plate down in front of Pittman. As soon as she left, he lifted a forkful of waffle to his mouth and began to chew slowly.

"The job," he repeated. "You asked me about my job. Mostly the job is just work. Routine."

My plate was hot and a faint cloud of steam rose from the eggs. I had not the slightest appetite. "What made you go into police work anyway?" I asked.

He thought about it a minute. "I like it," he said. "I like that rush of adrenaline when you're closing in."

I shivered. His was a taste I did not understand at all. The less adrenaline the better as far as I was concerned. "I wouldn't think you'd get many murders in a place like Bailey City."

"Shows how much you know. We get all kinds of murders. Last week we had a guy who killed his neighbor by throwing a brick at his head. Last night, a couple of migrant workers had a fight and one is on the critical list at the hospital, not expected to last the week. And we found a dead baby in a dumpster around Christmastime."

"Something interesting all the time," I said faintly.

"Of course, I have to admit we don't often have this class of murder. You know what I mean?"

"You mean, where the suspects are all in high-income brackets?"

"Yeah. And the fact is, it's usually pretty obvious who the killer is. Getting a conviction, that may be another thing, but generally we know who did it, and if it's not the victim's nearest and dearest, chances are the guy who did it was drunk. This one is different."

"You don't think this murder could have been committed by a drug addict?"

He regarded me with pity. "What gave you that idea?"

"That's what everyone's been saying."

He snorted. "They wish." He ate another bite of waffle. "Think about it. Unless you did it yourself—"

"I didn't," I put in hastily.

"Then somebody had to steal your tire iron on Tuesday and take it into the office the next morning to kill Miller. Does that sound like a drug addict?"

"Maybe that wasn't my tire iron, though. Maybe it was somebody else's?"

"You found your tire iron?"

"Well, no."

"Okay, then."

I saw that he was probably right about the tire iron. Still couldn't some drug addict steal my tire iron, stash it in the bushes, and then come back the next morning and—no, that didn't make any sense.

"What is it brings you to Bailey City?" asked Pittman.

I had a hard time wrenching my attention away from the question of the tire iron. "I don't know," I said. "I like the climate. It looked like a good place to get a practice going. It's within driving distance of a good university. Lots of workshops to go to and stuff. I figured I could keep up in my field more easily here than in some places."

"You're starting to sound like a brochure from the chamber of commerce, Dr. Fellowes."

"Well, I did get a brochure from the chamber of commerce. So what? What are you getting at? Why shouldn't I move to Bailey City?"

"Just wondered if you knew any of these people from before."

"I had heard of Miller," I admitted cautiously. "I even heard him speak once when I was a student."

Lieutenant Pittman did a passable imitation of a bird dog spying a partridge. His back stiffened and his nose twitched.

"But I didn't really know him at all," I added. "Not at all. Not in a personal way, I mean."

"What about Miller's ex-wife? Did you know her?"

"Never saw her before I moved here."

He pulled a small spiral-bound notebook from his pocket. "I just happened to notice that you went to school in New York City, the same school where Avise Miller had a part-time secretarial job during the time she worked as an actress." He licked the tip of his pencil.

I stared. "Lieutenant, that was seventeen years ago. Seventeen years ago I was a child of ten."

He produced a smile. "How did you know it was seventeen years ago that I was talking about?"

"I thought you were off-duty!"

"I am off-duty."

"Listen, I just happen to know that Avise gave up acting when she got married and her son is seventeen years old so that's how I figured it had to be seventeen years ago," I said triumphantly. "Basic math."

"Oh." He put away his notebook and his pencil. "My wife used to say I couldn't leave my work at the office," he said, looking a little embarrassed. "It made for problems between the two of us."

"I don't wonder." I looked down at the cold eggs and gelid bacon on my plate with regret. Under other circumstances I might have actually liked Lieutenant Pittman, I realized. But I found being a murder suspect amazingly distracting. "You know something, Lieutenant? I have not found this little chat of ours relaxing in the slightest."

"Sorry about that."

"I think I'm going to go home now."

He astonished me by putting his hand over mine. It was a large warm hand. "Don't go," he said. "Why don't we get Rudene to warm up that coffee of yours."

He raised his other hand to signal the waitress, and she came scurrying over. She shot a disapproving look at my plate. "Honey, if you don't eat any better than that you're going to end up nothing but skin and bones."

"Why don't you bring the little lady a nice fresh waffle, Rudene? Put some whipped cream on it. We got to fatten her up."

I started to protest, but the waitress was already dashing off to the kitchen.

"What is this?" I protested. "Do I have a sign on my back or something? Come one, come all, only bossy males need apply. Where do you get off deciding what I'm going to eat, Lieutenant?"

"Kinda sensitive, aren't you?"

I glowered at him.

"Maybe you ought to go into therapy," he suggested, deadpan.

When the waffle appeared, I began to eat it. What else could I do? It wasn't bad.

"How did you happen to decide to go into psychology?" Pittman asked.

I told him I was interested in people and wanted to do something worthwhile with my life. There didn't seem to be anything inherently damaging about that admission. The conversation while we ate was passably civil and completely unconnected with the murder. Lieutenant Pittman was, in fact, showing pretty obvious signs of having noticed my excellent legs. There was a certain softening in his manner, and a marked interest in me as a human being, rather than as a murder suspect. I could have relaxed and enjoyed it, I suppose. I like a little flirtation as much as anybody. But after a while, I suddenly found I couldn't stand it any longer.

"Tell me," I said, "are you guys getting any leads at all? I mean it sounds like you're doing an extensive background check on absolutely everybody. Have you actually come up with anything?"

He met my eyes. "You need to learn to relax some. Don't worry about the murder, okay? You do your job and I'll do mine."

Great. Thanks a lot, Lieutenant. He didn't seem to grasp that the purpose of this little get-together was for *me* to pump *him*. In fact, pumping him had proved to be a lot harder than I had anticipated. I sensed that the police had not made much headway, but that was no comfort to me. I wanted them to find that murderer and quit sniffing around me. I was not sorry to finish my waffle, claim my car in the parking lot, and drive home.

When I got there, though, I was too restless to settle down to work. A meal with Lieutenant Pittman was, I decided, no way to get that mellow feeling. I wondered if he had often had the problem of his job interfering with his attempts to get close to women. Probably not, unless he had a habit of limiting his social life to murder suspects.

I fell back on my usual remedy of a little housework to calm the nerves. I put birdseed in the feeder, vacuumed the downstairs, and then took out the trash. While I was stuffing the plastic trash bag into the garbage can, I heard a rustle behind me. Brannigan pushed aside some branches and stepped through the hedge, carefully avoiding the bees on the thyme.

"What do you hear from the police these days?" he asked.

"We are in constant communication, the police and I," I said sweetly. "They tell me everything."

"I hate sarcasm in a woman."

"The police asked me to identify the tire iron that was used to kill Miller. I couldn't tell them for sure that it was mine, but mine is missing. I suppose the murderer must have seen it in my backseat and taken it sometime before Wednesday." I couldn't bring myself to tell anybody about the weighted planter that had impressed Lieutenant Pittman so unfavorably. It embarrassed me even to think about it.

"The murder had to have been premeditated. That's what you're telling me."

"Yes," I said regretfully. "I'm afraid it's good-bye to the drug-crazed vagrant theory."

"Sorry to hear that."

"The police wanted to know who knew about

my tire iron being in the backseat."

"I knew about it. I saw you throw it back there when you had that flat tire. I wonder why you don't sic that police fellow on me." Brannigan's eyes met mine. I felt he was challenging me to admit that I felt a connection between us, a connection strong enough to make me willing to shield him from the police. But even if there were crumbs of truth in that notion, I was not ready to admit it.

"I think we suspects ought to stick together," I said lightly.

"Yeah, but they don't really suspect you."

"Don't they really? Lieutenant Pittman just way-laid me at the grocery store and dragooned me into going out for waffles with him."

"Maybe he likes you." Brannigan smiled. "I could understand that."

"Maybe, but he practically ended up giving me the third degree."

"About the tire iron?"

"No, now it turns out they're doing background checks. Somehow they came up with the extremely obscure fact that Avise worked part-time at my grade school ages ago. I guess they're wondering if we're in cahoots."

"Why would they think that?"

"Easy. Avise has a motive but she's got a great alibi. I have no alibi but no major motive either. That's probably the only reason they haven't arrested me. But together Avise and I would make a great team. I could have killed him for her while she played bridge."

"Nobody'd buy that. Why would you kill somebody for Avise?"

"They're probably trying to establish that we're lesbian lovers."

"How likely is that?" He was amused.

"Well, extremely unlikely," I admitted, "as the most cursory background check of my life would show."

Brannigan grinned.

"The point is, though, that they're desperate. If they had any real leads they wouldn't be going at it from such a stupid angle."

"They're stumped then. That's fine with me. Why don't you come on over. Want something to drink?"

I looked down at the garbage can. Why not? I followed Brannigan back to his patio and arranged myself on a chaise longue. There was a faint breeze and the sun sinking low in the trees had turned the surface of the pool to sequins of light.

When I refused a gin and tonic, he picked up the house phone and ordered two cups of tea.

"Calm down, Fran." He glanced at me. "You told me yourself the police aren't getting anywhere. As far as I'm concerned, whoever killed Miller did the world a favor. If the cops are getting nowhere, that's good."

"No, it's not good. It's awful. I'm a major suspect. Nobody's going to come to a therapist the police have under surveillance."

"You might get the odd ghoul."

"Very funny. This is my life we're talking about here. It's no joke. Not to me, anyway."

"I'm sorry. I take it back." He held out a handkerchief to me and I dabbed at my eyes, feeling like an idiot. "Look," he said, "it'll all die down after a while. Even if they don't catch the guy who did it, the story'll move to the inside page and then right out of the newspaper. Next thing you know it'll just be a bunch of papers in the back of that lieutenant's file cabinet."

Obviously he hadn't listened, as I had, to Owen Windersley's jeremiad on the aftereffects of scandal. I blew my nose.

The self-possessed lady on Brannigan's staff appeared and laid a silver tray containing two china cups of tea on the table before us. I wondered if this was the fabled secretary whose loyalty was beyond question. She forgot herself so far as to look curiously in my direction before she went back to the house.

Brannigan stirred two teaspoons of sugar into his tea. "Come on, Fran. It's not that bad."

I dabbed at my eyes with his handkerchief. He shifted his position in his chair. Before I knew it he had pulled off my shoe. I shivered a little as I felt the unaccustomed breeze on my foot and stared at him in surprise.

"Here," he said, "give me your foot."

"What for?"

"Foot massage. Very relaxing."

"I don't need relaxing," I said. "I need for them to catch that murderer."

"Hush." Brannigan began kneading the ball of my foot. I had to admit it felt delicious and before I thought it all out, I sort of melted back into the chaise longue. He flexed my feet, wobbled my Achilles' tendon some, forced his finger between each of my toes hard, and kneaded the ball of my foot again. At that point, I would have followed him anywhere. It didn't matter what I told myself about the necessity of getting my emotional life in order before I got involved with anybody again, when Brannigan touched me, I could feel my resolution getting fuzzy and soft around the edges. Too soon, he gave the sole of my foot a brisk pat. "Better?" His eyes were soft and sympathetic. He let his finger trail down my leg as if he wanted to go on touching me, but wasn't sure if he should. God knows, I could identify.

"You know, I didn't figure you were going to be like this," I said.

"Like what?"

"A nice guy."

"I'm not."

"Daddy!" Merris and Tim came galloping out on the patio.

"Hey, Dr. Fellowes," said Merris.

I tucked my naked feet self-consciously under my skirt. "Look, I'd better be going."

"Don't go," said Brannigan. "Hang around for supper. Isaacs has put on this big bouillabaisse."

"Not hungry. I've got to work, really." I felt such a strong pull toward Brannigan that if I gave in to it I would obviously go up in smoke. So much for my vaunted determination to get my emotional life straight before forming another impractical attachment. It wasn't enough that I was barely recovered

from being besotted with horrid Jason. Now I had to
be panting after a movie star whose reason for being
in town seemed obviously to be related in some way
to a brutal murder. I had to ask myself if a self-
destructive impulse was at work here. Indeed, considered from the point of view of sound mental
health, my love life was comical. But I was not much
in the mood for laughing. Under the circumstances, I
wasn't sure I was up to idle chitchat at the dinner
table.

I hooked my shoe with my foot and tried to
unobtrusively step into it. "I've got to finish this
report—" Uncomfortably conscious of Tim's presence,
I avoided speaking his father's name. "This report for
Feininger's," I finished lamely. "I've put it off as long
as I can, honestly. I've got to get down to it."

Refusing all further entreaties, I went back to
my house and got the folder with Miller's report in
it. Brannigan's features swam in my mind, drown-
ing out thought, and I shook my head to clear it. I
could still feel the touch of his hand on my foot.
From his manner, I would have thought that this
was a man for whom sex and breathing were virtually indistinguishable, a thorough-going pagan, a
connoisseur of the flesh. Yet the more I knew of
him, the more I felt his passions ran deeper than
that. I even found myself wondering if he had been
with a woman at all since his wife had died. "Don't
be ridiculous," I said out loud. "You're getting
soppy." It never fails to amaze me how sex does
that to a person. Want someone, and infallibly he
sprouts a halo. It was an interesting psychological

phenomenon, considered dispassionately.

Briskly I sharpened six pencils until they would have qualified as lethal weapons. At last, I had run out of excuses for not getting to work. I spread out all the papers on the dining-room table and began to try to decipher them. It was good to have solid material before me to grapple with. I was getting nowhere trying to make sense out of my own feelings. The only catch with getting down to work was that I knew the Feininger's people would be looking at my report and judging me on the basis of it. This did my concentration no good. Add that to the way Brannigan kept nosing his way into my thoughts and it was no wonder that my progress was very slow. After I had been at it awhile, my writing finger got a crimp in it and my back felt stiff.

It puzzled me that each test score had been neatly penciled with either an N for normal range or an A for abnormal range. That seemed odd. I would have expected Miller to have had the normal and abnormal ranges for the Reitan engraved on his heart. He should have been no more likely to label the test scores than to go around his office sticking on labels that said "lamp," "book," "pencil sharpener." It took me quite a while to review the scoring. And when I took everything apart and added it all up, I felt even more unhappy than when I had begun. Miller's conclusion of left hemisphere dysfunction didn't seem fully supported. I would have said rather that there were indications of schizoaffective disorder. Could he have gotten his diagnosis all wrong?

I felt momentarily unsure of myself. Miller was so much more experienced a diagnostician than I that I felt uncomfortable tearing up his conclusions and saying something completely different in the report to Feininger's. Had I overlooked something? Was there a subtle reason for what he had written that had escaped me?

I got up to turn on the lamp over the dining-room table since the light was growing dim. I suddenly realized that my head hurt and that I was hungry. I went into the kitchen to get a cheese sandwich and came back to the table with it. I ate it staring at Miller's report and wondering what I should do. My head hurt and my eyes felt like retreads. I should listen to my instincts, I reminded myself. Something was wrong with this report, and I knew it. I had to face the possibility that it had not been Miller but the murderer who had labeled those test scores and written that report. And if Miller hadn't written that report, then the time of death was much vaguer than we had assumed. The medical examiner had already refused to pin it down except within the range of several hours, at least if Lyman Finch's wife's bridge club was to be believed. That meant that now nobody's alibi meant a thing. It was as if all the cards of the case had been tossed up in the air. The idea gave me a cold feeling in the pit of my stomach.

Suddenly light blazed out from the open kitchen door and my head snapped around.

"Don't pass out. It's only me," said Brannigan.

"Don't you ever knock? How did you get in? I had a new lock put on that door."

He leaned back against the wall on his shoulder and folded his arms. "It would work fine, I bet, if you'd remember to lock it."

I fidgeted uncomfortably with the papers on the table. I didn't want to let Brannigan see the faulty report. Not until I had decided what to do with it. With him feeling the way he did about Miller, I wouldn't have put it past him to make a move to destroy the evidence. It was too late to hide the papers, so I had to hope he would not notice them.

"You missed some great bouillabaisse," he said. "What is it you're working on that's so important?"

"Just some stuff from the office." I stacked the papers and shoved them awkwardly back in their envelope. "A report Feininger's wants me to do for them."

Brannigan had moved over a step or two and was now standing with his back to the kitchen light. I saw him as a silhouette. The weak light over the dining-room table cast only a dim reflection on his face.

I wished he would go away so that I could call that lawyer Owen Windersley had recommended. I badly needed some impartial advice. I did not need Brannigan in my house looking gorgeous and muddying my thought processes.

Brannigan opened a kitchen cabinet and poked around among the glasses. I had never known a man to make himself at home so fast. "Can't you offer me a drink or something?" he asked plaintively.

"Gee, I'd love to," I said, "but I've got all this work and all—" Irrationally, I felt guilty. But I dared not get caught up in worrying about Brannigan's feelings just now. Urgent evidence pertaining to a murder case was burning in my hands. "This just isn't a very good time for me," I finished lamely.

"Okay, I can take a hint."

To my relief, he turned to leave. The light cast furrows at the corners of his mouth, and his eyes were lost in shadow. "Used and tossed aside," he said dolefully. "Like an old shoe. I'm going. You're not mad at me are you?"

"It's just my work! You've heard about work? It's what pays the bills?"

His eyes were drawn to the flash of color from the oriental carpet. "Sure," he said. "I know about work."

After I heard the door close, I went into the kitchen and carefully locked it. Brannigan gives me a foot massage; I kick him out of the house. No wonder I felt guilty. But what I had found out about the report couldn't wait. I needed to know what to do next. I was going to have to call that lawyer. And something told me that unless I was reading this all wrong, I was going to have to be calling Lieutenant Pittman, too. I shivered. Suddenly I couldn't bear the shadows in the room. I would have liked to turn on floodlights until the house was as brightly lit as a prison during an escape attempt. Instead, I switched on all the downstairs lights.

Feeling safer, I sat down in the kitchen surrounded by hundreds of footcandles of illumination and called the lawyer. I didn't expect him to answer his office phone this late in the evening, but he picked it up at once.

"Mr. Lenoir?" I began. "This is Fran Fellowes. Your name was given to me by Owen Windersley."

"Of course, Miss Fellowes. Mr. Windersley got in touch with me last week and told me to expect your call."

"Yes, well, there's been a new development. When can I see you?"

"I'm going to be in court all day tomorrow and probably the next day, too. How would it be if I came over right now and you filled me in?"

"Oh, you don't have to do that."

"I insist," he said, a smile creeping into his voice. "Owen Windersley would never forgive me if I didn't."

I hung up feeling uneasy. I had liked holding all the evidence in my own two hands, turning it this way and that, deciding what to do with it in my own good time. Telling Lenoir would be an irreversible step.

Within a half hour Robert Lenoir was standing at my front door, the porch light shining on his short-cropped hair. He wiped his feet on the mat and moved with deliberate steps into the foyer. He was a tall, thin man with a low voice and big hands—a physical type I associate with the West—but he was dressed in the conservative tailoring of the South.

He sat down on the couch. His gaze swept the room and finally settled on me. "Why don't you begin by telling me everything. Mr. Windersley was concerned that you might have said things to the police that you shouldn't have."

I told him about finding the body and about the tire iron.

"That doesn't sound so bad," he said. "You haven't talked to anybody but the police about this, have you?"

"I've told a couple of people about the tire iron," I admitted.

"What we've got here, as I see it, is basically a public relations problem. The police don't have a case against you. The crucial point is that the body was already cold when you found it. That doesn't fit with your being the murderer. And the idea that you might have been fighting off Dr. Miller's advances seems implausible, too. If that was the way it was, why would you have a tire iron in your hand? The tire iron means premeditation. People don't just waltz around casually carrying tire irons." He shook his head. "Nope, they don't have a motive."

With some hesitation, I told him about Miller's lewd letters and the buckshot in the planter. He made a face at that.

"I don't know what made me do it," I confess. "I guess he scared me, and I had the idea that if he ever tried anything again I'd have a way to defend myself."

"Of course, of course. That's simple enough to understand. The important thing to keep in mind is that he wasn't killed with your planter."

"Thank God. But going and getting all that buckshot—it does look kind of calculated." I winced a little. "Even bloodthirsty. I wonder if they don't think Miller had been harassing me in some systematic way and I decided to take care of him for good. Kind of a case of feminist revolt carried to an extreme?" I smiled weakly.

"But he hadn't been harassing you, had he?"

"Oh, no. There was just that one incident."

He smiled. "Naturally, I wish you hadn't had this, shall we call it, this Rambo-ette impulse to, uh, reinforce your office decor. But let's not lose sight of the facts here. What are the statistics on sexual harassment? Don't they say about half of the women in the work force have been harassed at one time or another? And nobody imagines that makes them dangers to society. They won't be able to find any evidence that Dr. Miller was continuing his assaults on you because it just wasn't so. I think the police can understand the momentary impulse to defend yourself that led you to, uh, load your planter. I doubt they'll make too much of it. Remember, they don't have you on the scene at the right time. I don't think we need to worry about charges being brought. I know Lieutenant Pittman—he'll wait until he has a good case."

"There is one other thing," I put in awkwardly. I pointed out that as far as I knew the police had not yet discovered Miller's grand plan to reorganize the office with me and Brack as his peons.

Lenoir smiled broadly. "Hey, I'd like to see Lieutenant Pittman arguing that Sanford Fellowes's daughter was desperate for money."

Apparently Owen Windersley had filled Lenoir in on my father's penchant for trust funds. "I have complete confidence in you," my father used to say to us even though all too clearly he envisioned his heirs donating their assets to some commune and ending their days standing vacant-eyed on street corners giving out flowers. "Perfect confidence," he would repeat in hollow tones. But then he fixed it so that Mom and I couldn't get our hands on any of our capital without the informed consent of First National City Bank and Trust.

"It just won't wash," Lenoir concluded. "There is no case. I think we can put that out of our minds. But you do have to be concerned about word of your involvement in the investigation getting out all over town. Unfortunately, the public is not as careful about what constitutes proof as the police have to be. We have to be realistic about the possibility of rumors going around. I don't guess the police have a lead on the murderer yet?"

I shook my head. "Every time I see Lieutenant Pittman, he's more grouchy. I think that must mean he isn't getting anywhere."

"That's too bad. It would be better for you if the police arrested someone. That would stop the talk."

"There's something else that's bothering me." I took a deep breath. "In fact, this is really why I called you." I told him about the report Miller had been working on and the anomalies I had found.

"It could be significant," he said slowly. "What you've found is evidence. It should be turned over to the police right away."

"You think?"

"I do. In fact, as an officer of the court, I insist on

it." He smiled. "And as your attorney, I must say it can't hurt you. You must see that if Dr. Miller didn't write that report, it points the hand of suspicion away from you. With your training in neuropsychological testing, you could have written a perfect report and it's hard to see what motive you could have had for writing a flawed one. On the other hand, from what you have told me, the ex-wife may have enough training to have written the report, if not quite enough to write it perfectly, and she would have had an excellent motive to do so—to create an alibi for her son. She could have written the report the night before, murdered Miller either with or without her son's help the next morning, put the disk into Miller's machine to be printed out, then hurried off to set up her and her son's alibi. I advise you to call the police tonight."

My body seemed instantly lighter, as if I had sucked in a sharp dose of helium. I realized that I had called Lenoir for the sole purpose of hearing those words. Of course, the person who had written that report had had some acquaintance with psychological testing. I had seen that at once. And that meant the police's attention would shift to Tim and Avise. I didn't like it. I would have preferred to shift suspicion to someone I didn't know. To some drug-crazed addict, for example. Certainly not to Tim and Avise, who had both been mercilessly tyrannized by Miller. Now, in the slippery way of casuists and moral cowards everywhere, I had handed the responsibility over to Lenoir. After all, I told myself, there's no use having an attorney unless you take his advice.

When Lenoir had driven away, I leaned against the door, feeling my heart beat. I knew I had to take Lenoir's advice, but I didn't feel as clear of conscience about it as I had hoped I would.

fifteen / / /

I went back in the house and called the police station. I left word for Lieutenant Pittman to get in touch with me, and he called me back right away. You might have thought he was on tippy toe by the phone waiting for the signal to sprint to my house. At ten he was on my doorstep with a timid-looking assistant cop in tow. Pittman had furrows of fatigue running from his nose to each corner of his mouth and his face looked gray and shiny.

He stepped inside. "You're telling me something is wrong with that report of Miller's?" He spoke between clenched teeth.

"I don't see how Miller can have written it," I said. It took me a minute to tell him why.

He shot me a look I had no trouble interpreting—he was angry at himself for not having had the entire test done over again by a neuropsychologist in the beginning, and he couldn't forgive me for making his oversight significant.

He shook a cigarette out of a pack, bit on it, flicked his lighter, and sucked fire into it. He exhaled

the smoke through his nostrils. I hadn't seen an unre-
generate nicotine addict at work in so long I
watched him with some interest. "You know what
this means?" he said. "It means if you're right, the
wife's alibi isn't worth a damn. The son's alibi isn't
worth a damn. I get to flip a coin between them." He
blew out a cloud of smoke and glared at me.

"Well, there are other people who could have
done it. Lots of them."

"Nobody with as good a motive though. The kid
comes in for a bundle just in time for college and as
far as I can tell Miller was making his ex's life a living
hell. She'd probably be happy to kill him just for the
fun of it, forget the money. Besides—" He stared at
me. "The whole idea of faking Miller's report is to
give somebody an alibi, right? So forget everybody
that doesn't have an alibi for the faked time."

"I can't see Avise banging on anybody's head
with a tire iron," I said stubbornly. "I don't care what
you say."

He waved that objection away with his cigarette,
distributing smoke all over my dining room. "Yeah,
but maybe the kid and her were in it together. She
writes the report. He does the bashing." He bent
over the table, scowling, and collected the pages of
the report. I had no idea whether he would be able
to make sense of the queries I had penciled in the
margin. Still sucking on his cigarette, he wrote me
out a receipt and left. I noticed that the young
policeman trailing behind him looked thoroughly
intimidated.

The dining room now smelled like a bar. I turned

on the kitchen ventilator fan and sprayed a can of Lysol around. It didn't help. After that, I double-checked to make sure all my doors were locked. I went up to bed with a bad taste in my mouth. And it wasn't just from the smoke. I felt like a stool pigeon.

When I woke in the morning, I realized I couldn't face going in to the office. For one thing, I wouldn't know what to say when Mrs. Smythe inquired how I was coming with the report. Should I tell her it would be a little later than I thought because I had to send it to the police first? But, no, the real reason I couldn't go in was Avise. I was sure that the minute she looked at me, she would know from my expression what I had done to her.

Okay, I won't go in, I thought. Simple. I sat at the kitchen table in my favorite old, thin pajamas, the ones fastened at the waist with a safety pin where the elastic had given way, reading the newspaper and drinking coffee. I tried to imagine Avise murdering Miller, tried to imagine her raising a tire iron and smashing it down with all her strength on the smooth, fleshy roundness of Miller's unsuspecting head. The image wouldn't jell. The action seemed altogether too decisive for Avise. It was out of character. But what about Tim? Despite everything Brack had said, I could imagine Tim as a murderer. I could imagine him striking his father in a rage. What I couldn't imagine was his planning it. Neither could I conceive of Avise doing the phony report to create an alibi for him. She would have had to know about it ahead of time in order to do the report and get the disk ready to plug into Miller's machine, and though she might have covered up for Tim if he had done something rash, I couldn't see putting their heads together and plotting the kind of cold-blooded, premeditated murder this was. I couldn't believe that Avise would have wanted Miller's blood on Tim's hands. She was too protective of Tim for that.

I remembered Brannigan grabbing the bumblebee. The thought of it made me faintly ill and I pushed my coffee cup away. I remembered Brannigan striking Avise—Brannigan peremptorily sending Merris out of the country before she learned of her mother's death. Brannigan would not have shrunk from killing Miller. It was his instinct to take drastic action.

Furthermore, Avise and Brannigan would have made the perfect pair for murder. She could provide the alibi for them both; Brannigan could do the killing. It only required me to believe that Avise and Brannigan still had some link, after all these years. And that was easy. The link could be as simple as Tim. If he were Brannigan's child, Avise might have turned to Brannigan for money when Tim's college expenses loomed ahead. What could be more natural that they should work together on this murder that so neatly solved both of their problems? Brannigan wanted revenge. Avise wanted freedom from Miller and she needed his money for Tim. She might have even figured she had it coming after all Miller had put her through.

When I considered the whole thing, I realized

that nothing was easier to imagine than Brannigan working in concert with a woman.

I poured myself a tall orange juice but it seemed no more appetizing than the coffee had. I left it on the kitchen counter and walked away. Solving the murder was Lieutenant Pittman's problem, I told myself. I should quit telling myself scary nonsense tales. Resolutely, I shook the local paper open. I noticed that it repeated its usual irritating formula, "The police have no leads." I read the entire newspaper from front to back, even the society pages and the obituaries. Then I lay my head in my hands and tried to figure out what to do with the long, empty day before me. What could I do to keep myself from thinking?

I knew it was pointless to try to go out and drum up business. Anyone I called on would want to talk only about the murder. For all practical purposes, I was unemployed. Only my father's money separated me from the people who eat at the soup kitchen. It was a depressing thought.

I got dressed and went to the bank. I needed to cash a check, and more important, it was something to do. The teller looked down at the name printed on my check, leaned forward and whispered, "Tell me, do the police have any leads yet?"

"I don't think so," I said. I stuffed the currency into my wallet and hurried out of the bank.

On my way home, as I drove past a street of placid suburban ranch houses, each closed up tight to contain air-conditioning, I fought the sensation that inside countless bridge clubs were busy dissecting the case against me.

The kitchen phone was ringing when I walked into the house.

"Hullo?"

"Fran? It's James. James Brannigan. Come over and have lunch with me."

I was absurdly glad to hear from him. I had seriously entertained the idea that he was a murderer and yet I was glad to hear his voice. I was that hard up for company. Or maybe it was more than that. Maybe on some crazy level I trusted my instincts more than my reason. "You aren't going to ask me if the police have any leads, are you?" I asked, recalling the bank teller.

"Sure, I am."

"Never mind. I'll come anyway."

I went out back and pushed my way through the hedge. We were wearing a regular path there. I noticed that a few diligent bumblebees were still at work in the thyme, weighing the blossoms down. The sun had bleached the sky over the Brannigans' patio. A blue beach umbrella was tilted at a rakish angle over the table where Brannigan and I had drunk tea together and heat rose from the paving stones. I rang Brannigan's back doorbell.

Brannigan himself met me at the door. I had expected to see his trusted bodyguard and major-domo, Isaacs. Brannigan had not shaved, and his stubble was much in evidence, but instead of making him look unkempt, it only made him look deliciously rugged, like a Portuguese fisherman. His bare feet, his very brief shorts—which showed a long expanse of thigh—together with a loose white shirt open at the neck gave an effect that could be called extremely casual or nearly nude, depending on how puritanical your point of view was.

The house was silent. "Where are your trusted aides?" I asked, craning my neck to look around.

"It's their day off." He padded in the direction of the kitchen. "Merris is at Tim's, so it's just us. Okay with you?"

I felt a seductive thrill and wondered if the house had been cleared of employees because Brannigan was planning a romantic tryst with me. It was a surprisingly enticing idea considering that I had just been telling myself he might be the murderer, but then my suspicions of Brannigan had an amazing way of fading whenever he faced me in the flesh.

But perhaps seduction was the last thing on his mind. I thought about the murder constantly, and I supposed Brannigan did, too. I followed him into the kitchen and watched as he dished out chicken salad.

"Potato chips, too?" he asked.

I nodded.

"I saw two cops going into your house late last night. What's up?"

"The investigation is continuing," I said primly. Ah! He was trying to pump me. I found I didn't mind at all. I was beginning to understand the perverse satisfaction Lieutenant Pittman derived from withholding information.

"So did they come to get something? To ask something? To give you something? Don't tell me they came by at ten o'clock just to pass the time of day?"

The front door was suddenly flung open with a bang. "Daddy!" came Merris's anguished cry.

Brannigan dropped his plate onto the table and rushed out. I followed him to the door. There I found Merris with her arms around her father. "The police took Tim and his mother away!" she wailed.

Brannigan shook her by the shoulders. "Are you telling me they've arrested them? Pull yourself together, Merris. What's going on?"

She snuffled. "They said it was for questioning. Since I knew I couldn't get hold of you, I just went along, too, and Tim and his mother went into the back of the station with these policemen and then I waited a long, long time out front. It seemed like hours. These people kept coming out and getting candy bars out of the vending machine there and nobody said anything to me and I thought I was going to go crazy." Her hands fell limply to her sides. "Finally this policeman came out and took me home."

"Why didn't you call me, nitwit?" he asked.

"I didn't think anybody was here. You told me you were going out!" She threw me an accusing look.

"Look," said Brannigan, "I don't think it's anything to worry about. It's just for questioning. It's nothing to get upset about."

"You weren't there. It was awful! They said they had new evidence."

Brannigan's gaze fell on me. "Fran and I were just going to eat lunch. Come on in and have some chicken salad."

"You think I could eat at a time like this?" Merris cried.

"Look, baby, starving's not going to help any-body. If Tim and his mom need a lawyer, I promise you we'll get them a good one, but being questioned isn't the same thing as being arrested. Practically everybody who knew Tim's dad has been questioned. Fran was there, and they let her go, didn't they?"

"So far no warrant," I agreed.

"I don't think this is like that," protested Merris. "When we got to the police station, everybody looked up at us—the people at the desk, all the other policemen, everybody. It was like they were excited and happy, you know—like those creepy people who watched all that guillotine stuff after the French Revolution. I think they've found something. What if something's the matter with Tim's alibi?" She gave a choked little sob.

"I'd better get you an aspirin," said Brannigan, eyeing her with misgiving. "You want to lie down or something?"

"If I only knew what was going on," she cried. "They were back there so long. What can they be talking about? Do they give people the third degree anymore, Daddy?"

"Nah," he said, sounding uncertain. "Look, we'll find out sooner or later what's going on. Why don't you just calm down and get yourself something to eat?"

He guided her back to the kitchen. He had opened the cabinet and was reaching for an extra plate when we heard the front door open again.

"Merris?" called a voice from the foyer.

"Tim!" Merris jumped up. "Tim! Daddy, they let him go!"

Tim strode in with his hands shoved deep into the pockets of his baggy jeans.

"Are you okay?" said Merris.

He didn't answer but looked past her shoulder at Brannigan.

"Is there a problem, kid?" Brannigan asked him. "Do you need a lawyer? I've got somebody good in L.A. who could be out here tomorrow if you want."

"I don't need your lawyer," Tim said coldly.

Merris drew back from him. "Dad's only trying to help."

"Sure." He snorted. "I don't need his help."

Brannigan viewed Tim warily.

"What's your blood type?" Tim spat at him.

"O. What's yours?"

"O. Coincidence, huh?"

I could see a vein pulsing at Brannigan's temple. "Most people have type O," he commented mildly.

"You know what I'm talking about. You're my father, aren't you?"

"I don't know what you're talking about," said Brannigan.

"The hell you don't!"

"Tim!" cried Merris, plucking at his shirt. "Daddy!"

"Leave me alone," Tim burst out. "The two of you, just leave me alone!"

He turned suddenly and ran out of the room. Merris went after him, calling his name.

Brannigan looked wryly at me. "Why do I have a feeling you know something about this?"

I heard Merris screaming "Tim!" Her voice came from upstairs. Brannigan was out of the dining room like a shot and tore up the stairs. I ran after him.

"Daddy!" Merris's voice cried from above us.

I glimpsed Brannigan a flight ahead of me, his face pale. When we got to the third-floor hallway, Merris suddenly darted out of an open door, nearly colliding with us.

Brannigan embraced her fiercely. "Are you okay, baby?"

"Daddy," she whispered, "he's out there! He says he's going to jump."

"Sweet Christ." Brannigan pushed her aside as he rushed into a large, sunny bedroom wallpapered with spring flowers. Tall French doors were open to the balcony.

"Tim!" yelled Brannigan. After an initial hesitation he approached the balcony.

"Don't come near me!" screamed Tim. "If you come any closer I'll jump."

"Do something, Daddy," pleaded Merris, pressing her fist to her mouth. "Stop him!"

Tim was out of my line of vision, but looking out the open doors, I realized that we were directly over the flagstone terrace.

"Tim?" I called. "It's Dr. Fellowes. Won't you talk to me?"

"There's nothing to say. I just can't take it anymore. I hate him! You can't stop me."

I edged closer to the doors. "Don't you want to tell me about it? Tim, be careful if you're sitting on the railing out there. You don't want to fall—you might not be able to draw anymore."

"It doesn't matter," he sobbed. "Nothing matters."

"I'm going to come on out there," I said. "And I want you to tell me all about it, okay?"

"Don't! I'm warning you!"

Brannigan caught hold of my shoulder, but I pulled away. I was frightened of moving toward Tim but it would be worse to do nothing. I counted on Tim wanting a sympathetic ear more than he wanted to kill himself. My guess was that he was more angry and hurt than seriously suicidal.

"Come on, Tim," I said. "Tell me about it. I think we can work this out." I cautiously inched out onto the balcony. I spotted a geranium blazing with irrelevant cheerfulness directly ahead of me in an urn-shaped masonry pot.

I saw Tim then, sitting on the thin railing, tears streaming down his cheeks. The wind ruffled his fair hair and his legs hung loosely. His beat-up sneakers were coming untied. He looked sixteen and desolate. He sniffled and wiped his eyes with the back of his hand. The shifting of his weight made him wobble a little bit on his perch in a way that made my heart stop. If he fell backward—but I wasn't going to think about that. "Tim?" I reached out to him, and to my relief, he suddenly slid to the floor and buried his face in his hands. I put my arms around him. "It's going to be all right," I murmured.

I took him back into the bedroom. There was no sign of either Brannigan or Merris and I realized why when I heard a siren in the distance. They had gone to phone for help.

At the sound of the siren, Tim raised his tear-streaked face and looked me directly in the eyes. It was a surprisingly adult look. "It's the police, isn't it?"

"No, I expect it's a fire truck and an ambulance. Merris and James were pretty panicked about you. They must have called them."

"I hate him," he said hoarsely. "What'd he ever do for me? He's rotten. He doesn't deserve to live."

A cold shiver ran up my spine. "You didn't kill your father, did you, Tim?" I asked anxiously.

"Which one?" He looked at me and laughed. "Hell, no, I didn't kill him. I'd been fighting with him for years. Why would I kill him now? The police don't believe me, though. They think Mom and I killed him for the money. I told them I didn't want his money. They didn't believe that, either."

Then I heard lots of footsteps on the stairs. The rescue squad had arrived.

An hour later I called Avise's apartment from Duval General Hospital lobby but got no answer. I was staring at the eye-rest green wall of the hospital lobby so fixedly that I had to remind myself to blink. Only with a distinct effort of will could I stop feeling that I was the cause of all this.

When I left Tim tucked in bed on the fourth floor, he had been quite calm, evidently soothed by the procedures of checking into the hospital. I wished I could say the same for myself. I turned from the phone and saw Merris standing a few feet away waiting for me. She looked pale, but whether it was from anxiety or from the fluorescent lights reflecting off of the green walls I couldn't be sure. Her eyes had a look of painful concentration, as if she were in the midst of a delicate task like juggling eggs. "Daddy's waiting outside," she said.

We walked to the car. The sun was fiercely bright and the heat rolled off the pavement like a punishment. "Is Tim going to be all right?" Merris asked me. "What did they say?"

"I don't think it's serious. As far as I can tell, he's only suffering from too much pressure—his father's death, the murder investigation . . ." I trailed off, and we walked the rest of the way without speaking. Brannigan was in his Mercedes with the motor and the air-conditioning running.

We drove home in silence. From the faces of the two Brannigans, I could see how much this near reenactment of their family tragedy had shaken them. They both moved with exaggeratedly careful and restricted gestures, as if they had suddenly discovered that their skins had shrunk. Brannigan groped for the air-conditioning control with an invalidish uncertainty that was not at all like him.

I wondered if the two of them had talked about Tim's accusation that Brannigan was his father. I suspected they hadn't. Brannigan had given out unmistakable signals that he didn't want to discuss it, and Merris, who did not seem to be given to confrontation, was unlikely to have ignored those danger signs.

I broke the silence. "I wasn't able to reach Avise."

"It's okay. I called her at the office," said Brannigan in a colorless voice. "She's on her way to the hospital now."

He pulled up into his own driveway. "Merris, honey, run along inside. There's something I need to talk to Dr. Fellowes about."

Merris got out of the car and with a single glance back at us turned toward the house. Brannigan watched her go in the front door, then looked directly at me.

"What did you tell the cops, Fran?"

I saw no point in continuing to evade his question. He knew that I had told the police something, and now that the police had questioned Avise and Tim, it was only a matter of time before he found out what it was. "The report Miller was supposed to have been writing Wednesday morning was a mess. The data were misinterpreted. It was a misdiagnosis."

Brannigan saw at once what I was getting at. "So the cops think he didn't write it, huh? So that's what happened to Tim's and Avise's alibi."

"I suppose so. You see, the report wasn't handwritten. The printer of his computer had printed it directly off the disk. There is no proof that Miller made the disk. In fact, anybody could have made that disk on his own computer and then just stuck it into Miller's machine. When I think about it, it's odd that Miller printed out just a paragraph of the report. Normally you write the whole report on the computer before printing it. You don't write one paragraph, print it out, then write the next paragraph and print it out. See what I mean?" I looked at him uneasily, trying to gauge his response to what I was saying.

But Brannigan was not looking at me now. He was gazing up past the house, above the line of trees to the sky beyond, as if trying to spot a plane in the far distance. "You think Avise killed Miller?" he asked finally. "Or do you think it was Tim? I thought I was your chief suspect the way you were talking."

"I don't know what to think. My lawyer told me I had to tell the police about that report, that's all." I reached for the door handle, but Brannigan's hand closed around my arm.

"You think this is some kind of game?" he said dangerously.

For a second I thought he was going to hit me. "Let go of me."

He released my arm. I got out and dusted off my skirt. Then, conscious of Brannigan's eyes on my back, I awkwardly made my way through the hedge and to my own house.

The worst of it was I could entirely see Brannigan's point of view. It wasn't as if Miller's death meant any great loss to the world. And when I told the police about the discrepancies in the report I had been motivated less by respect for justice than by the desire to preserve my own career. Brannigan thought I was the worst kind of troublemaker, and just then I sort of agreed with him.

sixteen / / /

To my surprise, Brack Prideaux was parked in my driveway waiting for me. I wondered if he had heard any of the scene between me and Brannigan. He got out of his car when I appeared and walked with me up to the door.

"I thought you might be sick," he said. "Why didn't you come into the office this morning?"

"Why shouldn't I sleep late?" I shrugged. "I don't have any patients." Brack didn't show any sign of knowing what had happened to Tim and I shrank from telling him.

"Where have you been?" he asked.

"Out," I snapped. I was not in the best of spirits and I had to exert all my self-control to keep from screaming "Give me some space!" But from some unsuspected reserve of strength I managed to produce a mature, detached voice for my next utterance. "Would you care for something to drink?"

Brack followed me into the room and watched me opening the liquor cabinet.

"Nothing for me," he said.

"Oh." I looked around the kitchen, feeling a little at a loss. One thing that can be said for fixing drinks is that it gives you something to do with your hands.

"I ran into Eunice Caruthers today at the Mental Health Association luncheon," he said.

"Who?" I should have been at that luncheon, I thought dismally, making contacts, doing my best to live down the murder rumors, and showing what a responsible professional I was. Of course, if I had gone to the luncheon, Tim might have dashed himself to bits on the Brannigans' terrace. But the point is, I hadn't even known about it, hadn't even joined the local Mental Health Association.

"Eunice Caruthers," Brack repeated. "She's a nurse over at Feininger's. She told me she'd met you, kept saying how charming you were."

Then I remembered Eunice, the nurse I had lunched with. I realized it was too much to hope that she had limited her remarks to a discussion of my charm. The woman loved to talk. Odd to think that at one time I had been grateful for that.

"Why are you shielding Brannigan?" asked Brack.

An ice cube slipped out of my hand. "I'm not shielding Brannigan!" I exclaimed, annoyed at myself for getting rattled.

"You knew he had a first-class motive for killing Miller. Are you going to deny that?"

Obviously, Eunice had given Brack the entire saga of Jessica's death. Why not? She had given it to me pretty readily.

"I had a motive for killing Miller, too," I said, throwing ice cubes in a tall glass recklessly. "In fact,

Miller's enemies would fill the Astrodome. He was a nasty little man."

"It's funny the way Brannigan hangs around here. What's in Bailey City for him, a guy like that? I'll bet he wants to keep an eye on the investigation. I've heard that murderers do that. I'll bet he's always asking you what the police have found out, isn't he?"

"Yes, he is. But so does the teller at the bank." I poured a fizzy soda over the ice. "I only wish I did know what the police were thinking."

"I think the police ought to be told about Brannigan," Brack said stubbornly.

I handed him the drink. "Give it up, Brack. He's got an alibi."

"He does?" Brack's eyes looked bewildered, like a cocker spaniel's.

"He was riding over at Dr. Carmichael's ranch and was watched at least part of the time by a breathless journalist."

"Shit," said Brack.

I thoroughly understood Brack's desire to pin the murder on Brannigan. He didn't know and like Brannigan the way he did me. Or Avise and Tim. As I remembered Avise and Tim, my gaze fell guiltily from Brack's face and rested on his tie. The impress of the lining showed through from too much cleaning and pressing, and its burgundy thread bore telltale signs of carpet lint from crawling around on the floor with little kids.

"Brack, there's something you ought to know."

His mouth twisted wryly. "You're giving up your career to seek fame and fortune in Hollywood."

"Very funny. No, I'm serious. That report, the one that was on Miller's desk? I don't think he wrote it. I had to call the police last night and tell them that. It was sloppy work. I don't think that patient had left hemisphere damage at all."

He was rocked by the news. "You're telling me the police think the murderer wrote that report?"

"I think so."

"But, my God, that means the murderer was a psychologist!"

"Somebody familiar with psychological testing anyway." I decided I needed a small drink after all. I pulled a bottle of white wine out of the refrigerator and poured some out into an orange juice glass. It was slightly vinegary, but all the better suited to the occasion for that.

"They pulled in Avise and Tim for questioning this morning, and Tim got so upset, he threatened to jump off Brannigan's balcony. He's over on Duval General's fourth floor right now."

"Tim suicidal?" He looked at me numbly. "I can't believe it. I never saw the slightest sign— My God, Fran, don't tell me you think there's anything to it!" He fell into a chair, looking staggered. "They've got it all wrong," he said. "Tim didn't kill his father."

"Who did then?"

"You're not telling me you think—"

"I don't know what I think," I said wearily. "All I know is it's all up for grabs now. Nobody's alibi is any good because the time of death can't be pinned down very precisely from the medical evidence alone. Anybody could have killed him, I guess, but the problem is only a few people could have cooked that report. And let's face it, Avise is the most likely one."

"The hell with 'likely.' I know these people, Fran. I've known them for years. It may be 'likely' but it's just not possible."

He caught sight of the kitchen clock and panic flashed over his face. "Good grief, and I'm booked up all afternoon. What a nightmare. I'm due back at the office in a quarter of an hour." He ran his fingers through his hair. "Look, have you talked to Avise yet?"

"Brannigan called her. He told me she was going over to the hospital."

"I'm not going to be able to get over there until after seven. Did Tim say anything? Did you talk to him? Why didn't he come to talk to me if he was upset? We're old friends. Or why didn't he talk to that art teacher of his at school. Something about this doesn't make any sense. Do you think this was a gesture or a serious attempt?" But before I could answer, he came at me with a new question. "Why did he go over to Brannigan's to pull this?"

"There's something else you ought to know," I said reluctantly. "It seems there's a chance that Tim is Brannigan's son."

He looked at me uncomprehendingly.

I threw up my hands. "I don't know anything about it, so don't ask me. But it turns out Brannigan is somebody from Avise's past."

"Are you telling me that that's why Brannigan is hanging around Bailey City?" he asked after he regained his powers of speech.

"I don't know, I don't know, and I don't know again. But I do know that if you've got a two o'clock you'd better move."

He glanced up anxiously at the kitchen clock. "Look, if you talk to Avise, explain to her that I'm all tied up, would you?" He groped in his pocket for his car keys. "This is the goddamnedest mess I've ever heard of," he exploded. The door slammed hard behind him.

I sat down at the kitchen table and drank my wine. Unfortunately, after I finished the glass I felt as sober as ever. I was debating whether the benefits of getting high were worth the pain of another glass when the doorbell rang. At first I thought that Brack had come back for something, but when I opened the door, Avise was standing on the mat. Her dark hair was swept back into a chignon that was coming slightly undone on the sides. That and a certain rigidity about her lips that suggested conscious control were the only signs that this was a woman in a lot of trouble.

"Avise," I said, starting guiltily. "Come on in."

She moved with slow stately steps into the living room. "I just came from the hospital," she said.

I would have been less wary if she had been more visibly distraught. "You're doing awfully well," I said, watching her. "I know you must be upset."

"I have to keep my composure for Tim's sake." She poised herself elegantly on the edge of the sofa. "It would only upset him to see Mamma worried." I wondered vaguely if the pale blue color that Avise wore so often symbolized her constant, futile quest for serenity. "Tell me what happened," she said in the same spooky-calm voice. "I didn't want to ask Tim for the details."

I felt dreadfully uncomfortable, but I recounted what had happened as faithfully as I could.

For a while she sat on the couch, her arms hanging at her sides as if she had forgotten about them. "I guess I must seem like an awful slut," she said finally. "But you know, it wasn't like that at all. I wasn't promiscuous. It was just a case of off with the old love on with the new. I was so devastated when James dropped me that I positively flung myself into Aubrey's arms. I guess that seems strange to you."

I made politely negative noises.

She pushed her hair away from her eyes. "You don't happen to have a cigarette, do you?"

It was easy to guess what made her ask for one. Lieutenant Pittman had blown smoke all over the place last night and the house still reeked. I was about to shake my head when I saw Pittman's pack on my dining-room table. I grabbed it and tossed it to Avise, and went to look for a match. A brief search in a kitchen drawer turned up a collection of business cards, memo pads, corn cob holders, and at last a pack of matches emblazoned Gaslight Bar and Grill. It had been Jason's favorite dive. At last I had something to be grateful to him for.

"Thanks," said Avise when I gave her the matches. "I gave it up, but—" She gestured helplessly. "I guess you can't even imagine what it would be like to find yourself in a mess like this."

"Oh, I've been in my share of messes," I assured

her.

"Not like this, though."

No, lady, my life has been one long yawn, I thought. But I didn't say that. The woman's life was in pieces all over the place. I figured she was entitled to be a pain.

Maybe it was just the cigarette that was making her look more visibly unglued, but now I noticed that her tailored blue shirt with its countless tiny pleats across the front was slightly rucked up on one side in an uncharacteristically untidy way. And the hand that held the cigarette was not entirely steady.

"It happened a long, long time ago." Her voice softened as she looked at me. "I thought James was the great love of my life. Can you understand that?"

I shifted uncomfortably in my chair. "Sure. He's an awfully good-looking guy." I hesitated. "He has a way about him, too."

"But you know, he wasn't nearly as good-looking then as he is now. Funny, isn't it? I loved him almost from the minute I saw him. We met in a traffic accident."

"A traffic accident?"

She laughed, and I realized it was the first time I had ever heard her laugh. "We both ran a red light somewhere out in Westchester County, and we met practically head-on. It seemed like destiny. There we were, standing in the rain exchanging insurance information, and it turned out that we had both just moved into the same building in New York. That seemed amazing." She stood up and began to pace the carpet, waving her cigarette about. No doubt I would have to have my place fumigated when this was all over. What the hell. It didn't matter.

"You know how it is," she said, glancing at me. "Or maybe you don't."

I opened my mouth to protest that I had had my share of love affairs, none of them exactly roaring successes, but she went on before I could speak. "James and I adjourned to a nearby bar, and that's where we found out we were both trying to break into acting. We sat there in all the smoke talking about our art and coughing and one thing led to another and we ended up living together." Avise seemed younger and happier as she talked. I began to think she might have been a pretty good actress because just at that instant, she looked almost triumphant, untucked shirt, shaking hand, and all.

"I felt terribly sophisticated and daring." Her voice took on an edge. "I had been brought up in Kokomo, Indiana, you see. But then he found somebody new." She lowered herself gracefully to the couch. I hastily produced a saucer and she stubbed her cigarette out in it. "It had never occurred to me, somehow, that he might. I suppose I wasn't as daring and sophisticated as I thought. I actually thought about killing myself. When you're young and that happens to you, you don't realize that somehow you'll survive." She flicked at the cigarette ash aimlessly with her finger. "That's why I understand how Tim feels, you see. You think it's the end of everything. You have no sense of how long life is, of how many years you have ahead of you." Her eyes met mine soberly.

"I don't think Tim was seriously suicidal," I said. "He was just upset."

"Sure he was. So upset he threatened to dive off a balcony." She lit another cigarette and inhaled deeply. "You don't have to try to spare me."

"It's just that he's found this confusion about his father kind of hard to handle."

She shook her head. "I never in a million years imagined—" She broke off and tried again. "It was just—well, Aubrey was a friend of my sister's." She caught my eye, pleading for understanding. "That's how me met."

I nodded, encouraging her to go on.

"He seemed to be so much in love with me and he was so *there*, if you know what I mean. He didn't know about James. Aubrey belonged to a different part of my world. I had seen him out at my sister's house in Larchmont, and we often went out to dinner together, the four of us. I was glad to have someone who didn't know what I had been going through, someone who hadn't seen my . . . humiliation, someone who still thought I was desirable."

"Of course," I murmured. "I can understand that."

Avise frowned absently. "I think he was surprised when I suddenly wanted to get married, but he didn't protest. I've wondered lately if that was why he got this fixation about Tim not being his." She pressed her lips together a moment, hesitating. "He remembered that I had been in a hurry to get married, you see. And he had so little self-confidence under all that bluster."

"That's what Brack said."

"Brack was right." She shook her head and lit another cigarette. "It was bad luck that Tim turned out to be such a different sort of person from Aubrey. When he was not much older than ten or twelve, he began making fun of Aubrey's peculiar little ways. That didn't help, you know."

I could see that a good-looking son making fun of the aging, ugly father could kind of undermine the bonding process.

Avise exhaled and her face was momentarily lost in a cloud of smoke. "I think Aubrey came to be jealous of Tim as he got older," she said. "Aubrey had had such a painful adolescence he couldn't even speak of it. When things started coming so easily for Tim, Aubrey resented it. It was as if he were trying to make life as hard for Tim as it had been for him. He continually criticized Tim, tore him down. He never seemed happy until he had driven him to his room in tears."

"That would be tough."

"Tough!" She laughed mirthlessly. "It had all been tough, but that was it for me. I mean *it*. I had been unhappy for years, but when I saw what he was doing to Tim—well, it wasn't as if I had much of a marriage anyway. I filed for divorce. That was when Aubrey began saying Tim wasn't his son. Maybe he had thought that for a long time. I don't know. He kept saying that he'd always suspected it, but I thought he was just trying to get out of paying child support. He was pathologically stingy. It never even occurred to me that Tim might not be Aubrey's son."

She plucked absently at the fabric on the couch. "One has a way of forgetting inconvenient things, you know." She paused and spoke in a quite different voice. "This smoke isn't bothering you, is it?"

I shook my head mutely. My eyes had begun to tear, but Avise was already looking away from me, seeing the past again, her voice softer.

"It was only when I saw James's daughter in the office that it came to me that there might be something to Aubrey's wild accusations." She stubbed the half-smoked cigarette out and lit another. "It was biologically possible, you see. The only thing I could think of was if it were true, how could I explain it to Tim? What would he think of me? When I came in one afternoon and found him and Merris going over my old book of clippings, I shriveled inside, I was so afraid they would piece together the whole story." She looked up at me. "I suppose I didn't handle it very well. I just ignored the problem and hoped it would go away. I'm afraid I have a way of letting things go, of hoping that somehow things will work out. If I had talked to Tim about it, maybe it would have been easier for him." She gave me a pleading look.

I tried to think of something comforting to say. "Probably nothing you said would have made any difference. You know, if the whole thing had come up at another time, it might have just been something Tim was curious about. His father's murder, the police investigation, meeting Merris—all that has made things so tough for him. It's a lot to handle, even without any mystery about his parentage."

"I know. The police questioned us for hours this morning. I couldn't understand why they were doing it, but it was scary." Her eyes grew moist. "How can they think I did it," she asked, "when I was at the bridge tournament the entire morning?"

I looked at her in dismay and found myself unable to speak.

seventeen ///

The following afternoon, I went to see Tim in the hospital. He was dressed in jeans and standing at an easel. He turned as the door opened and smiled warmly at me. My heart gave a strong thump of sheer relief. Since I felt responsible for his landing in the hospital, I wanted to think the damage was not permanent.

I went over and peered at the canvas—a bright acrylic, unlike the drawings I had seen. It was a painting of several faces that seemed to be swept around and around in a whirlpool of wispy, ill-defined bodies and traces of landscape. Only two of the faces were well defined. One had an open mouth. Its jaw sagged somewhat, its ice-cream-cone-shaped nose was icing pink and its eyes were very wide. The other had long greenish-blond hair and the serene, dreaming look of a sea creature. Around them I made out other, less clearly defined faces and what looked like some trees and turf that had fallen foul of an electric blender.

"Interesting," I commented.

Tim looked at the canvas with half-closed eyes,

then drew a black line at the corner of the eye of the creature with the ice-cream-cone nose. "It's kind of an experiment. Something along the lines of early Kokoschka. Kind of like Expressionism."

"You took the words right out of my mouth."

He grinned at me.

"Hey, wait a minute," I said, looking at the painting more closely. "That's Merris!" Tim's skill in caricature had carried over into his Expressionist ventures and after I had looked at the painting awhile, I made out some of the characteristic quirks of Merris's face—the slight shortness of the upper lip and the emphatic jawline. Once I had identified her, I had no trouble seeing that the other face was Tim's. The ice-cream-cone-looking triangle was the artist's depiction of his own sunburned nose.

"When are they going to let me out of this place?" he asked, touching up the pink of Merris's lower lip.

"When your insurance runs out," I quipped. "No, really, Tim, I haven't talked to Dr. Pickering, so I don't know. I don't think it will be very long. You're looking good."

"Maybe I shouldn't be in such a big hurry to get out," he said glumly. "The police will probably grab me the minute I check out of here."

I looked down, avoiding his eyes. I was afraid he was right. Remembering the quick interest Lieutenant Pittman had shown in the man with the supposed left hemisphere dysfunction, I knew he would have a decided partiality for a suspect residing on the hospital's fourth floor. It didn't cheer me up any to realize it was all my fault.

There was a light knock at the door, and Merris appeared holding a bunch of Mylar balloons. She brightened when she saw Tim. Brannigan trailed behind her with his hands in his pockets. I watched Tim's smile fade. He turned his back on the Brannigans and began carefully painting the inside of the boy's open mouth with a line of black that brought the color of the lips into bolder contrast.

Merris tied the balloons to the foot of the bed and darted an anxious look at Tim.

"I didn't know you painted," said Brannigan, going over to the canvas. "I thought you just did drawing."

"Oh, I paint, too," Tim drawled.

With astonishment, I recognized Avise's Eleanor Roosevelt act as interpreted by a sixteen-year-old boy. It came off quite well, I thought. It made Brannigan look by contrast like a bit of a cheerful ninny, which was no doubt the intention.

"I guess you have to have a pretty good feel for color to do that kind of thing?" said Brannigan, looking at him hopefully.

"Yes, I suppose so." Tim was clearly not interested in any comments Brannigan might offer.

Merris touched Tim's shoulder, imploring him with her eyes to look at her.

"I don't know if I should bring this up," said Brannigan, "but if you were any kid of mine, Tim, you wouldn't be standing there painting."

Tim frowned. "What exactly are you getting at, Mr. Brannigan?" he asked, provocatively drawing out the syllables of *mister.* Tim was leaping into a quarrel with Brannigan with a readiness that argued nostalgia for all those battles he had had with Miller.

"I'm color-blind," said Brannigan simply.

Tim stared at him.

"So what?" put in Merris. "I don't see what you're getting at, Daddy. What difference does that make? I'm not color-blind."

"Tim's mother is," said Brannigan softly.

Tim sat down suddenly on the bed, his brush leaving a trail of black acrylic on the sheet. "That's right," he said. "She is."

I wondered now why I hadn't thought of it. I remembered Brannigan's embarrassment when he ran the red light that day I had the flat tire, his apparent unconsciousness that we were driving into a built-up area. Rainy days present special problems for people like Brannigan since they drown out some of the visual cues that the color-blind normally use to compensate for their handicap. So it had not been quite accidental when Avise and Brannigan had run into each other at the traffic light that rainy day years ago. In that sense, Avise had not been wrong when she said that their meeting was destiny. There was a certain inevitability in color-blind people meeting at a red light. Now that I considered it, I could see that there had been some subtle cues that Avise suffered from color blindness. Her reliance on blue and nothing but blue as a color accent, for example, and the ugly carnivorous-looking flowers on her couch. No one who could see that couch properly would have chosen it.

"So Dad really was my father," said Tim.

Brannigan watched him anxiously.

"God, color-blind!" breathed Tim in the tone of someone who has suffered a narrow escape.

"Not that I wouldn't be happy to have a son like you," Brannigan said, tugging at his earlobe. One could imagine him sitting up at night puzzling over what would be a tactful and kind thing to say and coming up with this phrase.

Tim looked at him with something approaching amusement. "Sure."

Merris sat down beside him on the bed. "How are you feeling?" she inquired. I saw her sneak a worried look at the hermetically sealed window.

"Okay," said Tim irritably. "I'm not going to kill myself, Merris, so you can quit worrying about that." He frowned. "The first thing I've got to do when I get out of here is get a lawyer. The police aren't kidding around with this thing. Mom doesn't seem to see that. She thinks that as long as she can prove she was at the bridge tournament all morning, she's home safe. She doesn't catch on that all that's up in smoke. They must have changed the time of death somehow."

I had the odd sensation once more of the resemblance between Merris and Tim. They had the same worried, intelligent look to their eyes, the same tough line to their mouths. I realized now that it was emotional rather than biological kinship between them. Golden-haired, handsome, lucky, and clever, they had both been dealt lavishly generous hands by fate. But what showed on their faces was not just confidence but also a wariness that had come from firsthand knowledge that all the good fairies present at their birth could not protect them from hurt.

"Do you want me to get you that lawyer?" asked Brannigan.

"Okay," said Tim. "If you want. Tommy Hvidding's dad doesn't do criminal law it turns out."

There was another knock at the door, and Lyman Finch appeared carrying a large satin-wrapped box of candy. He handed it to Tim with a chuckle. "I think the girl at the candy counter thought I was going to eat it all myself. She looked most disapproving. It's interesting that practically the only meaning that the word *sinful* has retained in ordinary modern speech is as a description for chocolate. So how are we feeling, Tim?"

Tim flushed. "Okay. I guess things had been kind of getting to me. I'm okay now, though."

"Good, good." Finch rubbed his hands. "You know, we all realize you had your problems with your father, but it would be a mistake to take to heart the things he said in anger over these past months. It was plain to all of us that Aubrey wasn't himself."

Having defined the problem to his own satisfaction, Finch inclined his head toward me like a king granting an audience. "Edith Smythe just asked me again about that report Aubrey was working on. Of course, as I told her, it's perfectly understandable why you haven't got down to it, and in any case it doesn't matter. It's my firm opinion that all the reports Aubrey did in the past month or so should be redone. Retested. From scratch. The sad fact is, the man was decompensating and we must consider the possibility that his work had of late not been up to standard. I spoke to Jim Feininger about it this morning, and he agreed. When you're dealing with something as grave as the misdiagnosis of possible brain tumors, you cannot afford to take chances."

I felt acid burning dime-sized holes in my stomach as the implications of what Finch was saying hit me. Could it be that Miller had written that report after all but he had been falling apart so badly, he had made a mess of it? I had as much as told the police he couldn't have written it. I had given it as my expert opinion. Yet I had known Miller was coming unglued. Even if I hadn't been acute enough to notice it myself, Brack Prideaux had told me so flat-out. I could count myself lucky that Tim had not actually killed himself. What would that have made me?

"Yes, I think we all saw," said Finch, "that poor Aubrey wasn't able to handle it when Avise began seeing other men."

Merris popped a chocolate in her mouth. "I didn't know your mom was dating, Tim. Do you like any of them? Who is she seeing? Anybody I've met?"

"Dr. Prideaux for one," Tim said.

"Oh, I remember him!" she exclaimed. "The one with the broken nose. He was over at your house that time. He's nice, isn't he, Dr. Fellowes?"

"Oh, yes. Very nice." I looked at the whirlpool of Tim's picture, and whether through an optical illusion or an excess of acid in my stomach, it seemed to rotate around and around.

"Are you okay, Dr. Fellowes?" asked Tim.

"Forgot to eat lunch again," I said.

"I wish that would happen to me," said Finch sadly. "I never do seem to forget lunch."

Tim held out the open box of chocolates to me. I looked at them, feeling vaguely repelled.

Brannigan, who probably followed my thought processes, regarded me with something approaching satisfaction. "You'd better watch it," he said, "or you're going to end up with ulcers."

"I wouldn't be surprised," I said. "I'd better be going," I added. "I need to get over to the office this afternoon. I've got a lot to do."

I made my escape. There wasn't room enough in that entire hospital for me and all my guilt. Outside Tim's door, I passed a clutch of bright-eyed candy stripers and some self-conscious-looking pink ladies lying in wait to get Brannigan's autograph.

As I made my way across the steaming parking lot to my car, I realized that I had been unaccountably disturbed by the news that Brack was dating Avise. Why hadn't he mentioned it? But then why should he have mentioned it? Men don't normally wear a list of their current romantic attachments on their breast-coat pockets. No wonder Brack had been so aware of the reasons for Miller's falling apart. Had he been on the receiving end of one of Miller's outbursts of jealousy? I knew how strongly developed Brack's protective instincts were. Would they actually move him to murder? No. I could believe that Brack's interest in me was feigned, but his kindness seemed to run so deep, I couldn't believe it was an act. Or maybe it was just that I didn't want to believe it.

I spent a bad night, to say the least. I tossed and turned into the wee hours, thinking about what an idiot I was. Jumping to conclusions. Running off half-cocked. Maybe the Puritans had the right idea with their pillories and stocks. After sitting in a village square for hours with the legend "sluggard" or "scold" hung about their neck, Puritan criminals must have had a lovely sense of expiation. All the same, I had not exactly rushed to tell Avise and Tim that I was reponsible for unleashing the police on their heads, had I?

I made up for the night's insomnia by sleeping past noon. I woke up with a head that felt like cotton and a conscience that felt worse. I fixed myself a couple of boiled eggs, then called my lawyer. He was in court in Wilmington and wasn't expected back until the next day. It didn't matter. It was perfectly clear what I should do.

I would not make the mistake of jumping to conclusions again. Maybe Finch was right and Miller's work had been a mess for months. There was only one way for me to find out.

eighteen ///

"**O**h, Dr. Fellowes!" Mrs. Smythe exclaimed. I stopped suddenly. I had hoped to sneak by her window but I hadn't made it.

I stood there a second feeling awkward as she bustled over to speak to me. The chain clipped to her glasses jingled softly. She lowered her voice. "About that report. It's all settled with Dr. Jim that the entire thing will be redone by one of their own people."

"Uh, yes. Yes, that's fine."

The gravity of Mrs. Smythe's expression so ill-suited her cap of curls that for the first time it occurred to me that she might be wearing a wig and I found myself looking with interest for her hairline.

"So you don't have to worry about it," she said.

"Yes, that's great."

"And another thing." She smiled. "You got a referral this morning. A fourteen-year-old who ran away from home last week. I scheduled her for tomorrow afternoon. I hope that's all right. Since I hadn't heard from you—"

"No, no, that's all right. I mean, that's terrific. Good."

Any other time the news that a patient had fallen into my lap would have elated me beyond measure, but just then all I cared about was slipping inconspicuously into Miller's office. I wanted to check over the reports he had done in the past month.

Lyman Finch strode up the hallway, his shirt soaked with sweat. He wiped his dripping forehead with a handkerchief and muttered, "I'll never get used to this heat if I live to be a hundred. Inhumane, that's what it is. I vote for barges to tow a few arctic icebergs in this direction, where they'd do the most good."

I made way for him at Mrs. Smythe's window.

"Your three o'clock has already arrived, Dr. Finch," she said. "I sent him on back to your office since we have this little problem with our waiting room." Her eyes were drawn to the right where a broad strip of plastic emblazoned "Crime Scene. Do Not Cross" roped off access to the waiting room.

"Yes, yes, I'm sorry I'm late." Finch gathered his messages with plump fingers. "I ran into Dr. Pickering at the hospital and couldn't get away."

Standing behind Finch and waiting for the proper moment to slip unnoticed into Miller's office, I felt remarkably large and awkward. I took my address book out of my purse and studied it with a rapt frown until Finch had gone back down the hallway to his office.

I waited until Mrs. Smythe returned to her typing before I turned and tiptoed to the door of Miller's office. To my relief, there was no police seal on the door. Feeling faintly illegal, I went in. I gently slid open the top drawer of his filing cabinet and stared with dismay at the long line of manila folders. A number of them were fat with corners of blue and yellow sheets peeking out, hinting at the multiplicity of records within. It looked as if I would have to go through every file in his cabinet to find those that had been done in the past month. But then it occurred to me that anyone as methodical as Miller was bound to have a master list of the files. A rapid search of his desk drawers turned up the index to his filing cabinet. I flipped it open and breathed a deep sigh of satisfaction when I saw that every entry was dated. Now it would be a piece of cake.

I pulled out a file in which the testing had been done in the past month. Chewing on my pencil, I began reading over all the testing and the hospital records. It was going to take a while. I would essentially have to do the report over to check Miller's diagnosis. Outside, I could hear Mrs. Smythe rattling her keys.

After I had read the hospital records, I confronted the test scores. I noted with satisfaction that they had no A or N beside them. Now I needed a scale listing the normal and abnormal ranges because even if Miller had all that stuff down by heart, I did not. On one of the bookshelves I spotted Golden's casebook and the new clinical guide by Reitan. I reached for them, but in my nervousness the Reitan book slipped out of my fingers. It bounced off the filing cabinet and landed facedown on the carpet. The noise sounded to my ears like cannon shot and I gritted my teeth.

Behind me, slowly, Miller's office door swung open. I turned around and smiled sheepishly at Mrs. Smythe. "It's just me, Mrs. Smythe. Checking on a few things in Dr. Miller's library."

She leaned against the open door, pressed one hand to her chest, and began fanning her face with her other hand. "My dear, you gave me such a fright, I can't tell you. For a minute there, I thought you were a ghost. Not that I believe in ghosts, of course."

Finch passed, carrying his trimline briefcase. Spotting us, he backed up and put down the briefcase. He stood beside Mrs. Smythe in the doorway and directed an eloquent questioning look at me, his eyebrows raised, his blue eyes lively with curiosity.

"I thought about what you said," I confessed, "and I decided to check over those old reports of Miller's. Just to be sure."

Mrs. Smythe pulled the office keys out of her pocket with a jangle. "Of course, if Dr. Miller's ghost had come back," she said, "I expect I would know just where to find it. With its hands in the blueberry yogurt, that's where! Not a thing has disappeared from the refrigerator since the murder and that just goes to show you."

"Hadn't you better quit for now, Fran?" Finch said kindly. "Now's the time for us all to go home, put our feet up and relax, huh?"

"You're right. I'll finish this one file, then head for home."

"We'll leave you to it, then," whispered Mrs. Smythe, ostentatiously closing the door.

I could hear sounds of departure outside. I struggled with the test scores. I heard a phone ring, then Brack Prideaux's muffled voice spoke briefly. A door closed and I heard keys. Finally there was silence.

After thoroughly working over the file I decided I couldn't find any flaw in Miller's diagnosis of Pick's disease. On the Weis subtests, S was exceptionally low, well below the verbal mean, which was by itself a flag suggesting possible dementive process, and on the Reitan, the very poor performance on the Tactual Performance Test pointed to a circumscribed frontal-lobe disease. Miller's diagnosis looked on target.

One down, I thought wryly. Heaven only knew how many complete batteries Miller had worked on in the past month. I slipped the file back in the filing cabinet and decided to quit for the evening. If I kept at it until I got really tired, my judgment might get erratic, which would negate the worth of the check.

Closing Miller's door behind me, I went to fetch my briefcase. Mrs. Smythe had left on the air-conditioning and the hall light as well as the light in my office. I switched off the air-conditioning as I passed it and a sudden silence fell.

I ducked into my office and saw a note on my desk, a small square sheet of paper with just a couple of typed lines on it: "Couple for marriage counseling. Can only come in evening and the husband commutes. I gave them 8:30 tonight. Edith Smythe."

I supposed Mrs. Smythe hadn't wanted to disturb me with the message. Marriage counseling wasn't something I had much experience in, but I couldn't help but be buoyed up at the thought of a new case. Two—count them, two—referrals in one day! Maybe I was going to make it after all.

I went out by the rear door since the front entrance was still roped off with the police tape. The office parking lot was empty. Nobody in the neighboring offices seemed to be working late on this summer evening. The construction site across the street was deserted—stacks of concrete blocks stood there by the heaped-up dirt, the abandoned shovels, and a couple of dusty trucks. The air was so still, I had the sensation of being in a terrarium.

As I drove home I kept looking behind me. I wasn't sure why. I should play a little tennis, I told myself. Take vitamins. My nerves weren't what they had been. I was getting jumpy.

The tall hedge cast its broad shadow over my driveway. As I drove up into the shadows, Brannigan appeared through the gap. He had to have been waiting for me. Slanting sunlight glimmered on a dark bottle in his hand.

"Champagne?" I asked. I personally was not in a champagne mood.

"I'm feeling good. Humor me."

"I think I'd better eat something first. Care to share an omelet?"

He followed me inside and put the champagne in the refrigerator. While I rattled pans under the cupboard, looking for an omelet pan, he sprawled at the kitchen table, his blue-jeaned legs apart, his shoulders hunched over. "What a day."

"Do I gather that you are happy about something?" I asked. I produced the omelet pan with a triumphant flourish.

"Right. I am happy about something."

"That Tim is better?"

"That Tim isn't mine."

"He's a nice kid," I said reproachfully. I broke some eggs into a bowl and began beating them.

"Sure he's a nice kid. But there's a lot of difference between *nice kid* and *my kid*. You know how it is. They bring you this little baby to hold. It's all red and looks squashed up and puffy, and you think 'yuck.' But it grows on you. Next thing you know you wouldn't trade anything in the world for that kid. What I'm saying is, I don't feel like Tim's father. I mean, I don't like to think I'm a complete heel, but I didn't want to be anybody else's father. I got my hands full the way it is. And what would I do about Merris? She and Tim all the hell over each other all the time. Great setup I'd have there if Tim were part of the family."

"But you thought maybe you were Tim's father, didn't you?"

"Let's just say I've never been so glad to walk in and see somebody holding a paintbrush in my life!"

I poured the beaten eggs into the omelet pan, tilted it to cover the bottom, and watched the edges congeal and turn pale yellow.

"I think Tim's alibi is going to hold up, too," he went on. "I saw the look on your face when that guy Finch started going on about how Miller was unglued. I could follow what you were thinking. So Miller loused up a report? No surprise to me. The guy touted himself all over the place as a great expert, and people swallowed it. Doesn't mean it was true."

"You thought he killed Jessica, didn't you?"

"He did," said Brannigan, his voice hardening. "Now he's got what was coming to him. And about time."

The omelet was nicely brown. I slipped it onto a plate. "He didn't kill Jessica. It was all a mistake. Poor old Miller was such a snob, he fell all over himself trying to please important people. You've seen him do it. That day you brought Merris in, he was practically polishing your shoes with his nose. That's the way he was. And that's the only reason he let Jessica move to the top floor. He was trying to please the famous Mrs. Brannigan."

"That's your opinion." Brannigan pulled the bottle out of the refrigerator with a clatter and put it on the table.

"He couldn't have killed Jessica to get back at you," I said. "He didn't know about you and Avise. Avise never told him."

Brannigan popped the cork. His dark eyes burned at me out of a pale face. "What?"

"Avise told me that Miller never knew about you two."

"I don't believe you."

I sat down and began eating with some difficulty. My mouth felt unaccountably dry. I wondered if Avise had inveigled Brannigan into the murder by feeding him tales of Miller's murder of Jessica. I had envisioned Brannigan as the moving force in the murder and somehow the idea hadn't quite made sense to me. In my gut it didn't make sense. But Avise. It would be so like her to get a man to do something for her. "The tyranny of the weak," a professor of mine used to say. The giveaway was that they had overplayed the estrangement bit. Was it natural that after eighteen years ex-lovers wouldn't be on speaking terms? That was laying it on a bit too thick.

"Don't forget the champagne," said Brannigan.

Sure, the champagne. I got up and got some glasses. Avoiding his eyes, I watched his hands as he poured. All my well-thought-out suspicions came together with my gut feelings and suddenly I was afraid. I could feel cold sweat beading on my back. Was I in the presence of the murderer? He had long, pale fingers, and I had to force myself to quit looking at them. I stared instead at my glass. The bubbles clung to the sides of the glasses but one by one released their hold and floated upward. I could feel the faint pinging of them exploding against my nose as I drank. It was crucial, absolutely crucial that I give Brannigan no clue to what I was thinking.

He put his half-empty glass down and pinioned my hand under his. "I think you're telling me the truth. I haven't caught you in a lie yet."

"Why should I lie about something like that?" I said hoarsely. "Ask Avise."

He snorted. Then, keeping his fingers entwined in mine, he slipped out of his chair and came up behind me, touching his lips lightly to the small hairs at the back of my neck.

I shivered, feeling the attraction in spite of myself. A sort of warmth began to spread to my limbs.

"I've always liked you," he murmured. He gently lifted my hair and kissed my neck again.

Suddenly it seemed impossible that he could have anything to do with the murder. I couldn't feel this way about a murderer, could I?

"I've got an appointment at the office at eight-thirty," I murmured. The sound of my own voice seemed to startle me. My eyes opened wide. I didn't know what I believed anymore. I only knew that I was afraid.

He laughed softly in my ear. "Truth?"

"Truth." I scooted my chair back suddenly, bumping into him.

I turned to see him looking at me from under his thick lashes. His brow was high, and the symmetry of bone and flesh and shadow was beautiful. Lucifer, son of morning. I could feel the tingling that comes when your body is screaming "Fight or flight" and instead of doing either you just stand there. I had to look calm. I had to look as if he was the last person I suspected of being in league with Avise. God, they were good actors. Even standing there regulating my breath, feeling fear like bitterness in my throat, I could see that.

Brannigan leaned against the kitchen counter and folded his arms. His dark eyes looked at me with a slightly puzzled expression. "If you're in a hurry, leave all this. I'll clean it up."

I grabbed my purse and ran out the front door.

I was in a state of mind where I fully expected the car wouldn't start and the doors wouldn't lock, as in a nightmare. I felt a soft jolt of surprise when the locks slipped smoothly into their grooves and the engine obediently leapt to life.

I backed out of the driveway, looking at the house ablaze with light against the violet summer sky. Brannigan would wait for me. Let him wait, I thought, clenching my teeth. I could spend the night in a motel.

What would the police say if I went to them with what I had? And what did I have? A telltale look of shock on Brannigan's face when he was told that Miller couldn't have deliberately murdered Jessica?

Brannigan knew I was going to the office. I had told him so. What if he guessed that I knew he had killed Miller? I was no actress. If Brannigan couldn't tell when sexual attraction turned to cold fear, he was denser and less experienced than I thought. I caught my breath sharply. I had left him, but I hadn't really made a clean escape at all. There was nothing to stop him from coming after me. He could still silence me for good. But how could I go to the police? I had no evidence, nothing solid to give them. Only a look of shock when he realized he had murdered a man for nothing. Miller was just another of the many stupid people littering the world. Miller had never been out to get Brannigan. He had never murdered Brannigan's wife. It had all been a mistake.

Brannigan should realize that I had no real evidence against him, I thought. But murderers are quick to panic. They have too much to lose. For all I knew, he could be following me now.

I decided to cruise around the block once before going into the office. If I spotted his tan Mercedes, I would drive away and go directly to the police station to give them my disjointed story, silly though it was. The marriage-counseling couple would just have to cope without me.

I turned onto Veringer Street and drove past the hospital and the fire station and the upholstery shop. A woman who had been working late was loading samples into her car. I cruised slowly past the office building. Williamsburg-style lamps shone weak illumination onto the pavement of the empty parking lot. There was still light in the sky, but night was waiting in the shadows of the streets and the gutters. Soon it would rise and engulf the violet of the sky. There was no sign of Brannigan's Mercedes. I was beginning to feel slightly ashamed of my panic. Even if Brannigan was the murderer, he knew I was going to meet clients. I had told him so. There was no reason whatever to think he had stalked me to the office. Why should he when he could have so easily strangled me in my own dining room?

I went around to the back door, casting an involuntary glance over my shoulder. When I closed the door behind me, I left it unlocked so that the couple could get in. I switched on the hall lights and the air-conditioning, not because it was a particularly hot evening but because I wanted the comfort of the unit's faint shuddering sound. Then I went into my office and switched on its lights.

The most astonishing thing about murder, I reflected, is that it leaves no mark on the murderer. Such a deed by rights should leave traces. Yet experience tells us that it doesn't. A prim accountant murders his wife and three children, lays their bodies out in the living room, withdraws the family savings, and calmly begins life over as a cook in Butte, Montana. A teenager stabs a stranger in the subway and then goes dancing afterward.

I stood on tiptoe and straightened my Ph.D. diploma. They must have been out of alignment ever since the police had searched my office. Then something clicked in the back of my mind. Finch had no diplomas in his office. That was strange. If I hadn't been so preoccupied with my own problems, I would have realized before how very odd it was. True, Finch's office was pared down and elegant, probably done by an interior decorator, but no decorator on earth could have persuaded me to take mine down. They represented too many years of hard work. Nor was I alone in feeling this way. Brack Prideaux had his diplomas up. Diplomas and certificates covered an entire wall of Miller's office. In fact, now that I thought of it, I had never known a psychologist who didn't display his diplomas. I wondered if there was something suspect about Finch's degree. Possibly he had some sort of non-APA-approved internship that he was ashamed of. Or perhaps he had a nonstandard degree, something from a mail-order college or something run by California astrologers. If his training was faulty, then he wouldn't have been able to write up a decent neurological. Was that why Brack had laughed when Mrs. Smythe had suggested Finch as the person to rewrite Miller's last report? Was Brack aware of Finch's shortcomings in neuropsych?

Finch. I turned him over in my mind, amazed that I had never considered him before. That disk in Miller's computer had provided alibis for several suspects with very visible motives. But I had not noticed that it had provided an alibi for Finch as well. First he had been on camera and then he had carefully arranged to be in the company of a horde of young witnesses until well after lunch, by which time I had discovered the body.

Suddenly, I heard something in the hall, and stuck my head out. It was Lyman Finch. I smiled automatically in his direction but he didn't seem to see me. His hand on the brass knob, his graying head was bent as if he were listening intently for something. I was feeling a little embarrassed about entertaining suspicions of such a benign character when suddenly I realized he was turning the key in the dead bolt lock. He dropped the key into his pocket with an air of finality, and I saw he was holding a crowbar.

He turned and began walking toward me slowly, the crowbar gripped in his right hand. He was looking at me with an odd, almost-sad expression. I seemed to choke on my own breath as I instinctively stumbled backward into my office. I kicked the door shut and flicked the little lock. It was a solid-core door—the office was soundproofed—but the lock was flimsy, and the doorframe was an ordinary interior one. It would soon give way if a man as heavy as Finch threw his shoulder against it. In my terror I gulped for breath, but I did recall that my office door opened outward. That might make it hard to ram open. I heard a slight splintering sound from the other side and realized that Finch had no intention of ramming the door. The sharp tongue of the crowbar was being forced into the crack between the door and its frame.

I glanced frantically around my tiny office. It was a perfect trap. There was no window, no other door. I dived for the phone on my desk. A loud splintering sound made me drop the phone. I knew I would never have time to dial 911 before he got into the room. I grabbed the arms of my big blue chair and forced it in between the desk and the wall. But the door suddenly swung open. Finch was framed in a rectangle of light, blinking, looking momentarily disoriented. The phone—I had to get to the phone, but the office was so small I was within reach of his crowbar even now. I cringed against my bookcase, pressing my body hard against it as I inched back toward my desk. Then I jumped toward the receiver. There was a flash of movement, and an ashtray on my desk shattered as the crowbar hit it. A shard of flying glass stung my arm. I looked frantically around, as if willing an escape to open for me. Then I saw the philodendron.

There was a sudden flash of burning pain as the crowbar hit my arm. I dropped the phone and leapt back, cringing against the wall. Quickly, I stretched to the other side of the desk, grabbed my philodendron with both hands and hugged it to my chest. I stared at him, mesmerized by his contorted face with its halo of graying hair. He was like a grotesque parody of amiability as he raised the crowbar over his head. Hardly knowing what I was doing, I raised the planter over my head. My arm burned painfully where the crowbar had struck it, and I knew I only had one chance. My gaze steady on him, I threw with all my might. He crumpled and fell behind the chair that blocked the door. I could see only his legs sprawled out behind him. I seemed to be screaming but the sound was coming from somewhere in my head.

"Fran! Fran!"

I sensed vaguely that another voice was calling my name from farther away, at the front of the office, but nothing seemed to matter to me except the phone. I picked it up with my left hand and gasped into the receiver, but my tongue suddenly felt too large for my mouth.

"Yes, please?" said the operator's tinny voice.

"Operator," I cried, "get me the police!"

nineteen ///

The next morning found me lying on my living-room couch doing a passable imitation of Camille in the last stages of decay. The paleness, the languor, and the artistic disposition of the skirt of my flowered negligee were intended to recall Garbo at her most poignant. The only jarring note was the substantial white bandage the emergency room had insisted on wrapping around my arm. I wiggled my fingers for the hundredth time to reassure myself that nothing was broken. It certainly had felt broken, but the X-ray technician assured me it was not.

I had taken some care with my toilette because I fully expected visitors to come check on my well-being.

The doorbell rang, and over my shoulder I called, "Come in."

Brack Prideaux appeared in the archway to the foyer. "You ought not to leave your door unlocked like that."

"It doesn't matter. Finch is in jail, so we're all safe, right?"

He took the chair at the foot of the couch. "Tim's getting out of the hospital today. I just talked to Avise."

"He's sick to have missed the excitement, I expect."

"I can't believe it." Brack shook his head. "I can't make sense out of it. I went over to see Amy Finch this morning. She's completely bowled over, poor woman. Lyman won't even see her. He won't say anything. He won't explain anything. The only thing the police have got out of him so far is a demand to see his lawyer. The kids are coming in from school this evening, and Amy's mother is with her now."

I felt a little ashamed that I had forgotten the human dimension of the solution to the murder. It was so like Brack to check on Finch's family.

"Of course, Amy didn't believe it," he went on heavily. "I had to tell her I came right in on it—you barricaded in your office and Lyman out cold with a crowbar in his hand."

"Lucky for me I hit him with that planter. He would have gotten me with the next whack and all the time I was raising the philodendron over my head I kept thinking that I was always the last one picked for volleyball. What if I'd missed?"

"Well, I had my key, and I'd have been right there in a minute."

I shuddered. "It wouldn't have been soon enough."

"I know." He sighed. "Poor Amy keeps insisting that it's a misunderstanding, but I think on some level she's starting to understand what's happened."

"She's ahead of me, then. I would never have figured Finch for a murderer. Never. I mean, even though I had started to put two and two together and had actually begun to suspect him, it still doesn't seem quite possible."

Brack rested his hands on his knees like an old man. He shook his head.

"You didn't suspect anything either, then?" I asked.

"Hell, no. I was so sure it was—"

At that instant Brannigan strolled into the room from the kitchen. "Making my entrance again with my usual flair," he commented. "The old man's looks may be going, but his timing's still in good shape."

"Don't you ever knock?" snarled Brack.

Brannigan considered the question as he threw himself into a chair with his usual carelessness. The woman who married him would do well to reinforce the furniture. "Sure I knock sometimes," he said. "Say if I figured you and Fran had something going in here, I would have knocked, right?"

Brack gave him a nasty look.

"I was sure glad to see you two last night," I said hastily, and to my relief Brack's attention was diverted from his transparent desire to rearrange the chiseled perfection of Brannigan's face.

"We could have been a bit hotter off the mark," said Brack wryly. "You almost got killed."

"Ah, you forget my trusty planter."

"Yeah." Brack looked a little puzzled. "I was surprised it knocked him out like that."

I blushed a little but said nothing about the buckshot.

"I'll have to get you a new philodendron," commented Brannigan. "Looked to me like the one you had got pretty much totaled last night."

"Why did you two come to the office, anyway?"

Brack looked uncomfortable.

"You should have seen Prideaux when he came over last night and found me here," said Brannigan, putting a foot up on the coffee table. "He didn't believe me when I said you'd gone to the office."

"Mrs. Smythe never schedules anybody for the evening unless she can be there," Brack explained. "Ever since an incident over at Feininger's when a borderline accused her therapist of attacking her in the office, we've stuck to that rule as a protection for ourselves. But I knew that Mrs. Smythe wasn't going to be at the office because she had told me she was going to a play at the Arts Center that her granddaughter is in."

"So Dr. Prideaux wasn't happy," said Brannigan. "And I don't know, I suddenly got this weird feeling about it myself." He shot me a curious look. "At first I thought maybe you wanted to get out of here for some reason you didn't want to tell me about, but it sounded like the truth when you said you had to rush off to the office."

We were approaching dangerous ground. I preferred that Brannigan not know I had almost been convinced he was the murderer. I changed the subject. "You know, the one bright spot in all this is that now at least I won't have to check over all those reports of Miller's. Obviously they were okay. That's what Finch wanted to keep me from finding out. That flawed report was written by Finch, not Miller. All that stuff he said about how Miller was too unglued to write a decent report was baloney."

"I don't see what Lyman hoped to gain by killing you," said Brack. He was gently massaging his temples as if to erase a headache. "You had already told the police about Miller's not writing that report."

"Yes, but Finch didn't know that. He evidently thought I hadn't looked at the report yet. I hadn't come into the office. He probably thought the report was still in my locked office waiting for me to get around to it. After all that business with Tim, I felt so guilty about talking to the police that I didn't mention it when we were at the hospital. Also by then I was beginning to have some doubts. I realized I should check over the rest of Miller's work and see if it squared with my idea. Finch was obviously awfully shaken when he saw me in Miller's office checking over his old reports."

"Why?" asked Brack. He closed his eyes. "Why should Lyman murder Aubrey? It doesn't make any sense unless he was completely around the bend. How can you work with a man for years, eat lunch with him day after day, talk about cases and the price of eggs, and have him be that crazy without your knowing it? I've been thinking about it all night. Could he have been in some sort of fugue state? But that doesn't fit with the premeditation. None of it makes any sense."

"Does it sort of shake your faith in these mental health types?" inquired Brannigan solicitously. "I mean, maybe it crosses your mind that none of you know what you're talking about, huh?"

Brack didn't appear to have any fight left in him. Instead of rising to the bait, he leaned back in his chair and sighed. He looked at Brannigan. "To tell you the truth, I was sure it was you."

I coughed softly. Considering how kindhearted Brack was, he was amazingly short of tact. "I guess we all had a lot of theories," I murmured.

"Oh, I thought of killing him, all right," said Brannigan, not a bit offended. "I came down here with the idea of working out a way to do it. Maybe a convenient accident, I thought. Something like that."

I stared at him.

"Don't worry, Fran." He smiled a little. "Killing Miller turns out to be the kind of thing that makes sense when I'm lying awake in bed at two in the morning, but then I see the creep in the flesh—"

"Yeah, you see him in the flesh and then what?" I asked, propping myself up on my good elbow.

Brannigan looked embarrassed. "I start thinking it's not a fair trade, this jerk for Jessica. I start thinking that just for this guy to live ten minutes as himself was punishment right there. You see what I'm getting at?" He looked at me appealingly. "It was like if I hated him the worst thing I could do to him was to let him go on living."

"He was a pretty pathetic person," I agreed.

"One of the worst excuses for a human being I ever saw," agreed Brannigan with feeling. "Except for a few agents I know, maybe."

"I never thought you did it," I lied, sinking back onto the couch. "Actors have too much empathy to be good murderers."

Brannigan shot me a glance that was at once skeptical and amused. "Thanks. But I don't think it's that. I think cold-blooded murder is a lot harder than you'd think. I mean, when it came right down to doing it, the whole idea made me sick to my stomach."

"Finch didn't seem to have had that problem."

"I don't know," Brack said dully. "None of this figures."

"I know," I said. "I feel the same way. I can't put together what I know of Lyman Finch and come up with a raving maniac."

"Well, look, I've got to get back to the office," Brack said, rising wearily from his chair. "I just came by to check on you. Mrs. Smythe has been shuffling my appointments all over the place, but I've got a one o'clock coming in that she hasn't been able to reach."

The doorbell rang, and again I called over my shoulder, "Come in!"

When Lieutenant Pittman's long pale face appeared at the archway, flanked by a uniformed police officer, Brannigan took one look and quietly faded away through the kitchen door. He could appear and disappear with the unearthly ease of the Cheshire cat.

"I've come to take your statement, Dr. Fellowes,"

said the lieutenant, "if you feel up to talking."

I was pleased to see that Lieutenant Pittman's face could take on a cheerful look when he had a murderer in custody.

After Pittman left, I tossed and turned on the couch. I didn't feel like getting up and doing much of anything. In fact, I had a conviction that if I had to do anything more difficult than soak a tea bag in hot water, I might burst into tears. What I kept coming back to was that Finch's murder of Miller didn't make sense. Even apart from the impressions that Brack and I had of Finch, it didn't jibe. If Finch was so crazy he didn't know what he was doing, how could he so cleverly construct an alibi?

I reached for the phone and dialed Duke Medical Center. "Dr. Macon Sherwood, please," I said. It took a minute or two to put the call through, and then I heard Sherwood's quiet voice on the other end. "Dr. Sherwood? This is Fran Fellowes. We had lunch together on Monday."

"Of course, I remember you, Dr. Fellowes. Have you had any luck with your investigation?"

There was an awkward pause as I thought of the meaning of the word *luck.* Was it luck that Lyman Finch was in a jail cell today deprived not only of razors but also of sheets and of any other means by which he could end his life? I supposed as criminal investigations go, that was luck.

"Dr. Fellowes?" said Sherwood, imagining we had been cut off.

"Excuse me. I'm here. It's hard to know where to begin. The police have arrested Lyman Finch."

"A mistake!" exclaimed Sherwood. "Believe me, there's been some mistake!"

"It's no mistake. He attacked me last night with a crowbar. I came close to ending up on a morgue slab. You could have been reading about my murder in tomorrow morning's paper."

"Lyman Finch! No, I can't believe it." His voice was troubled.

"You never had any feeling, then, that he was unstable? There was no history of that sort of thing?"

"Goodness, no. A gentle sort of man with quiet self-confidence. Could he have had a recent head injury, perhaps? A drug problem? When I knew him. . . why, we went camping together one summer, spent weeks together. That sort of thing brings out the worst in people. Tempers get short and so forth. But Lyman had a perfect disposition. And a very open man, too. Not secretive at all. I don't understand it. I really don't."

"Well, he isn't being very open now. In fact, he isn't talking at all. All he does is demand to see his lawyer."

"I'm afraid I'm still staggering from the shock of all this," said Sherwood. "One doesn't envision—I mean, someone that one knows. Of course, I knew him long ago. I wonder—speaking as a Canadian, you understand—if the racial prejudice in the South could not have somehow distorted—"

"Racial prejudice?"

"Yes. I was surprised to learn that Lyman had settled in the South, frankly. Of course, things have changed here a great deal, but—"

"Are you telling me that Lyman Finch is black!" I yelled. "Black?"

For a moment I think Sherwood believed I had gone around the bend myself, but after he repeated himself slowly, the dust began to clear.

Lyman Finch, Ph.D., a native of the Bahamas, a graduate of the University of Toronto, a track star and an athlete, was indeed black. Suddenly, other odd things about Finch clicked in my mind. A native Bahamian who "couldn't get used to the heat"? A natural athlete who had turned into pure pudge? I should have suspected that "Finch" was not the man he claimed to be. After I hung up on a confused Macon Sherwood, I called Lieutenant Pittman right away and gave him Sherwood's number. The doctor, I told him, would be able to tell him something that might interest him.

Pittman called me back the next day to let me know that subsequent police investigation revealed that the real Lyman Finch was not only alive and well and in good trim but was still playing a murderous game of squash. On a hunch, Pittman had the operator check the telephone directory in Freeport. Finch, it developed, was practicing psychology there. Pittman had talked to him.

Although our own "Lyman Finch" steadfastly refused to speak, Lieutenant Pittman's police work later turned up most of the story. "Finch's" real name was Roy Gilcross, and while he was a classmate of Macon Sherwood's and Lyman Finch's, he had flunked out of the premed course. His career hopes disappointed, he had then worked for a time as an orderly at Topeka State Hospital, but with the coming of psychotropic drugs, the hospital's population of chronic mental patients had drastically declined and his job was axed. Never one to approach life cautiously, Gilcross spent his severance pay on a vacation in the Bahamas and while there had had occasion to see the shingle of his old classmate, Lyman Finch, Ph.D., Psychologist. Like an inspiration, it had come to him—he would simply assume Lyman Finch's credentials and go into private practice. From his work in the psychiatric ward, he had some familiarity with the jargon of the field, and he no doubt figured that his chances of running into anyone who knew either him or the real Finch were incredibly small. North Carolina is a long way from both Kansas and Canada. And anyone who cared to inquire after Lyman Finch's academic record in Canada would find it sterling. It is doubtful, however, that anyone ever inquired.

As the years went by and Gilcross became more and more established in Bailey City, he must have come to actually feel he *was* Lyman Finch. He attended workshops with the laudable goal of increasing his general knowledge of his field. As it turned out, this could have proved his undoing. He so easily could have been tripped up by running into Finch's old friend, Macon Sherwood. Gilcross, it seemed, had underrated the mobility of members of his chosen profession and also, perhaps, had underrated his fellow countrymen's desire to escape the

Canadian winter. But maybe the threat was not so great, after all. Even though Gilcross and Sherwood had attended the same workshop, in looking for Finch, Sherwood had of course looked for a black face. If he had seen his other classmate, Gilcross, he had not recognized the now much fatter man. When Gilcross spotted Sherwood's name on the registration roster, he had no doubt removed his name tag and made a quick exit from the conference.

I was able to add a bit to Gilcross's story myself. Lieutenant Pittman finally thawed enough to hand me some real information. After I checked over my typed statement and signed it, he invited me for a cup of coffee at the café across the street from the police station. The place had yellow plastic napkin holders and paper place mats decorated with maps of North Carolina. Lieutenant Pittman pleased me by staying true to type and ordering black coffee. I had always imagined that was what police detectives drank. I filled my own cup with coffee whitener and emptied six little paper packets of sugar into the cup. My appetite had miraculously returned.

Pittman leaned back, looking pleased with himself. "Miller was on to Gilcross, I figure. That's why he had to go."

"Nah," I said derisively. "If Miller had found out that Finch was a fake, he wouldn't have let an hour go by without trumpeting the news all over the office and then the town. Not him! He would have turned Finch in at once.

"No, Lieutenant, Miller took Finch at face value,

just the way everyone else did. Miller's mistake was in telling Finch, as he had told me, his plans to cut a deal with Continental Health. It wasn't Miller that Finch was afraid of but Continental Health. They would never have taken Finch at his own valuation. They would have run standard credential checks. Finch's background would have been checked and rechecked from every angle. It was a risk he obviously couldn't take. But what were his choices? If he refused to cooperate, he faced, as Miller probably told him outright, the prospect of his practice being virtually wiped out. And he had a very high standard of living to maintain. But if he did cooperate, his imposture would be discovered, and not only his comfortable living but also his standing in the community and the entire life he had built on the deception would have been destroyed at a stroke. It must have seemed to him that he had to kill Miller."

When I remembered how "Finch" had actually called my attention to the fact that Miller's death meant the end of the Continental Health scheme, his audacity took my breath away. From start to finish, the impersonation had been the work of a daring man, and in the end he had not hesitated even to dare murder.

"Tell me," I said, "did you really think I had done it?"

"Nah." He smiled. "Oh, you were one of the prime suspects, officially. But when you told me outright that you had loaded that planter to hit him with it, well, I knew right then you hadn't killed him. I mean, admitting something really bad like that—I figured you had to be innocent. Personally, I mean. Officially, you were still on the list." He studied my face. "It did cross my mind that maybe you were shielding somebody, though."

"Nah. Never." I hoped I was not blushing. "Always eager to help the police."

"Sure. Sure, you are. What I don't get is that Finch got away with it for so long." Pittman looked at me over his coffee cup. "How could anybody think he was a psychologist?"

"He never did any testing or diagnosis, never saw kids or did any play therapy. He was able to structure his practice so he never had to do anything tricky. He just did that 'executive potential' stuff for those two big companies, which is a joke. Then in the afternoons I guess he listened to people's troubles and looked sympathetic. He was good at that." I thought a little sadly of how much I had liked him myself.

Lieutenant Pittman picked up the check for both coffees when we left and actually smiled at me. I began to think the man had a few human qualities, after all. He tapped me on the shoulder as we left. "Hey, let's stay in touch," he said. "Maybe I'll take you to a few Little League games."

I smiled. "Sounds like fun." I had discovered that I actually kind of liked Lieutenant Pittman. But I wondered if I ever could look at him without thinking of Miller's murder. Being a police officer must have severe social disadvantages.

When I got back to the house, Brannigan

brought over a bottle of Dom Perignon for lunch. He put it down on the kitchen table with a loud clunk. "I say we keep celebrating until we get it right," he said.

"Okay." I was feeling a little shy of Brannigan still because of that awful night I had almost decided he was the murderer.

He unpacked a paper bag. "Caviar, boiled eggs, black bread, strawberries, and thou beside me singing in the wilderness? Tim and Merris are off having a picnic, so I got Isaacs to pack us up a picnic, too. Merris is playing major tragedy over potato salad somewhere. She's all upset because we'll be pulling out of here soon."

I felt a twinge of sharp disappointment. I had gotten used to seeing Brannigan glide in and out of my house, and I would miss him. Face it, I had grown attached to him in spite of myself. Life would go flat on me, I was afraid, like leftover champagne, after he disappeared taking his beauty and his infuriating ways with him.

Outside a couple of jays protested the presence of a cat prowling through the hedge. I glanced out at them. The sun was bright on the holly leaves, and even the grass looked full of air and sunshine. "Are we going to picnic, too?" I asked.

"We can picnic right here."

"Here?"

"If you want someplace different," he said after some consideration, "I'm open to suggestions. We could try the bedroom."

I have never done a good moral indignation. I

was thinking that as one of the few women in the history of the world to have ever turned down a pass by James Brannigan, it was nice to have a second chance.

Janice Harrell received her M.A. and Ph.D. from the University of Florida. She is the author of numerous young adult novels and currently lives in North Carolina.

 HarperPaperbacks *By Mail*

Ambition—
Julie Burchill—
Young, gorgeous, sensuous Susan Street is not satisfied with being deputy editor of the newspaper. She wants it all, and she'll do it all to fight her way to the top and fulfill her lust for success.

The Snow Leopard of Shanghai—*Erin Pizzey—*
From the Russian Revolution to China's Cultural Revolution, from the splendor of the Orient to the sins of a Shanghai brothel, here is the breathtaking story of the extraordinary life of an unforgettable woman.

Champagne—
Nicola Thorne—
Ablaze with the glamor and lust of a glittering industry, fired by the passions of the rich and beautiful, this is the sizzling story of one woman's sudden thrust into jet-set power in a vast international empire.

Kiss & Tell—
Trudi Pacter—
Kate Kennedy rises from the ashes of abused passion to become queen of the glittering, ruthless world of celebrity journalism. But should she risk her hard-won career for what might be the love of a lifetime?

Aspen Affair—
Burt Hirschfeld—
Glittering, chilling, erotic, and suspenseful, Aspen Affair carries you up to the rarified world of icy wealth and decadent pleasures—then down to the dark side of the beautiful people who can never get enough.

Elements of Chance—
Barbara Wilkins—
When charismatic billionaire Victor Penn apparently dies in a plane crash, his beautiful widow Valarie is suddenly torn from her privileged world. Alone for the first time, she is caught in a web of rivalries, betrayal, and murder.